Piggyback

Piggyback to Paradise

SARAH BAILEY SOUTHWELL

© Sarah Bailey Southwell, 2016

Published by New Tortue

All rights reserved. No part of this book may be reproduced, adapted, stored in a retrieval system or transmitted by any means, electronic, mechanical, photocopying, or otherwise without the prior written permission of the author.

The rights of Sarah Bailey Southwell to be identified as the author of this work have been asserted in accordance with the Copyright, Designs and Patents Act 1988.

A CIP catalogue record for this book is available from the British Library.

ISBN 978-0-9955051-0-0 (Paperback)
ISBN 978-0-9955051-1-7 (ePub)
ISBN 978-0-9955051-2-4 (Mobi)

Book layout and design by Clare Brayshaw

Cover design by Sue Bracewell

Prepared and printed by:

York Publishing Services Ltd
64 Hallfield Road
Layerthorpe
York YO31 7ZQ

Tel: 01904 431213

Website: www.yps-publishing.co.uk

For Russell

1
June 1986, DAY 1 – Midnight, Lindos

The girls sang in unison, striding in time to whatever music drifted out from the bars they passed. Anna linked Sally's arm, driving the pace. As they turned the corner it was 'West End Girls' that came through the next doorway, the pace was perfect for walking, but Sally still had to skip to keep up, her high, black suede heels clunking rhythmically. They managed to keep walking in time together at that steady pace, until Sally went for a theatrical 'punching the air' kind of jump. She landed awkwardly and noisily on the paving stones, Anna just managed to keep her upright.

"We've come the wrong way!" Anna said.

"I know," replied Sally, grinning. "Shhlould we turn round?"

"Shhlould we?" mimicked Anna.

"'Ey, you! . . . Actually, I do feel a bit squiffy. My face feels really rubbery." Sally said this, pulling her bottom lip out with her thumb and finger. Anna reached over and pinched Sally's cheek.

"Feels rubbery to me!" Sally shouted. They both doubled over in the street, laughing, Anna slapping her thigh and stamping her foot. Sally, half in a squat with her legs crossed. "Don't make me laugh Anna, I need a wee." Sally laughed so hard she collapsed in a heap, her smile transformed into a horsey grin, with lips drawn back to reveal more gum than teeth. Her laugh was an open mouthed silent one, Anna's guttural.

"Come on Sal," Anna said eventually, offering a hand to help pull her friend back up. "I think if we continue up here, the Acropolis is over there and we will be able to get back round." She pointed as she spoke.

"Smells of poo down here anyway." Sally said unfolding herself.

"I thought it was just a wee you needed!" They fell in a heap again. Sally just managing to utter the words "Donkey poo!"

Sally made a retching sound.
"Sally?"
"Yes."
"What was that noise?"
"Nothing."
"Sal! What was that noise?"
"It was just a little bit of sick . . ." Sally moved to open her clenched hand.
"Sally, that's disgusting. Get rid of it!"
"I did just." Sally grinned. "I feel much better now."

As the first day of their holiday drew to a close Anna and Sally were already feeling settled in Lindos. Pushing the boat out just a little too far, the girls had celebrated the start of the holiday with a meal at Manolis restaurant. Finding their spirits lifted by the hordes of good looking men there, they continued the celebrations in and around the many bars of Lindos.

They decided to go to the beach. Inebriation had been their first hurdle. The second was negotiating the labyrinthine alleyways, every junction looking like the last. The initial 'aim for the Acropolis' plan did not work. For a while to help them choose which direction to take, Sally had tried the 'ip dip sky blue, who's it not you' rhyme, but that didn't work either and so finally decided to just keep going downhill, presuming that they would eventually come to the sea and Sally would be able to wash her hand.

*

The light seemed odd; strong, crisp white moonlight liberally illuminating the path, made a mockery of the yellowy flickering lamps in the village, like a child's torch in the daylight. The moon and lamps joined forces, intensified by their white surroundings, to give an eerie glow that cast a range of shadows, some long and dark, others moving and dancing. Mist blanketing the bay added to the atmosphere and limited the view ahead. The bars had been hot and the village felt muggy as it had last night when they arrived, but moving away from the buildings, dropping down towards the beach, the air became cooler and more comfortable. The pathway was narrow, dusty and in need of some repair, it followed a stone wall, crossing over it at one point at a makeshift stile.

Tentatively, Anna and Sally made their way. It had seemed like such a good idea at the time, the alcohol fuelled romantics inside them, took them by the hand to drag them down to see the beach by night. Right now the cautious side of Sally was pulling her back by the lime green sweatshirt, playing to her sensible side, telling her to *'get to know the place before you go roaming about in the dark'*.

As they approached the beach, the air was filled with the scent of the trees. Clumped around the periphery of the beach they form a welcoming shelter in the heat of the day, but at that moment, they took Sally and Anna into dark shadow. Anna grabbed Sally's arm and they stood motionless, their eyes struggling to become accustomed to the darkness. Then they heard voices close by.

"What do we do now?" Sally whispered.

"Don't panic. Just wait a minute." Anna reassured. The beach went quiet again.

"I preferred it when I could hear them; at least I knew where they were then!"

"It sounds like there are lots of people. It will be fine. Let's go and see what they're doing."

"Hang on." Sally waited, hoping to hear the voices again.

"Come on, Chicken!"

"Is that a term of endearment . . . . Ferret?" Both girls laughed, a silent breathy laugh.

Singing and then laughter filtered through the trees and so the girls moved a bit nearer. They managed to stay hidden in the foliage, though Sally was regretting wearing her lime green sweatshirt. The light level and the mist which aided their camouflage also hindered their view of what was going on. It appeared to be a group of people they had seen in the restaurant earlier that evening. Sally thought that she spotted her 'Bruce', but could not be sure. There were about fifteen of them and one of the holiday company's reps; he was trying to organise some games. The rep shouted out "last one in buys the drinks . . ." his voice trailed off as his naked bottom disappeared into the sea. Suddenly, it was like a jumble sale, clothes flung everywhere, as they all stripped off and ran into the sea. Something landed close to the girls in their hideout.

"What do you reckon, Sal, fancy a dip?" Anna asked.

"I think I'll give this one a miss."

Anna decided to stay with her friend. As they watched the splashing frenzy created when they all entered the water, they noticed that Eva the little Greek waitress was with them and had been left sitting amongst the clothes strewn on the beach. She watched and smiled momentarily as they ran into the sea, but did not look very happy.

After hiding for over fifteen minutes, the girls began to sober up. Sally hated the fact that she did not have the nerve to go naked and run into the sea. She considered what she had to lose and 'nothing' was the answer, but she still could not do it. She knew Anna would have been there in a shot if it wasn't for her.

"If we stay here, that bloke will spot us when he comes over to pick up his shirt, or whatever it is. Should we throw it back over?" Anna suggested.

"Go on then." Sally encouraged, and so Anna set off, moving in an exaggeratedly stealthy manner. As she got close to the garment, she reached out, but then jumped and ran back to the bushes, as quickly as she could.

"Oh gosh!"

"What?"

"It's a dead cat."

"Don't be daft" said Sally.

"It is. It's a dead cat, go see for yourself."

"Why would he be wearing a dead cat?"

"Well, I don't know! Maybe he was just carrying it." Sally stared in disbelief. Anna's face softened and she snorted in amusement. It set them off giggling. Just at that moment people began to emerge from the water.

The majority of the swimmers came out of the sea and the nucleus of the group collected around a boat which lay stranded on the beach. They were much closer to Sally and Anna now. Some of the others continued the games which involve couples lying in the sand, but a small blonde girl standing by the boat complained loudly about not having a partner, the skinny dipping had obviously done little to sober her up; someone soon obliged. Their wet naked bodies' embraced as she leant against him and the boat. The kiss became prolonged and they slumped onto the sand. Within a short space of time he'd moved on top of her. The others around the boat looked down at them in disbelief and then drifted away awkwardly.

Anna and Sally felt increasingly uncomfortable – especially as they were hiding in the bushes – so decided it was time to go. It had seemed like a bit of fun, but now the mood had changed. Too late – someone was walking straight towards them. They both held their breath. Wide eyed they watched a large, bald gentleman walk to within inches of them. Sally gripped Anna's arm so tightly that she had to prize her fingers open. The man picked up the dead cat. Anna gasped. Sally covered her friend's mouth. He shuffled the cat about a little bit and then put it on his head, turning to walk back towards the group. The girls sighed in unison.

"Was he in the restaurant earlier?" Anna asked, as soon as it was safe to speak.

"Yes, except he has no hair." Sally said flatly.

"How bizarre! The dead cat must have been a wig."

"Unless, of course, the cat was just sleeping on the wig."

"Sally stop it, you'll set me off again. Come on, we better be making our way back."

They fumbled their way out of the darkness under the trees and found the path back up to the village.

"Do you really think they were having sex?" Sally whispered, once she was sure they were out of earshot.

"I'm quite sure they were!"

"But that's disgusting!"

"I don't think she'll remember much about it in the morning."

"What! And that makes it OK does it? How could they, with all those people watching?"

"No, it doesn't make it ok, but some people like that kind of thing!"

They walked in silence for a while.

"He reminded me of a giant turtle, with his wet, slimy, green body sliding on top of her like that." Sally pulled a turtle face as she spoke and then both of them sniggered.

"I don't think the blokes body was green, Sal!"

2

2002, DAY 1 – Rhodes Town

Sally MacFaddyan held her stomach as the nose of the aeroplane tipped downwards beginning its descent into Rhodes Town. She grasped her husband's hand, but the humming in her ears and increasing engine noise made it impossible for her to hear what he was saying. She smiled, fleetingly. Will MacFaddyan squeezed her hand and reached across to kiss her affectionately. Then, as Will watched the lights and buildings of the airport approach at speed through the small oval window, Sally considered the acrobatics going on in her stomach – she was not sure whether they were caused by the apprehension of landing, or the excitement of returning to the island. Only when the wheels bumped onto the runway and the plane had come to a stop, did she release her husband's hand. Within seconds all the passengers began to clamber out of their seats.

The MacFaddyans and the Howards stood patiently in the aisle, waiting to disembark. The doors of the plane opened with a reassuring blast of hot air. Sixteen year old Algie MacFaddyan breezed down the steps of the plane; he muttered 'cool' at the warmth. Slinging his hand luggage bag over his shoulder, he switched his music on again and pushed the headphones back down into place to listen to the Turin Brakes track.

In the Terminal, Will MacFaddyan ensured that the baggage collection went smoothly; he organised, and the others did as they were told. Jo, Will's twelve year old daughter, waited close to the conveyer belt so that she was ready to grab the bags when they appeared. A girl with style – her French plait still looked tidy after hours of travelling, apart from a few stray wisps of fair hair around her face. Algie towered over Jo; he hovered behind ready to give a hand with any heavy cases. She elbowed him in the stomach. "What!" he exclaimed, shoving her. After she regained her balance, she told him that he sounded stupid singing with earphones on, but he could not hear her. He pulled an annoyed and puzzled expression, so she impersonated his singing, exaggerating the words, holding her hands over her ears like headphones – then laughed a loud raucous laugh. "Freak!" he replied.

Will and Sally watched from a distance, laughing to themselves. Sally looked up to check that Will had seen them; the expression on his face said it all. She studied his face. *'How does it say it all?'* she thought. It is an expression reserved exclusively for his children: It was there the day that a six year old Jo had learned to ride a bike. It was there at every school concert; for saxophone and recorder solos, for the Tea-towel-wearing-shepherd and one of his Sheep-in-pink-tights, for the Maths prize recipient and for the ballet dancer. It was there at Will and Sally's wedding, when an excited bridesmaid had vomited at the altar because she was so nervous and a twelve year old best man had astounded all the guests by giving an entertaining speech. It had been there, just the other day, when driving home from town they had spotted Algie helping Mrs Simpson carry her bags back from the corner shop. In the baggage collection hall Sally noticed that Will looked tired – ready for his holiday, but his bright blue eyes sparkled. *I don't think I could capture that expression in a painting, it is so subtle,* she thought and then she remembered that it's probably not a good idea to paint him.

Anna Howard sat close by, dressed simply and elegantly in navy and white. After hours of fighting to stay awake, Hamish, Anna's six year old son finally slept on her knee and Anna began to relax. Their flight was the only one waiting for baggage and the majority of passengers stood around the conveyor belt keen to get on their way. The baggage reclaim hall seemed tatty, Anna thought, but also familiar. She remembered her own excitement in exactly that place, almost sixteen years earlier, barely able to wait for her bags before bursting through the doors to be met by Vasilis. She pictured the athletic, handsome Greek, with his long dark curls and sweet smile and then for some reason remembered his sandals – she smiled to herself, covering her mouth, as if people might read her mind – those sandals that looked as if he had walked around the globe. She slid her hand into her bag, unzipped the inside pocket and took hold of the item she found there. Turning it over and over in her hand she felt the silky smooth texture. Her eyes prickled and she quickly blinked away the tears.

One by one the suitcases were piled onto the trolley. Pushing the trolley through Customs, they declared nothing.

"Move along, People, no standing on the top deck." Will said jovially, in a bad cockney accent, directing everyone to their seats in the car. Forgetting that it is left hand drive, Will ushered Sally to the driver's side.

"I'm not driving this great big thing!" Sally said.

"Only joking my old sparrow." He shuffled her into the front passenger's seat.

Out of the airport in record time, they headed due south, towards Lindos. The route was unfamiliar, but straightforward.

First light began to unveil the surroundings. Sally felt disappointed to find that the scenery seemed unremarkable, but kept this to herself. She had a nagging doubt that nothing would live up to the memories she has of summer 1986.

Everyone was tired.

Their journey took them through the outskirts of a town. Lights pulsed, but the music had stopped. A drunken young man staggering through the street stepped out in front of the car. Will managed to stop the car in good time and then they all watched and waited whilst the young man got his bearings. He swung around, looking into the car and then pointed down the street, either to indicate to them where he intended to go or in order to direct himself. His rebellious body took him in every direction except the way he wanted to go. Will manoeuvred around him.

In less than an hour they were pulling up the last hill. Sitting in the front Sally caught a fleeting first glimpse of Lindos; breath-taking, especially at dawn. She looked for somewhere for them to pull over, but Will did not want to stop. So when they reached a long open straight stretch in the road there was finally time for them to take in the view. "Look" shouted Sally, pointing and waving, not wanting anyone to miss the view. "Amazing!" she said under her breath.

The huge rock rising up from the sea, stood with the Acropolis apparently growing out of the top. Sugar cube buildings and the village lights swept around the base of the rock and twinkled like pearls on the train of a wedding dress, the mist a veil. The orange and pink rays of sunrise gently bathed the scene, then sporadically flashed laser-like reflections in village windows. Sally's heart flipped, unable to contain the excitement, her earlier disappointment forgotten.

*

Striding purposefully, Manolis made his way through the village. He groomed his moustache subconsciously and then, in a well-practised manoeuvre, swept an undisciplined clump of curls back onto the top of his head. Uncharacteristically, he had woken at dawn that morning and found himself in the street an hour earlier than usual. He stopped to make way for an attractive woman, twenty years his junior; smiling, he nodded his 'cali mera'. As he set off again, he almost collided with a smaller gentleman walking towards him.

"Away, you scruffy waster." Manolis shouted, swinging his arm as if to knock him out of the way, the vernacular Greek he spoke was barely comprehensible. The small man ducked briefly and went on his way. Manolis continued along the street, visibly he sniffed the air and muttered to himself ". . . mushrooms."

3
2002, DAY 1 – Lindos

Emerging from the kitchen in the corner of the courtyard, Sally carried a glass of juice and made her way towards the table. Something moved and caught her eye. She stood motionless, riveted to the spot, her eyes hidden behind dark glasses, frantically scanned the length and breadth of the courtyard. There! Something moved again and the second time she spotted it. She had disturbed a small lizard basking in the morning sunshine, on the koklaki flooring. The lizard darted between the terracotta tubs, scurrying through to the safe shelter of a wide crack in the crumbling garden wall.

Koklaki flooring covered the courtyard like a carpet. It was formed by small, round grey stones laid in a mosaic which continued up the steps into the rooms. Each room directly off the courtyard contained a small symmetrical pattern in a central area, the most elaborate being in the main 'sala' where the stones were black and white, as well as grey and formed a circle with a star inside.

Sally pulled out a chair and sat at the table, half watching the wall in the hope of seeing the lizard again. As she glugged the orange juice, she slipped off her sandals and felt the pebbles under the table; like the hands of a reflexologist, they felt smooth and cool, but firm and reassuring.

She wanted another look at the lizard and so set off back towards the wall. Away from the shade of the table the temperature of the sun-warmed pebbles took her by surprise. Again she stood in the courtyard, this time sliding her feet backwards and forwards over the pebbles, savouring their silky smoothness and warmth. In a line between gate and door, the pebbles had been polished to perfection. Sally pushed the tips of her toes down so that they tapped rhythmically against the stones as she moved her feet. She imagined herself laying at the Beauty Therapists and considered whether she would pay for the sensation – *quite possibly.*

"Sal?" Will called out from the bedroom window. Sally jumped. "What are you doing?" he laughed. "Are you looking for inspiration?"

"Just feeling these pebbles, they are really hot."

"So are you, in that skirt." He smiled. Sally performed a sweeping bow with her back to him, knowing that she would flash her bottom in the little skirt she was wearing. Her husband wolf-whistled.

"Is it ok if I go to meet Anna and Hamish?" Sally asked.

"Aren't they in bed?"

"No, they've gone down to the shops. I said I would meet up with them, once I've woken up properly!"

"No problem. It will be a while before the kids are sorted. Will you wake them up before you go?"

"I think your whistle probably woke them– but I'll go and see." She slid across to the first window.

The shutters rattled as she unfastened them. "Come on Jo, it's a fantastic day. Wakey wakey!" A slim band of sunshine lit up the room.

"Too bright," came back the reply.

"Come on girl" Sally said. "Get up; you're on your holidays now. I'm going into the centre with Anna. Your Dad's already up."

Jo came to the window, screwing up her eyes. "What an incredible blue sky! Wait for me, I'll come with you."

"No, I won't be long; you get dressed and get some of this sunshine on to that peaky white body of yours. See you in a bit."

She moved down the courtyard to the next window.

"Algie," she shouted.

"Euh?" came back the reply.

"Algie!" Sally repeated and again she got a similar mumbled reply. "I need to hear a proper word." There was a long silence, then just when she thought he had gone back to sleep, back came the reply.

"Chicken."

"Oh very funny" she said, beginning to open the second set of shutters.

"Oh no, shut it Sally! . . ." silence ". . . The shutter I mean."

When Sally picked up her sandals, she noticed that Will was still at the window watching her.

"Do you know where you're going?" he asked.

"I think so. Hopefully I'll be able to find my way – I'll soon be back if I get lost!"

"I think you might be hours if you get lost." Will grinned a boyish grin.

"I'll be fine, I'm confident I can find Yolanda's Bar. See you in a bit."

"Bye, Funny Lady."

Leaving the courtyard Sally tugged at the door, jumped over the threshold and walked down the steps. The door creaked, then banged as it closed behind her. She glanced back towards the villa as she walked away, making a mental note of the way it looked and its surroundings, so that she would be able to recognise it on her way back.

Sally could not help but smile. She was more than a little bit excited, but kept telling herself *'it's just a place, like lots of places'* but it felt special. She did not understand why it felt so special and sixteen years had passed since she had been there.

When the way to Yolanda's Bar was not quite as she expected it to be, Sally began to wonder if she had taken a wrong turn. Her attention became focused on her surroundings. The streets were narrow and paved, more like pathways, so – no change there – not that they are likely to change in sixteen years, they have been like that for hundreds of years. High white walls bordered all the streets. Some of the walls formed parts of buildings, some enclosed gardens and courtyards, but all of them had huge doorways. Sixteen years before they all looked old; flaky, dry and battered. But over time more of them have been cared for, but only a few more – it takes a lot of time and care to counteract the effects of that scorching hot sun, day after day, month after month, year after year. She became nosy, peering through any of the doors that had been left open. Many of the ladies from the houses were sitting in the doorways, either preparing vegetables, or making lace. Those big old doors gave nothing away; she found immaculate homes concealed behind scruffy old doors.

When she compared the Lindos before her to the one she had encountered years ago, she concluded that little had really changed.

The streets were busy enough to be interesting, but not so busy as to be uncomfortable – many of the locals had been up for hours, making the most of that cooler time, doing whatever Greeks do between seven and ten in the morning. As it was still what Sally considered to be early, she was surprised to feel the sun burning her skin. She rooted around in her bag to check that she had brought sun cream. Within a few steps she was rummaging in her bag again, this time to check that she had money. Every now and then she pulled down the back of her skirt as she walked to ensure that it stayed in place. Sally is not one of the world's graceful movers – she is too self-conscious, especially when she walks alone. She knows she does it, but the more she is aware, the more it happens. She loves and understands the phrase 'dance like nobody's watching'. Age has not made Sally any less self-conscious. Perhaps not quite the gawky teenager that was too proud to walk into town after school with her glasses on, even after she had waved at a bunch of flowers in her friend's front room window, but still awkward. Sally loves to dance; she does this in the living room at home with the curtains shut, the only exception to this being when she is drunk. She always hopes that one day there will come a time when she doesn't care what anyone thinks.

Anna and Sally had been friends for more than twenty years and although they did not see each other very often, as they lived some distance apart, they spoke regularly on the phone, usually once a week. When Sally had suggested that Anna and Hamish should go away with them, Anna had seemed keen until Sally suggested Lindos. She took some persuading, but Sally was so persistent, eventually she'd won her over.

They found a variety of villas on the Internet and after a good deal of deliberation they had chosen a traditional old Lindian villa with three bedrooms that nestled on the lower slopes of the Acropolis, just big enough for both families.

Sally was amazed how busy the streets were without cars. She could hear the donkeys in the distance and then suddenly they were there and she was in their way; each one clip-clopping up the road to the Acropolis, carrying another tourist – poor little donkeys with their skinny little legs – it was no wonder they made such a racket! She moved out of their way and then waited to let the suitcase-delivery-man go past on his buggy and trailer. The suitcase-delivery-man drives just about the biggest vehicle you're likely to see on a street in Lindos, *maybe that's why the place is special, no cars!*

Sally felt sure that she was heading the right way. To confirm this, when she turned the next corner, she knew where she was. *'Now then, if my memory serves me well, I go down to the bottom here – yes, I remember this leather goods shop, so just around this corner should be Yolanda's Bar.'* And there it was, the same as ever, in the shade of the big tree.

A number of tables were taken so Sally picked one in the corner at the back and sat down. Yolanda's Bar was positioned at a kind of crossroads. From the table she could see up three of the five streets that criss-crossed around the bar and hoped that this would enable her to spot Anna, fairly easily, when she arrived.

The area around Yolanda's Bar always seemed like a meeting place. There, many of the old people of the village – especially the men – congregated. They perched on the stone benches set into the old white walls that looked as if they had been there forever, mind you, so did some of the men.

The gentleman who came to the table to take the order, looked very familiar to Sally. Maybe he was there sixteen years earlier; a little plumper, a little less hair maybe, but she was convinced that she had seen him before. She did not know his name and if she had seen him anywhere else, she would not have been able to put a place to the face, but seeing him there, she was certain that it was the same man.

Sally skimmed through her phrase book as she waited for the coffee. She practised a Greek accent in her mind; trying to make that throaty 'gh' sound – which was, of course impossible, without speaking the words out loud. A young lady dressed in bright pink entered the bar. Without thinking, Sally said "cali mera" to her as she walked past, then immediately felt stupid, seeing the girl's reaction to the over exaggerated Greek accent. She was still recovering from this when Anna appeared.

Looking casual and confident, Anna Howard sauntered down the hill towards Yolanda's Bar. Watching her from afar like this, Sally looked at her objectively; she looked rounder than Sally imagined, voluptuous even; she looked fantastic! Anna was the sort of person who could throw on a simple T-shirt dress and look great; on this occasion the T-shirt dress was red. Hamish walked close to Anna, putting an extra skip in his step every now and then to keep up with her, clutching her hand just to be sure. Like his mother Hamish had thick glossy blonde hair, but that was where the similarity stopped, as Anna's fell in long streaky layers down her back; Hamish's hair sat in springy curls that framed his face. He was cherubic, but with designer T-shirt and sunglasses, he was one cool dude of a cherub!

Sally waved and Hamish started to run, darting around the tourists in the street. But his dash across was halted by the donkeys on their way back down. They brayed loudly, making him jump. Recovering, he giggled and dodged his way around the tables and chairs, greeting Sally with a donkey bray.

"Hamish, my little man, how are you doing?" she said, fiddling with his beautiful curls. "You need a hat."

"I know Sally, Mummy said we can get one this morning."

She tapped the seat of the chair beside her. "You sit here look Hamish, what do you want to drink?"

"Orange please, Sally" he said, struggling to get on the chair. Anna arrived at the table, so they ordered drinks and then spent the next half an hour comparing notes on Lindos 2002.

Anna had also noticed the girl in bright pink, but that was not surprising, as she stood out in the crowd just because she was so good looking. The girl was tall and slim, her hair, straight and dark, hung over the back of her chair. With a deep sun tan she looked quite exotic. They tried to decide whether she was Greek, until they overheard her speaking with a southern English accent.

"Is she famous?" Sally asked, "She looks familiar."

"I know what you mean, but I can't think who she is, she certainly looks glamorous."

The girl sensed them watching her and turned around. Automatically they both looked away, but she was still looking at them when Sally glanced back. Anna coughed, stifling a giggle and choked on her coffee.

Hamish had made friends with a little boy at another table and he seemed to be playing happily, so they order more coffee and chatted about things back home.

Anna would be forty soon, in fact they had timed the holiday to coincide with her birthday. Her on/off relationship with Hamish's father had fallen to pieces four years before, when Hamish was two, leaving Anna a single mum. Her optimistic outlook temporarily deserted her and she dipped into the depths of despair. Over the last two years Sally had watched Anna, slowly but surely, come back to being probably the happiest she had ever seen her. She seemed content on her own, although she had become a bit grouchy with men generally these days. When she was younger she always seemed to fall head over heels in love and then fall just as quickly out again! On the previous trip to Lindos she had fallen hopelessly in love with a local.

"Coming back here has brought it all back to me, more than I expected, it really seems to have stirred up some old feelings. Don't mention Vasilis, I don't want to talk about him," she confided.

"Maybe he's still here," Sally said, thinking it might cheer her up.

Anna replied curtly "I said I didn't want to talk about it!" she held her lips in a tight, straight line.

They sat quietly for a while until Hamish pulled them out of their thoughts. He was standing in the street shouting at a young girl walking past. They could hear what Hamish was shouting, but could not hear her replies.

"Where did you get your ice cream from? . . . But you can't have!" He sounded angry, his little cheeks were red and he was standing with both hands on his hips. "I don't believe you; mummy said they don't have ice cream in Lindos." Anna looked sheepishly at Sally.

"You didn't?" Sally said.

"Erm, I might have, I thought it might stop him asking all the time. Well it worked for a while!"

"Yes, must be all of one hour, Anna!"

Anna called him over and he stamped his way back to the table.

"You told me . . ."

"I know, Hamish. Yes, I'm sorry; they didn't use to have any here. It must be a new thing." Sally began to collect their things together. "There weren't any ice-creams here last time were there Sal?" Anna looked at Sally when she got no response. "Sal . . . ?"

"Don't look up!" Sally ordered.

"What?"

"Shush" she whispered "get your stuff and follow me into the bar."

"What are you doing mummy?" Hamish said loudly.

"Shhh," they both replied.

Quickly they scooped up all their things, including Hamish, and darted into the bar then back out of another door.

"What is going on Sally?" Anna pushed her face just a little too close to Sally's.

"Hey, don't panic! Didn't you see?"

"What?"

"Just go and have a peep" Sally said, directing her with a nod of the head. But then she grabbed Anna as she started to move. "Look at the bloke sitting with Mrs Glamorous Pink Lady . . . and look at the back of his leg under the table." Anna looked puzzled, but did as she was told.

She came back shortly. "Oh my Gosh, do you really think it's him?"

"Well it looks like him . . . and that scar is in the right place."

"You're right. I'd forgotten all about his leg."

4
1986, DAY 1 – 9pm, Lindos

The day-trippers had all gone and for a while Lindos seemed calm and quiet. Anna and Sally wandered the streets looking for somewhere to eat. It was warm, but the searing heat of the day had reduced to simmering. The shadows began to creep up the white walls, as the sun dropped down in the evening sky and left a slither of bright glowing light in a line at the top of each wall. Even now the sun was hot, so the girls were enjoying the breeze that had picked up. They quickly found the coolest places to linger, where the high-sided narrow pathways channelled the wind. The two pale faces that had arrived in Lindos in the early hours of the morning were now lost under freckly cheekbones and glowing red noses, the tell-tale signs of a first day dash to the beach to make the most of the sun. They were not alone; the Wednesday night flight arrivals were out in force.

Sally wiggled her slim and shapely ankle and shouted to Anna to wait. Turning around, Anna found her friend struggling desperately to free the narrow heel of her shoe stuck between the cracks in the uneven paving stones. Sally felt so embarrassed; it was bad enough the first time, but to happen again! She felt her cheeks flush and cringed, remembering how red they were to start with.

She looked worried, but Sally often looks worried; it is her natural expression. Her eyelashes are long, wispy and straight, somehow giving her a gentle, thoughtful look; her cool grey-blue stare, hints at sadness. Her nose is straight and larger than average (character building her mother always said) and altogether she has, what can only be described as a plain face; her dry sense of humour and the well-practised deadpan look that goes with it, mean her smiles are rare; and if ever a face needs a smile, it is Sally's. When she smiles, the broad display of even white teeth, transforms her face. Her lips are full and sharply defined. Something Sally obviously appreciates, as she takes lipstick application to a Fine Art.

"I told you those shoes wouldn't be suitable." Anna said, laughing.

"You're so clever; who do you think you are, my mother?" Sally replied. "These are fine, I've just been unlucky. Anyway, I've only got little legs – I'd look stupid in flat shoes."

'*Yes,*' Anna thought, '*you have incredibly short legs and an enormous bottom that you need to hide under a sweatshirt, in this heat!*'

Sally nibbled her bottom lip in concentration, hopping from time to time whilst Anna pulled at the shoe. She did not see the young man running around the corner. He flew into them, muttered 'sorry', then turned around and walked back. Sally and Anna stared at him; he was wearing a suit jacket with a shirt and tie – which in itself looked odd – but he had no trousers on, just boxers. "Strange!" they said in unison. Anna continued to work on the shoe. They got it free just in time to get out of the way when the same man ran into them again.

"Sorry. Hopefully that's the last one!" he said and disappeared again. As they walked around the corner it became clear that he was an actor and they were in the middle of filming. The film 'High Season' came out the following year.

"What about this one Sal?"

This was the fifth restaurant they had looked at, hunger was taking over and so they were ready to settle for anything. The other places had been too busy, too small, too expensive and too Greek. This place was all those things.

"Hello ladies, I am Manolis. Welcome to my restaurant. A table for two?" A portly Greek gentleman gestured to the girls to go into the restaurant. Anna gave Sally a 'not this one either' look, and they began to walk away.

"Don't do this to me ladies, we have too many young men in here tonight, we could really do with a couple of pretty faces!" His heavy Greek accent had disguised his now obvious, command of English. Sally gave in to her hunger and followed him through. Anna showed her displeasure in the usual way; it was always the same, she raised her voice slightly and her answers became short, sharp and blunt, to the point of being rude. Sally dug – what was left of – her heels in and positioned herself in the corner of the room where without too much trouble she could see what was going on in the restaurant around them.

Anna's rant was longer than Sally expected, she almost gave in and got up to leave – almost. She half listened, but felt that Anna's original grievances – which were justified – had grown and transformed into an epic lecture guaranteed to prove her wrong. This was out of character for the normally optimistic Anna, but when Sally thought about it, Anna was, on occasions, prone to righteous ranting if she felt someone was going against her sound advice and wishes. So Sally continued to nod, and 'yes' and 'no' with the odd 'uhha' in hopefully the right places, but began to surreptitiously glance around the restaurant.

Anna was right; there were great clouds of steam bellowing out from the kitchen every time anyone walked through. People were smoking, and the smoke did seem to be combining with the steam to form a kind of smog in the room. It was very hot. Any breezes making their way through the main doors were well and truly stifled by the time they got through to where they were sitting in the back. The ceiling fans couldn't waft a whisper – Anna's words. It was noisy, the place was buzzing and so Anna's voice became part of the general hum in Sally's head. Sally viewed her surroundings quite differently: she heard the sound of fun and laughter. She saw, a romantic hazy warm glow, formed when the smog hanging around the tables diffused the light from the flickering candle flames. As her eyes became accustomed to the low light level, she noted that Manolis was right, the place was full of men; one large group in particular. This was the kind of place they had come on holiday for!

Sally scrutinised the men in the large group from the holiday company '2OS' – she hated that advert, she could hear it now 'Go wild for less, with 2OS'. The men certainly outnumbered the women and there were a few that Sally thought looked very promising. One in particular, ooooh, just as she noticed him he looked at her, she quickly looked away. Checking back to see that Anna was still talking she dropped in a nod and an interested look. She could not help but look over to the 2OS table again. He is definitely a 'Bruce' she decided. The term 'Bruce' came about when Sally was at school. It was a girls' grammar school, set within 200 yards of the boys' school. On the daily trip into town after school Sally worshipped the boys from afar. It was always one at a time and she rarely got to know any of the boys she desired. An overheard Scottish accent sparked the nickname 'Bruce' among Sally and her friends. 'Bruce' never knew of Sally's affection for him, despite valentine cards three years in a row. However, 'Bruce' turned out to be David a local farmers son, later vet, whose Yorkshire accent and love of 'Iron Bru' never left him. From their time at school and also through university the term 'Bruce' continued to be used by Sally to mean someone she fancied but did not know. Lindos 'Bruce' had short dark wavy hair, slightly longer on the top; his eyes dark. He looked at her again and she looked away. Sally found it harder to concentrate on what Anna was saying – *is she really still ranting?* When Sally looked over to him yet again, the waiter was in the way. When Lindos Bruce peered at Sally from around the waiter she did not look away and couldn't help but smile.

Sally noticed that Anna was staring at her, mouthing the words 'What are you smiling at?' and realised that she must have been nodding in the wrong places too. Then she had to laugh, just because Anna looked so grumpy.

The waiter brushed past Anna nearly knocking her out of her seat.

"Pardon" he said, but kept on walking.

"Excuse me." Anna jumped out of the chair after him. "Could we have some drinks?" He raised his eyebrows, thrusting his head back. "Err, fizzy water." Anna replied. He repeated the gesture. "Fizzy water." Anna repeated. The waiter nodded and went on his way.

"Well he was a bit rude wasn't he?" Anna said and then turned around to find him standing next to her.

"One water?"

"Errrrm, two fizzy waters, please."

"Two pissy waters?" Vasilis asked.

"Fizzy" Anna corrected. She began waving her arms about, puffing out her cheeks and making popping noises. "Fizzy, we would prefer fizzy water."

The girls managed to keep their faces straight just long enough for him to get into the kitchen.

"I can't believe that you just tried to do an impression of fizziness." Sally roared with laughter. They were still laughing when he came straight back out with their drinks. He looked so serious that their smiles dropped instantly.

"Two fizzy water." He pulled a notepad from his pocket. "Would you like to order?"

"Please can we have a menu?"

"Sorry, of course." He slapped the side of his head as he said this.

"Anna, are you starting to relax a bit?" Sally asked. "Have you seen this lot over here?" She pointed out the blokes over on the other side.

"I'm in love." Anna replied.

"Which one? I've already picked my Lindos Bruce, so hands off."

"Not that lot! I mean the waiter." As Anna said this, two menus appeared in front of her.

They pondered the menu for a long time. Unable to understand the Greek, they joked about what they were ordering, deciding eventually to 'just pick' and hoped that they had chosen a special traditional Greek dish – secretly feeling really adventurous.

A young girl came to take their order. She was petite, with a neat figure, an olive complexion and long dark curly hair. Like a lot of the local girls she was very pretty. She kept her gaze low; large hazel eyes fixed on her notepad. Momentarily she would look up, not quite grasping what they were saying, struggling with the English, her long thick eyelashes sweeping her cheeks. Her nose and mouth were small and perfectly formed, like a doll. She was softly spoken.

Swiftly and efficiently she took the order and despite the over exuberant attention she received from the large group of males across the room, she remained calm and professional, making the girls feel welcome in what turned out to be her father's restaurant.

"Tomatoes!"

"I like tomatoes!"

"That's lucky, considering you have a plate full of tomatoes" said Anna, giggling.

"Mind you, when I ordered tomato salad I didn't expect to get just tomatoes. And look at yours! What did you order, a 'mainly tomato salad'?"

The waiter brought out their main course. He struggled to find space to put things down among an array of empty glasses. The girls moved quickly to make space and he placed the food in front of them. Anna and Sally looked at each other and then again at their food. Both dishes looked the same even though they had ordered different things. Sally's looked like a plate of tomatoes; Anna's looked like a plate of tomatoes, except there were small strands of spaghetti peeping out from under the tomatoes. Anna picked up her fork. Cautiously she lifted a tomato from the edge of her plate; she brought it up to her nose and then placed it back on the plate. She started to giggle.

"At least you have some pasta." Sally said, struggling to contain her laughter.

"I'm not sure about that. You don't think they might be Greek worms do you?"

"Do you want any more fizzy water?" The waiter asked.

"Or more tomato perhaps Sally?" Anna joked, before doubling up with laughter.

"Sorry?" the waiter said, looking hurt. "I can bring more tomato, if you like."

"No thank you, this is fine." Anna managed to say.

"Enjoy your meals" he said and disappeared into the kitchen.

"We shouldn't be rotten" Anna said, "he looks gorgeous!"

"He looks exactly like the waitress, they must be related."

"I think we'd better get him back, I want more pissy water! Oh Gosh! I think I'm going delirious, it must be the heat."

"Or perhaps the gas, or come to think about it, have you ever had an overdose of tomato? Maybe tomato sends you delirious!"

Whatever caused it, they were extremely giddy. After futile attempts to eat the meal, whilst laughing, Sally inhaled the tomato sauce. Her tramp-like coughing drew lots of unwanted attention. Their giggling, comments about tomatoes, and the ingratitude shown for all their efforts, apparently offended the waiter Vasilis and his father Manolis, although that was not their intention.

Anna's attempts to woo Vasilis back to the table, so that she could have another close look, were in vain. They got up to leave the restaurant; both happy to have spotted a Lindos 'Bruce'. Whether they would ever see them again, was another matter. The little waitress, who never lost her cool, responding promptly to increasing demands from the 20S group, had disappeared into the kitchen. As Anna and Sally made their way out, it became clear that something was brewing. Behind the scenes, voices were raised and doors were slammed. Eventually the little softly spoken waitress came back out. She shouted three words through to the kitchen and walked out of the door, followed closely by an irate Manolis. 'Eva' he was shouting and he clearly did not want her going anywhere! Shortly afterwards, the 20S group finished their meal and left.

5
2002, DAY 1 – Lindos

Sally sat alone. Anna and Hamish had gone to buy a hat after making their furtive exit, taking the long way round to reduce the risk of being spotted. Sally perched on a low wall outside Yolanda's bar, deep in thought, she had lost all track of time. The hustle and bustle of Lindos went unnoticed. Locked in her thoughts, her sparkle gone, two strong vertical lines etched deeply between her eyebrows; her mind was in turmoil. *'It's no good'*, she thought *'I'm going to have to go and speak to Lou'*.

Sally walked back into the bar and stood quietly on the steps overlooking the terrace full of tables; she could see Lou chatting to the gentleman on the table next to him. She collected her thoughts, but her mouth was dry and her heart beat loudly. *'Get a grip!'* she bullied herself. Then just as she had mustered up the courage and began to move off the step, she overheard them and stopped in her tracks.

"I believe you're staying in the apartment next to us. I'm Lou and this is Emelda. We've just arrived," Lou said to the man. "We're here for two weeks." It was just the excuse that Sally needed. Turning on her heels, she walked out of the bar and straight up the road towards the villa.

As Sally sauntered up the street, her heartbeat slipped back to that quiet unobtrusive thud, the furrowed lines between her brows melted away and she smiled to herself – *it's great to see him again.* She could not wait to speak to him, but hoped that she would have some time to collect her thoughts before she did. *He still looks good – the bastard!*

6

2002, DAY 1 – Lindos Beach

Sally

The sea before me, as flat as a lake; tiny waves making their way up the gentle slope of the beach, breaking with the enthusiasm that I feel in the baking heat of the afternoon sun. An outcrop of rock on my right, forming a natural conclusion to the beach, rises sharply to the white walls of the village, then higher still to the Acropolis above. In places, I can just make out the winding donkey path that forms the main route from the village to the top. The semi-circular beach sweeps beneath me from the rocks, carpeted with people, intermittently protected from the sun with the all-too-regimented rows of parasols.

I can hear laughter intermingling with the waves; the rhythmic patter of bat and ball; the splashing of cold water, inducing gasps and shrieks; unfamiliar words, accents and voices; in the distance, snoring; birds overhead; a donkey braying; an occasional speedboat, momentarily interrupting the waves natural rhythm.

I feel the sun beating down all over my skin; it quickly dries the seawater sitting in beads on my suntan-oiled body. The sand moulds to my body through the towel. I lift the silky top layer and let it slip through my fingers, or I can burrow into the hot sand with my hands reaching down to the cool, damper sand beneath. I relish the breeze, not cool in itself, but cooling, stroking and massaging.

Occasionally it lashes out by bringing with it the sand, just to make sure I'm still awake.

Sally went through the visualisation in her mind. She did this as she has always done, only now the focus is sharper, her senses able to revise this picture that she has carried in her mind all these years. "Picture yourself," the Psychologist said "in a place where you feel happy and relaxed." Lindos beach was the place she chose every time.

The peace and serenity of the moment was shattered by ice-cold fizzy pop poured onto Sally's stomach. She doubled up in shock. Opening her eyes she saw Hamish running away, as if his life depended on it. Reaching what he believes to be a safe distance, almost falling over in fits of laughter, he turned to watch her reaction; seeing her watching, his face dropped. He looked to Will and then to Sally, backwards and forwards reassessing his situation, but in the process he gave away the identity of the instigator. A beautiful picture of innocence, Sally had to smile he looked so hurt.

"Good one Hamish!" shouted a chorus at the water's edge.

"What's he up to now?" Anna asked, looking up from her book.

"Nothing much, just my family putting him up to tricks."

"Hamish!" she shouted.

"Leave him Anna; it's only a bit of fun."

"You're lucky you know."

"How's that Anna?"

"Having Will."

"I know. Apart from certain little tricks he plays, I count my blessings every day."

Sally

I feel so proud of the kids. What right do I have to feel proud of them? They're not mine. I think back to our first holiday, full of tension. I made plenty of mistakes, but I was just so frightened of getting things wrong. Looking at Jo I can hardly believe how quickly they change and grow up, almost before my eyes, it seems. This last year, especially, has seen her grow into a young woman. The metamorphosis is riveting. Is it just me that sees so much of their mother in them, or does Will see it too? But then just lately they seem more like Will. I don't know if my 'rose coloured spectacles' are picking out those features that are more like Will. They are both good looking; I believe that I can say that, without the biased view of a natural parent. We have a family joke that Jo looks like me, we all know it's impossible but the similarity is there. Of course it could be that people grow to be like those close to them, the way adopted children sometimes do; possibly it's something to do with mannerisms. Maybe, it is that their mother and I are similar; I can't see that myself!

*

Algie could not believe that the others had managed to get down to the beach before him. He was sure that he could have chosen a more picturesque place to sit, not surrounded by these repulsive 'grannies' with their saggy bodies. *How on earth am I going to be able to watch those gorgeous babes further down the beach?* He thought about asking Anna and Sally if their cameras had zoom lenses, but decided that they might suss what he was up to. He glanced around, noticing the woman sitting directly behind him; she was old – at least forty, but had extremely large breasts. Turning over on to his stomach he immediately felt uncomfortable looking right up between her legs, so he turned back round to hide his embarrassment. After what he considered to be an acceptable time, he leaned backwards slightly, sneakily trying to watch her using his peripheral vision and the reflection on the inside of his sunglasses. *Are her tits the biggest I've ever seen? Could both my hands actually reach around one breast? Theoretically of course – I wouldn't want to touch them!* Bringing his knee up towards his chest he measured his own thigh with his hands to compare, trying to decide how much more they would squash up. A woman two parasols down looked at him in a strange way and he realised that he was sitting in a rather bizarre position. As he moved back to a more normal sitting position, he became aware of his erection. Casually he tried to hide it by covering it with his hand, inwardly he felt embarrassed and devastated that this 'old' woman had aroused him to such an extent. He considered how to get rid of it – *'if I can get to that nice, freezing cold water, then that could just do the trick. I could go for a swim and assess the day's talent before depression sets in'*. He considered whether to use the bat to hide it, or whether bending over and brushing sand off his knees would work. He chose the bat, but then found his next problem – how to get to the water's edge without burning his feet or having to resort to wearing those disgusting flip-flop things Sally bought. His theory was to walk slowly and scream inwardly. This theory lasted only a few steps, transforming his cool strut into a skipping kind of Greek-sand-dance, popular in Lindos at the middle of the day. At least he did not squeal and just for a moment he was thankful that his closest audience were the old birds.

After scouring the full length of the beach for his gorgeous babes, a game of bat and ball with his dad, and half an hour of body surfing with Jo and Hamish, Algie relaxed in the shallow water. Lying on his back, sculling, he allowed himself to be rocked by the gentle waves that now lapped the shore. He took pride in the way he could float and the way he could guide himself around wherever he wanted to go, with very little movement of his hands which he kept close to his body. He felt the top of his head make contact with something in the water. Opening his eyes, he found his head nestling gently between somebody's knees.

"Watch where you're going!" she said, towering over him. Struggling with water in his eyes he just managed to focus beyond her glistening brown thighs and the gentle curve of her belly, onto her fantastically large tits. It was turning out to be a good day for breasts, he thought.

"Oh sorry" he replied. Realizing that he could not even see her face in that position, he rolled over in the water and kneeled in front of her, sitting back on to his heels. Here was his gorgeous babe! They looked one another over for a moment. He liked what he saw, this girl was beautiful; a bit old for him, she must be at least twenty-five, but a young boy needs someone to show him the ropes.

"Call yourself a swimmer?" She asked, her tone abrasive.

"I can swim, if that's what you mean," he sounded offended.

"Sorry" she said, suddenly serious "I've been looking for someone who might be up for a race, but I can see I've obviously disturbed you."

"What kind of race?" Algie said, never being one to miss a challenge.

"I've been watching you and you look like a fairly proficient swimmer to me. I was thinking we could race over to the jetty, near the yacht on the other side of the bay."

Algie looked at this vision before him – *'she's been watching me!'* He had developed a cocky manner in recent months, following a surge of interest in him from girls at school, but this girl – no, woman – was out of his league. Standing there in front of him, radiant and wet, like one of the cover girls from a men's magazine he occasionally managed to cadge from one of his mates. But then again, how could he turn down a proposition like this?

"I'll leave you to it, then," she said, after waiting too long for his reply.

"No. No – I'll beat you!" Algie panicked and dived into the shallow water. He swam urgently, ploughing his way across the bay. More of a challenge than he had thought, she was by his side all the way and she just managed to touch the jetty before he did. They both clung to it, struggling to catch their breath.

"Not bad for a girl!" Algie said with a large intake of breath.

"Oi, cheeky! I'm guessing you didn't notice that I beat you?"

"I'm not so sure."

"That's outrageous!"

"Your word against mine, I'm afraid." Algie started laughing; he laughed long and loud, until a large wave swept past them both turning his laughter into coughs and splutters.

"God looking down." she said smugly. "Serves you right for lying . . . and laughing." She smoothed her hair back from her face. "I'm Mel by the way, what's your name?"

"Algie."

"Algae – we better not tell the locals they've got algae in their water!"

"Al – gee!"

"I beat Algie!" she shouted towards the beach.

"I can't believe you just did that." he said, shaking his head.

"I'm only joking. No one can hear, over here, anyway."

The majestic Yacht now within a hundred yards of them, sat gracefully in the water.

"Looks fantastic, doesn't it? I wonder how you get to stay on there." Algie changed the subject.

"I don't know, but it looks fab."

"You probably need to be rich or famous, or both!"

"Probably, and I am neither," said Mel.

"I'm going to have to go back now."

"Me too."

"Race, Alggeee?" She said, grinning as she over pronounced his name.

"Nar, you go on head."

"Ah, you know when you're beaten!" Mel gloated. "Maybe see you for a drink sometime?"

"Yes – see you later."

Algie became aware of how close their bodies were in the water and as they moved away from the jetty towards the shore, he felt something brushing over the front of his body, but was not quite sure if it was intentional, or in fact, imagined.

"Not such a big boy now." She said and was gone.

7
2002, DAY 1 – Lindos Beach

Hamish had settled down to look at a book so Sally seized the opportunity, grabbing her sketchbook from her bag. As she watched him closely, amazed at how still he was sitting, she rummaged around for a pencil. Hamish followed the words with his finger and spent a long time studying each of the illustrations. Knowing her time was limited Sally set to work quickly. She looked at him, carefully checking proportions; by narrowing her eyes she could see the areas that were lighter, she left those paper white, then quickly filled in medium and then darker tones.

"What's that word Mummy?" Hamish asked without looking up.

"She's gone in the sea, Hamish. Let me have a look." Sally replied, leaning forwards. "Spell out the letters."

"B-r-o-w-n."

"Ok, put those together."

"Brown," Hamish said, pronouncing it to rhyme with 'own' but then instantly recognized the word and shouted it out. "Brown!" He smiled, displaying square, gappy teeth which Sally quickly captured in her sketch.

"That's right, good lad," she said, catching a whiff of strawberry shampoo as she ruffled his hair. The ends of his hair still wet from swimming earlier, now fell in tight corkscrew curls. She finished off the sketch with a suggestion of shoulders, arms and the book.

*

As the sun began to drop down towards the horizon, Sally decided to round up the troops. Anna was not feeling well, Jo and Hamish had had too much sun for their first day and she thought the lads could maybe do with a bit of male bonding time. The suggestion did not go down very well with either Jo or Hamish, who both presented brilliant arguments as to why they must stay that bit longer. Sally suggested to Anna that when they got back to the villa, she and Jo would help to keep Hamish amused, so that Anna could have a lie down.

"I don't need people to keep me amused!" Hamish piped up, spitting out the letter p in people, to emphasize his horror at such a suggestion.

"Well, we certainly know that, Mr. Independent." Anna said, tired. "Come on, Hamish, you might just catch the donkeys."

"Ok, ok. Let's go, Jo!" Hamish said, taking her hand. Jo gave in without too much fuss, but pulled a face.

They said goodbye to the lads, then set off up the tiny steep steps at the village end of the beach.

Half way back, Sally stopped to wait for the others. She sat on a low wall overlooking the bay. She had got ahead of them because she was lost in her thoughts and had not realized that they had dropped behind having been distracted by the donkeys yet again! They were making very slow progress a long way below her. She was disappointed to be missing her favourite time on the beach. This quiet, cooler time that brought back memories of long, late afternoons dozing and dreaming on Lindos beach. It had been usual on her last visit to Lindos, for the locals to appear at this time, and as she surveyed the scene she saw that nothing had changed. Since they'd left the beach, approximately ten local lads had arrived strutting across the sand to begin a casual game of football. A number of Greek girls were lying close by, watching and talking. She could see Will and Algie deep in discussion just where she'd left them. About twenty yards further along the beach was Lou, the other reason she had suggested that they should go back to the villa. Sally had seen him arrive with three small boys about half an hour ago. She knew she was not quite ready to speak to him yet and so had prompted their trip back to the villa. Lou and the boys had joined the woman they had seen him with in Yolanda's bar. Sally presumed that it must be his wife. Although it seemed strange that she had been around on her own all day. She looked far too young for him, too. But then it was not a totally outrageous thought, he wouldn't be the first fortysomething to marry a twentysomething!

*

"Have you had a proper look at our room Sal?" Anna said as she stepped from the courtyard into the main 'sala' at the villa. "It's amazing."

"Look Sally the pavement comes right inside." Hamish commented excitedly at the koklaki flooring in the room. "It's as high as a house in here and there's an upstairs and a downstairs all in the same room!" He ran up the short wooden staircase onto the Lindian platform, behind the banister railing, plonking himself on a cushion on top of one of the wooden sofas. He came back down, then dashed up the longer narrow staircase that ran up the side of the room, throwing himself on to the small mattress at the top. His mother watched him with her heart in her mouth. "This is my bed," he said.

"I love all the wooden panelling and it is so cool in here, the walls must be very thick."

"I think it's cool too Sally." Hamish said. Anna and Sally laughed.

The kids had showers and then pottered in the courtyard. Sally and Anna settled down to a cup of tea and a chat.

"So what did Will say about Lou then?" Anna asked.

"Not a lot."

"He must have said something."

"I haven't told him yet." Anna raised her eyebrows enquiringly. "Well there's not really anything to tell, is there?"

"I just thought you might have mentioned it. What if you bump into him when you're with Will?"

"It's no big deal. It was a long time ago and really, what is there to mention?"

"Come off it Sally, it meant a lot to you at the time."

"Maybe at the time but like I said, it was a long time ago. You were the one with the big holiday romance."

Anna stopped her questioning immediately and put on her 'that's the end of that conversation' look, changing the subject. "Do you remember that outfit I made out of Tesco bags?" They both laughed.

"How can you make an outfit out of Tesco bags?" Jo shouted from the doorway.

"Well, Mrs. Big-ears, use your imagination" said Sally, annoyed that she had been listening.

"I used two bags, Jo. I cut the bottom off the first one, which became a strappy top. For the skirt I used another bag, cutting the handles off and then part of the bottom so that it fitted my waist."

"Cool!" said Jo.

"It was clever how it just fitted. I don't think I'd manage to get into one now!"

"You can get 'bags for life' they're quite big Anna."

"Thanks for the tip, Jo."

They chatted for a while reminiscing about their previous visit. Anna had fallen ill on their last holiday and had had to spend a day or two in the apartment. They decided that she must have some kind of allergic reaction to Lindos.

Hamish – In the courtyard

I don't actually need anybody to watch over me. I think that Jo is in the kitchen. Mum and Sally are talking again! Boys are much more interesting than girls; they always find exciting games to play, or things to see. Jo's not bad for a girl, but Will is the best, I wish he was my dad. Sally said she saw a lizard in that wall, I think I'll go and have a look for it. I'd better get my shoes first; this floor is a bit lumpy for my feet. These flip-flops of Jo's will do for now. If I was a lizard, where would I go? I think he must have gone in that little hole near the bottom. If I move a few stones he might run out.

Donkeys! I can hear the donkeys. I'm off to see, no one will notice, I'll just stand in the doorway, if I can get this great big door open. Hhhhuuerr! I did it. Hiya donkeys! You're my favourite, Mr. Chocolate Brown in the front, you're just like the one Mary and Joseph went on. Hey Mr. Stick Legs, watch they don't snap! What are you doing Big Belly Bunter? Why have you stopped? He's stopped to see me! Oh no don't have a poo there! . . . Ha! . . . He had a poo, he had a poo! . . . Ha, ha, ha, ha . . . Mrs. Donkey at the back, don't tread in it! . . . Ha, ha! . . . It's steaming! What a hot poo! . . . "What are you doing Mister?" he shouted out to the man. "Oh I don't believe it, mummy won't believe it! He's sweeping it up" he muttered this to himself, but laughed out loud again . . . "Ha, ha, ha, ha, ha, ha! . . . You need a pooper-scooper, a really big pooper-scooper! . . . Ha, ha, ha! . . . Don't forget to wash your hands!"

*

It was the sound of laughter that halted Sally and Anna's conversation; lilting, melodic chuckles drifting in the window, Anna immediately recognised it as Hamish.

"Where is Hamish?" Anna asked, dashing to the small high window in the room, but her view was a panoramic one of the sea, it was impossible to see the street below.

"Jo, where's Hamish?" Sally shouted "Isn't he with you?"

"No!" came back the reply. They bumped into Jo on their way outside; she was just titivating the supermarket carrier bag outfit that she was now wearing. "I've been busy."

"We can see that now."

Anna stopped at the large door leading out to the street, smiling she gestured for Sally to take a look at Hamish. There he was standing in the street, his little body rocking back and forth with laughter. Flinging his head back with his mouth open wide, then curling forward and stamping his foot, he pointed at the donkey which had obviously just left a steaming deposit on the pavement. What Hamish appeared to find funniest was the fact that the poor old man had to sweep it up.

The donkeys and the donkey man became a focus for Hamish. Left to his own devices for any length of time he would sit on the steps to the villa waiting for the train of donkeys to pass on their way up to, or back down from the Acropolis. He pestered the donkey man whenever he saw him.

*

Will was enjoying this time alone on the beach. It was quiet and cooler than earlier. He was surprised that Algie had been asking his advice about women. At least he got the impression he wanted his advice. He'd been doing one of those hypothetical 'if you were approached by an attractive older woman when you were only sixteen' lines. Will had told a story about when he was nineteen, stressing that the woman had been much older, but certainly was not attractive; he'd been frightened to death. Will had been surprised to hear that Algie thought he might also be frightened to death, but that he quite liked the idea – "if she was attractive of course," he'd added. Algie had gone for a walk leaving Will dozing and contemplating the different outlook he and his son had. Algie just seems so much more confident than he himself had ever been, he'd always got on very well with women, but it took a long time for him to feel really comfortable with a woman in an intimate sense, particularly if they were very attractive. On the other hand, Algie, for all his hang-ups and minor insecurities was really very confident to the point of being cocky, although Will knew to a large extent this was all 'front'. He fell asleep picturing the kind of woman he would like to be approached by.

When Algie set off on his walk along the beach, there were plenty of people left for him to scrutinize. If he was honest with himself he was looking for Mel; the whole incident had been so unreal he was beginning to think that maybe he had dreamt it. He often fantasized about women he might meet and today's encounter had fitted in fairly well with one of his fantasies . . . but he knew that it had really happened, as ridiculous as it may have seemed. Wrapped up in his fantasies he was oblivious to anything going on around him on the beach. When he got back to Will he spotted a woman leaving who looked very much like Mel – but with more clothes on. Screwing his eyes up did not help; he just couldn't quite see well enough to be sure.

For a while he just sat by a sleeping Will, watching the pathetic excuse for a game of football going on. *Call themselves footballers? They're just too hot-headed to concentrate long enough to conduct a game of football,* Algie thought. Bored by the shambles he saw before him, his attention turned to the crowd; this consisted of three girls sitting in the vicinity, roughly along the edge of the imaginary pitch. One girl in particular caught his attention. She was clearly Greek; *she just looks Greek* Algie thought; then spent a while trying to work out what a Greek look really was. He decided it was rich tones in dark curly hair, wide arching brows and a strength that he could not describe. This girl was all those things, but unlike the other girls he'd seen she was extremely sweet. He decided that this was maybe due to her slightly large front teeth which gave her that cute chipmunk look, or possibly it was the sprinkling of freckles across the bridge of her nose and her cheeks, but primarily because she was so incredibly tiny.

"You do go to extremes Algernon!" said Will, who had been watching his son for a while.

"What do you mean, Oh Wise One?"

"Well, earlier you were considering the advances of older women, now you're after some poor innocent child."

"Firstly, what I said earlier was hypothetical; secondly here's no harm in looking and lastly, and most importantly you're forgetting I am a child."

"Yes, but only when it suits you." He tapped his son's shoulder affectionately. "Come on, let's go! We'll be getting in trouble."

8
2002, DAY 1 – Bedtime, The Villa

Both tried to get out of the bathroom door at the same time and they clashed in the doorway. Will jostled to get through the doorway, so Sally did too and they pushed through together. They both made a run for the bed. Will got there first, stepping up on to the Lindian Platform. Sally nudged him just as he threw himself on to the mattress like a child.

"Aghrr" Will cried, clutching his back.

"Sorry." Sally said unable to stop the giggles.

"I think I've done my back in."

"Well you shouldn't play daft games," Sally said still laughing. "Let me look at it, where does it hurt."

"I'm sure there's nothing to see . . . You could scratch my back though." Will said, seizing the opportunity.

"It's too hot for back scratching. And anyway, I'll end up scraping all your sunburn off. Did you actually put sun cream on today?"

Will grabbed Sally. "Come on, snuggle up."

"It's too hot for snuggling."

"We better get somewhere with air-con then." Will suggested. He gently bit Sally's shoulder.

"'Ey, no biting!"

"It was just a love nibble."

"I don't need nibbling, I just need the love." Will took hold of her hand as she rubbed her shoulder. He kissed her thumb. "What are you doing?" Sally said, snatching her hand away.

"I just kissed your thumb!"
"That's weird because I couldn't feel it."

They lay still for a while, intertwined, their sheet still neatly folded at the bottom of the bed. Noisily the extractor fan buzzed through the open bathroom door. Sally settled, comforted by the warmth where their bodies touch. She began to drift towards sleep.

"What's best, a kiss that you can't feel, or a bite that you can?" Will said.

Sally smiled.

9
2002, DAY 2 – Lindos Beach

Sally

The sea before me, as flat as a lake; tiny waves making their way up the gentle slope of the beach, breaking with the enthusiasm that I feel in the baking heat of the afternoon sun. An outcrop of rock on my right, forming a natural conclusion to the beach, rises sharply to the white walls of the village, then higher still to the Acropolis above. In places, I can just make out the winding donkey path that forms the main route from the village to the top. The semi-circular beach sweeps beneath me from the rocks, carpeted with people, intermittently protected from the sun with the all-too-regimented rows of parasols. I can hear laughter intermingling with the waves; the rhythmic patter of bat and ball gets louder and louder and is really annoying me. The children close by, splash me with the cold sea water, inducing gasps from me and shrieks in my head. I go through the visualization in my mind. Then, I give in. Birds overhead and a donkey braying begin to grate. The speedboat that momentarily interrupts the wave's natural rhythm moves my lilo across the water and I feel anything but relaxed. I slide my legs around into the water, so that my bottom folds the lilo in half. By stretching out my arms to hold the lilo flat, I can sit higher in the water. I use my feet like flippers to propel and direct me. Turning around, I panic. Lou is close by me in the water, playing with his children. I didn't want to meet him like this, but it's too late now to get away. My heart begins to race. I imagine his children being deafened by my heartbeat pounding through the water as they snorkel. 'Keep calm!' I tell myself. I pretend I haven't seen him; then he spots me. Pulling an 'it can't be you' face, he smiles warmly, and then sends the kids back to the beach. Whatever will I say? For a moment I wish that if I let the air out of the lilo it would jet propel me across the bay; but part of me wants to stay, just my curiosity. Sixteen years, where did they go. I suppose I've thought about him from time to time; firemen on the telly, holiday programmes to Rhodes, or when anyone mentioned Oxford. I've wondered how life has treated him. And now I get to find out! . . . or do I? It's like finding the missing pages from the end of a book. As he moves towards me, I make the most of this closer view, scrutinizing him quickly. He looks just the same, slightly heavier if anything, although more handsome than I remember.

Excited and nervous, Sally scolded herself for behaving like a schoolgirl at forty, then instantly felt frumpy.

"Ever get that feeling of déjà vu? It is you, isn't it?" he said, smiling.

"It-it is me." Sally stuttered the words out.

"Unbelievable . . . Didn't we meet exactly here the first time? . . . Astounding!" he said. "It's good to see you." Reaching forward as he spoke, he touched Sally's shoulder gently and kissed her cheek. She had an urge to hug him, but in swimwear it seemed far too intimate.

They chatted in a hesitant, stuttering fashion, Lou never seeming to recover from the shock. They made promises to go for a coffee to catch up on sixteen years, but made no firm arrangements. Lou caught sight of his son putting sand into somebody's bag so he made apologies and dashed off.

Sally ploughed through the water back to the others and settled down to sunbathing.

"So?" asked Anna.

"So what?" Sally replied.

"What did he say?"

"What did who say?" piped up Jo.

"Sally's just met up with an old flame!"

"Thanks for that Anna." Sally added sarcastically.

"Well?" said Will.

"Which one is it?"

"God, what is this, twenty questions? It's that chap over there, with the snorkelling children."

"He looks nice Sal!"

"Thank you Jo. That's his good looking wife there . . . well, she was there a minute ago!"

"What did he say?"

"Not much. Married, three children, same job, still lives in Oxford."

"Pretty boring then, 'ey?" said Algie.

"Exactly. Now, can I get back to my sunbathing in peace, please?"

*

Algie was keen to stay on the beach again. He had detected an atmosphere brewing amongst the others and did not want to be part of any arguments. He had a feeling that his father would stay down with him for a while. When he asked him, he was not as keen as he'd expected, but he agreed to one quick game of footy when the beach had emptied. Algie's theory for the evening was to get involved in the football game with the locals, so that hopefully the little Greek girl would notice him.

Things went to plan, up to a point. He managed to get into their game; the little Greek girl showed up and took her seat with the other two girls; the problem was that he played football like a clown. It was almost as if his feet had grown three inches in minutes. He began to focus on the girl and her reactions – the more she appeared to be laughing at him, the worse he played. The worse he played, the more she seemed to laugh. *'Oh well, at least she's got a sense of humour'* he thought. He did not think that things could get any worse – until he spotted his father chatting to the girls. *'Emergency!'* he thought and feigned an injury over a non-existent tackle. Will had noticed. He left the girls and ambled over to collect his limping son.

"Thanks very much Dad!"

"What for, Son?"

"I was being sarcastic."

"What have I done now?"

"Showing me up – chatting to the girls!"

"You don't need me to show you up; you were doing a pretty good job of that all by yourself."

"It was the sand . . . Anyway, what did they say?"

"We were just chatting."

"Withos youros brilliantos Greek . . . os."

"One of them speaks reasonably good English, actually."

"Which one?"

"The little one. Her dad is a DJ and her mum's family have a restaurant in the village. She works there most evenings."

"Oh." Algie didn't dare say anymore.

10
1986, DAY 2 – Lindos

Any mist left hanging about from the night before had burned off in the early hours of morning sunshine. On the previous day, the sea and sky fused, the join made indistinguishable by the haze and heat, but today the clear blue sky stretched from the back of Lindos village over and round to a sharply defined line where it met the sea. This infinite expanse of blue was broken only by the serpent-like trail from a holiday jet that was long gone, whipped into a wispy 's' by lofty breezes.

Across the bay, the Pallas beach continued the curve of the main beach. The slither of brown land separating the sea and sky appeared to be moving, as a stream of people walked from Pallas beach along the jetty to board a boat for a day trip to Rhodes Town. The main beach was still fairly quiet, but with a trickle of people arriving from three different directions, it was not long before the sun beds were full. Their late arrival yesterday meant that Sally and Anna had spent most of the day on towels in the sand. Today they were up early. After calling into a shop for beach mats and sun tan lotion, they were positioned on their sun beds ready for a serious days sunbathing. Both of them had books, and every intention of reading them, but the intense heat quickly coaxed them into dozy submission, laid without a care in the world. Almost.

Sally was torn. Being part of a large family, she had always compared herself to the others and somehow just never seemed to measure up. This left her with a complex about her body. It wasn't all bad – people had always said that she had nice legs and she knew she was slim, but her perception of her bottom was warped and the idea of baring her breasts in public left her in turmoil. She had not really bothered about it yesterday, knowing that she had to take it easy on her first day in the sun. Today she wasn't quite sure what to do. She was beginning to feel like some kind of freak; looking around the beach she could not see anyone else with their top on. She just couldn't bring herself to do it. Eventually, mortified but driven by her fear that people would think that she was strange, she lay on her front undoing the straps at the back of her bikini top – that was okay, she could handle that. Within twenty minutes she was starting to burn – it was time to turn over. Sally turned over and removed her top, then covered her face with a hat to shield it from the sun, but also so that she did not have to look at her chest. This was perhaps done with the reasoning of a three year old who thinks that they cannot be seen when they hide behind their hands and can't see the person in front of them. For just fifteen minutes Sally Bailey bared her breasts to the world, it seemed like forever; gripped by her anxiety, Sally could not relax; her senses became heightened by the stress – her body flinching in an overreaction to the minute messages it received when an insect or small particles of sand landed on her skin. She tried to take her mind off it by studying the inside of the hat. Weaving the fibres in her mind she completed the production process in no time, it was simple! She turned her attention to colours, comparing the cream of the hat with the blue of the sky visible between the lattice. After a short while she could stand it no longer; peering out from under the brim, the sight of these two fried-egg-like objects perched on her chest was enough to convince her that fifteen minutes was in fact a life time of breast baring – never again did Sally show them to the world. She spent at least another fifteen minutes contemplating the evidence to back up this decision. She considered the idea that things seem more exciting when you cannot quite see them. Then when she noticed that the Greek women never go topless she became content in her decision and thought little about it after that.

"Tu ghandred drachma pleece."

Anna rolled over on to her side, propping her head up with her hand under her chin. Her hair, thick and the colour of straw, hung in a shaggy shoulder length perm and large cornflower-blue eyes gazed out from under the mop of hair. Her face, broad with a square jaw and high cheekbones, looked warm, friendly and proud – like a lion. Sally always said she should have been a Leo, not a Cancerian. Holding the other hand up to her eyes to cut out some of the glaring sun, she squinted up at the young man casting the shadow.

"Sorry?" Anna looked puzzled.

"Tu ghandred drachma, for san bed pleece." He spoke slowly; his voice harsh with an air of arrogance. His face never softened.

The sun radiated out around the silhouette of the man in front of Anna. In her mind she likened him to Tarzan – it was the large bulging thigh muscles – her subconscious mind took over, she smiled and there was a brief hint of a flutter in her eyelashes. "Sal, we need some money for the sun beds." They paid the gentleman. He nodded sharply without smiling, put the hundred drachma notes in a large leather money bag hanging just below his stomach, then moved on to speak to the people at the next pair of sun beds. His body almost hairless and extremely shiny had clearly defined muscles, big legs, broad shoulders and a deep brown tan. Wearing the tiniest of swimming trunks, he had a certain 'he-man' look. "He's got a big pouch, don't you think Sal?" Anna whispered, as they both continued to examine him somewhat furtively.

"He's not my type," replied Sally, pulling a face.

"See you later, Fillipos." The girls on the next sun beds said, clearly impressed. He strutted off down the beach; it was a frog-like strut, his knees and feet thrown outwards, obviously developed to allow him to walk quickly in the deep soft sand; his beach sandals flapped loudly against the soles of his feet.

"I think I've just gone off Mr. Fillipen-Floppos!" Anna said, and turned back to her sunbathing. Sally watched him for a while; he did not stand any messing – those who could not pay were thrown off the beds.

It was getting to the hottest part of the day now and so people sat huddled under the parasols trying to escape from the searing heat, others found respite in the sea. Sally nipped up to the kiosk for sandwiches and drinks, whilst Anna rearranged their sun beds so that they could sit out of the sun for a while. Sally returned in an excited state, a big smile on her face, practically throwing the food and drinks at her friend.

"Guess who I've seen?"

"Mr. Fillipen-Floppos with a smile on his face?"

"No."

"You'll have to tell me. It's not someone from home is it?" Anna asked, giving in quickly.

"Bruce from the restaurant. He's a bit further along the beach with his mates. I saw him at the kiosk."

"Bruce from the restaurant?"

"Yes, Bruce from the restaurant last night!"

"Ah yes! I know who you mean." She hesitated. "Just remember Sally, he was also on the beach last night and it looked like he was with someone to me."

"You never said."

Sally went quiet. Anna often withheld little snippets of information, which she strategically dropped into a conversation later knowing they would cause maximum hurt; this infuriated Sally. It was ages since she had seen anyone that she really fancied. She always seemed to end up in one-sided relationships and so was understandably getting apprehensive about making any first moves. She felt miserable suddenly. Picking up her lilo she went into the sea to cool off. Anna lay oblivious to any upset she may have caused.

'Why does she do that? She must have known that I would want to know if Bruce was with someone. How come I didn't notice? I was watching him the whole time . . . well almost, there were a few distractions. I don't understand why she does that. Maybe she was making it up, to put me off. But then why would she want to put me off? Maybe she just doesn't think.' Sally was lying on her back on the lilo in the sea. She heard something land in the water just by her and immediately after, felt the shock of the cold spray. *'Stupid kids, I wish they'd go and play somewhere else'.* She was aware of somebody collecting whatever it was, and so she paddled with her hands to move farther away. *'I suppose the fact that Bruce is on a 20S holiday should tell me something! He's obviously out here for a bit of fun; what is it they say, Sun, Sand and Sangria? No that's Spain. Sun, Sand and S . . Sex . . . well someone got some last night didn't they. I don't know how people can sleep with someone they've only just met.'* This

time the splash was bigger and an arm almost knocked her off her lilo. Her face got splashed with the salty sea water – she hated that. Sliding off the lilo into the sea, she turned to face the kids, ready to give them a piece of her mind. But there in front of her was Bruce.

"I'm really sorry" he said. He grabbed the Frisbee and went back to the game. Sally was left standing in the water looking dumfounded. '*Why didn't you speak? You just had your big chance and you blew it . . . mind you, I don't think he even noticed me.*' She climbed back on to her lilo, but no sooner had she got back on, then it happened again.

"Look, I'm really sorry" he said. And this time he was very close . . . and smiling; but smiling with a questioning, guilty look. Unfortunately he couldn't stop himself from laughing. Sally's heart sank. He straightened his face and spoke again. "My mate's idea of a joke. Honestly, I'm really sorry." He spoke with a deep, soft southern English accent. Sally felt as if they were laughing at her. Her mind went blank, but eventually she managed to smile.

"Oi, Beany!" He threw the Frisbee far out over the water.

"That'll keep him busy for a minute. How long have you been here, not long judging by your tan?"

Sally found it incredible that he could be so rude when he'd only just met her. He continued to smile, so she presumed he was not intending to be too malicious. "We've just arrived – Wednesday, this week. What about you?"

"We've done over a week now. Watch Beany, he's almost back! He'll be worn out; I bet he'll want to stop." He whispered this to Sally, as his friend got nearer.

"Let's call it a day Lou, I'm whacked!" Beany shouted across to his friend.

"He's so predictable!" Lou said.

"It sounds like you know him very well." Sally said managing a smile.

"Too well, I say!" Lou replied. Sally smiled again. "Right I'll leave you to your floating, don't strain yourself. Maybe see you later."

"See you."

'*Lou*' Sally thought. '*My new Bruce is Lou.*' She watched him go back to his friends. He was tall and well built. Sally thought he had lovely legs. The lads jeered as he re-joined the group. Sally supposed that she would not stand much of a chance with him. She stayed in the water thinking about him until Anna came out to see her, by which time her skin was going wrinkly.

11
1986, DAY 2 – Lindos

Manolis Estathio stood chatting in the entrance to his restaurant. He had spotted Anna and Sally further down the street, so kept an eye on them without appearing to lose interest in the conversation with his friend. He prided himself on his ability to do this and saw it as one of his skills. He always said he could tell if anyone had any news for him by the way they walked; he could entice snippets of juicy gossip from everyone and he always knew who was making eyes at his son or daughter in the restaurant – one of these girls was, he was sure. Yes, they would walk past, but they would be back. He smiled at them, bidding them a good evening and just as he predicted they kept on walking.

Manolis was ready for them on their return. "A table for two?" he smiled, his arm gestured for them to go through. The restaurant was much quieter than the night before, so they were a little surprised when he handed them over to Vasilis, who put them at an extremely small table, tucked away in a corner at the back near the kitchen again. They accepted this at first thinking that there must be a large party coming in. But no one arrived. To make things worse, every time Vasilis walked through the door to the kitchen and passed their table he accidentally nudged Anna's shoulder because the gangway was so narrow.

"Excuse me!" Anna said, trying to get his attention. "Excuse me!" she repeated louder.

"One moment please."

They waited a while but he did not come back to them. When he finally appeared Anna tried again, fluttering her eyelashes. "Excuse me!"

"Yes?" Vasilis stood in front of her, as he said the word he thrust back his head in a tutting fashion. He looked very serious.

"Could we move to another table?"

"Sorry?"

"Could we move to another table?"

"Sorry, I no understand. You ready to order?"

"Could we . . . . Oh, Yes, yes, OK!" Anna said, giving in. They gave him their order and sat quietly, things didn't seem quite so funny tonight. Anna went off on another rant and they both considered leaving, but neither said. He was soon back.

"You want fizzy water?" he asked.

"Yes, please" said Anna, still unable to stifle a smile. "Two."

Their drinks and meals arrived very quickly. Vasilis brought them on a large tray then made a ceremony of presenting them on the table. Firstly two large glasses, much larger than the night before, full of ice; then two large bottles of water dressed up with serviettes. Sally and Anna glanced sideways at each other. He placed their meals on the table. Anna was given one large plum tomato. It was peeled and it was warm. Carefully placed in lines radiating out from the tomato were pieces of penne pasta. On Sally's there was a little pile of cherry tomatoes, encircled by a single strand of spaghetti. They had to smile, but Vasilis didn't.

"Enjoy your meals" he said and was gone.

"A joke, and there we were thinking he didn't have a sense of humour!" Sally said, laughing.

"Good joke." Anna said sarcastically, poking the tomato.

"Maybe it's stuffed."

"Well I'm certainly not going to be, after eating this!" She poked it again, then looked inside a tube of Penne. "Oh Sal, I'm starving."

"You'd better get eating it then."

"Maybe we could go somewhere else for a main course."

Vasilis appeared as if by magic. "Problem?"

"No . . . thank you." Anna could not help but flirt. Vasilis bowed and went back into the kitchen. "What should we do?"

"Just eat it Anna. We can sort something out later."

"Crepe?"

"You're not wrong!" Both girls giggled. "Do you want a drink? I'll be mother." She picked up the water bottles wrapped in serviettes.

"Yes please."

"Anything wrong ladies?" Vasilis was right behind Anna.

"Erm, this is fine . . . actually, is this a starter? It's not what we were expecting."

"Not what you were expecting?" he raised his voice. Both girls watched in disbelief as the young man flipped. "Is this a starter?" he shouted. Sally thought how fortunate it was that the place was quiet. A wide manic grin spread over his face and then he began to spout endlessly in Greek. The girls just looked at each other.

"What do we do now?"

"I don't know." Vasilis was still shouting and began pacing backwards and forwards. Sally decided to speak to Manolis and got up out of her chair, Anna was right behind her but Vasilis invaded her personal space to the extent that she just sat back down again.

"So you say he brought you the wrong meals and then when you told him, he went mad?" Manolis tried to assess the situation.

"Yes" confirmed a worried Sally. They made their way back to the table. Manolis watched Vasilis for a minute. At this point Vasilis had stopped shouting, but was banging his fist on the table in front of Anna, the large bottles of water wobbled precariously.

"These young ladies are a little worried."

"Yes?"

"They say you have gone mad." Manolis spoke in English but then added in Greek. "You do a good impression of a mad man my son!" They both began to laugh.

"Thank goodness for that! I actually thought he'd gone mad."

"I'm not convinced that he hasn't." Sally looked scared, but they both laughed in relief once they realised that it was just an elaborate joke. Vasilis suggested that next time they don't understand the menu, they should just ask and he would translate. He moved them to another table out near the front, but not before Anna photographed their meals. He waited on them attentively and threw in a bottle of wine on the understanding that they could buy him a drink later at the Kamiros disco.

12
2002, DAY 3 – The Villa, Lindos

After a night of intermittent sleep, Sally woke up in Will's arms. Dozing she savoured the moment. The donkeys clip-clopped past on their first trip of the day. A door slammed and the patter of tiny feet in big flip-flops was heard across the courtyard, followed by the rattle of the key, the latch and creaking as the door opened. Then the donkey bray from Hamish the donkey impersonator.

"Who said we'd need an alarm clock!?" Will joked.

"Hamish, get yourself back in here now!" Anna shouted from one of the other rooms.

Sally came out of the shower. Standing in front of the Lindian platform she considered what to wear. A mixed array of clothing had accumulated on the rail at the end of the bed. She put on espadrilles, readjusted the towel on her head and then peered out of the door into the courtyard to gauge the weather. She noticed that Will was not singing and that he was soon out of the shower. They dodged each other in a well-practised fashion, adapted within the last couple of days to their new surroundings.

"So who is this old flame you saw yesterday?" Will said 'old flame' in a way that told Sally that this was not leading up to one of his little jokes.

"Lou. I've told you about him before."

"Remind me."

"I met him here sixteen years ago, had a very brief holiday romance and haven't seen him since 1986."

"And you just happened to bump into him in exactly the same place sixteen years later?"

"Yes." She thought for a while, pulling on a pair of shorts and brushing the knots out of her wet hair. "I know it sounds like too much of a coincidence, but it is a coincidence. She flung her head forwards so that her hair was hanging upside-down, scrunching the hair in her hands. But . . . for all we know he might have been coming back here every year since 1986. Lots of people go back, time and time again, to the same place. People often even have the same weeks off each year."

"You've obviously thought this through."

"Not really, although, since I bumped into him I have considered the odds of us meeting up again. It would be interesting to know whether he's been back since 1986. If he hasn't, that's amazing. Aren't there people that have gone out of your life that you've thought about? Wondered what happened to them and what they're doing?"

"I suppose so." They continued to move around each other in the small space between the bathroom and the bottom of the bed, finishing hair, brushing teeth and reloading pocket contents. "Are you going to see him again?"

"I might do." She was about to say they were going to meet up for a coffee but thought better of it. "Is it a problem?"

"No, that's fine." He changed the subject. "What do you want to do today? Do you fancy Rhodes town?"

"Sounds good to me!"

*

In the centre of the village two well know local figures passed in the narrow Lindian street.

"Stupid fool" muttered Manolis.

"Oaf" replied the other.

*

'Our rest day' Anna called it. Hamish did not like the idea – he thought that it sounded like the time at nursery when they make you go to sleep when there are too many interesting things to do. Hamish pestered her relentlessly to let him go with the others, but she did not give in. She knew that the Macfaddyan family should have some time on their own. They stayed close to the villa. Hamish was miserable – apart from when the donkeys went passed. It was shaping up to be anything but a rest day.

*

"Where do they get all the sponges from? They're all over the place." Jo asked, as they walked through the market in Old Rhodes Town.

"The sea," replied Will.

"I thought so."

"They grow in the sea."

"So there are sponge catchers?"

"That's right. Well, catchers . . . harvesters. To the Ancient Greeks, sponges were known as Zoofitan meaning half plant/half animal . . . and it takes up to twenty years for a sponge to grow big enough for use in a bath."

"How do you know all this stuff?" Jo exclaimed.

"I just read it on that sign there." Will pointed.

*

Anna quickly threw beach necessities into a bag whilst Hamish stood out on the step watching donkeys. She was enjoying having Hamish to herself. Her fingers caught the stone in her bag. She turned it over and over in her hand, smooth, silky and endless. She decided that it would be better if they spent the afternoon on the beach at St Paul's Bay.

*

The lad's desire to keep wandering was wearing Sally out and Jo was getting a bit crabby. She grabbed a table at one of the restaurants in the square. Algie and Will kept walking.

"Go get your Dad, Jo – I'll save the seats."

"Be a bit more adventurous, you can have pizza any time." Will said.

"Yeah, but I know if I get Pizza that I'll like it," replied Jo.

"You won't starve if you don't like it."

"Well what should I try?"

"Spanakopita?"

"What's that?"

"A kind of cheese pie, cheese and spinach. Or you could have Swordfish or Souvlaki, which is a bit like kebabs or Kalamari which is squid."

"Yuck! Can't I just have pizza?"

Will sighed in resignation. "I guess so, Chuckie."

*

After playing in the sea for almost an hour, Hamish fell asleep on Anna's knee. They were both in the shade of the parasol. Anna did not dare to move. She decided that it was probably best if he had a little sleep, because he was going to bed so late at the moment and always woke up early no matter when he went to bed. The logistics of eating the remainder of her lunch with Hamish on her knee seemed impossible – without waking him. She watched a young girl swim across the bay towards the jetty. It was a bit of a struggle but the girl managed to climb out of the water, up on to the jetty. Anna noted that she was sitting where she herself had sat with Vasilis. A man seemed to come from nowhere, he stood on the jetty by the girl. He was athletic and tanned, with long dark curls. Anna froze and her heart began to race. *Surely it can't be him?* It was too much of a coincidence. The couple walked along the jetty together hand in hand. Anna came to her senses; the young man was twenty at the most. Vasilis must be in his forties. '*Long dark curls – he's probably bald!*'

*

The MacFaddyans sat engrossed in the menus – well all except Algie, he knew what he wanted, Swordfish. His face dropped and his jaw fell open as the waiter walked towards them. The waiter stood, pen poised over pad, glancing in turn at his customers. Algie could not take his eyes off his nose, he was sure he had never, in all his life, seen a nose as big as that. Fleshy and hooked, Algie had seen prettier plastic false noses. He noticed the short black hairs that grew out of the end, they wiggled as he twitched impatiently, nostrils flaring. Glaring at Algie, who dutifully ordered, the waiter turned to take Sally's order. Algie watched as the nose swung round over Will's head. "Duck!" he shouted to Will. They all looked at Algie, but there was no way Algie was going to explain that one.

They waited. "Erm . . . any chance you have Duck?" Algie asked. "Actually no, don't worry I'll be fine with the swordfish" he quickly added, hands raised apologetically. His face turned crimson.

Once the waiter was back in the building they all pounced on Algie. "What was that all about?" "What are you talking about?" "Algie . . . !"

"Well didn't you see his nose?"

"You meant duck down didn't you, Alge?" Jo said laughing.

"Yeah, I thought he was gonna knock Dads head off. It was massive."

"Your nose isn't what you'd call tiny." Will said.

"I know that . . . I have character . . . character, not cartoon character. Shush he's coming back."

"I think it's you who needs to shush."

*

Anna contemplated the chances of Sally and Lou meeting up again after all these years and it crossed her mind that fate may be playing a hand for the second time and that this time she better not mess with the hand of fate. If she was honest with herself, before they came out here, she had considered the fact that she could quite possibly bump into Vasilis. She imagined him running the restaurant, married, hundreds of children. But seeing Lou really was a big surprise.

*

"Why do you think some people have such big noses? What's the point of a big nose?"

"I'm not sure." Will contemplated the question posed by his son.

"And are people with small noses disadvantaged? Like Jo for instance, her nose is stupidly small, how does she get enough air!"

"My nose isn't stupid!" Jo exclaimed.

"Stupidly small I said, not stupid. Maybe small people don't need as much air."

"It's the . . ."

"Shush you two! I don't think Algie meant that your nose is stupid, just that it is small. Think about your question Algie, what might a long or small nose do?"

"Do you know?"

"I have theories, but you have a go first."

"Is it to do with sensitivity to smells, like if you have strong smells around you, you need a longer nose to keep the smell away, so in countries that have lots of spices they need longer noses? Or, maybe you need a longer nose with more sensors in it to pick up subtle smells."

"Well my theory is that it might be to do with a long nose warming up very cold air, or moistening very dry air in very hot climates." Will said.

"Noses run in our family." Sally said and they all laughed.

"Sally may have a point. We tend to have noses like our parents."

"I know, I was meaning like genetics. We did that stuff at school about eye colours. You know how blue eyed people can't have brown eyed children."

"In fact blue eyed people can have brown eyed children. Genetics is a complex subject, so they have to simplify it for GCSEs."

"Don't put doubt in my mind Dad, I have to pass my GCSE yet!"

"Let's leave it at that then."

"Thank you, I thought I was going to die of boredom." Jo said.

13

2002, DAY 3 – The Villa, Lindos

Fumbling up the three creaking wooden steps on to the platform, Sally was careful not to wake him. The regular rhythm of Will's breathing told her that he was asleep. The old lamp close to the bed threw out just enough light to illuminate her way and formed a circle of light on the bedside table that reflected up on to his face. *'People look so angelic in their sleep'*, she thought. She studied this face she knew so well. The lines on his face had softened but the scorching sun had highlighted the shape of them around his eyes and brow. He is a natural smiler; the extreme corners of his mouth turn up easily in all but a few of his facial expressions. Even sleeping he appears to smile. *'How handsome he looks'* she thought. But he had hidden his most dazzling feature, those piercing blue eyes.

It was a sticky warm night – too hot for body contact, but she felt the need to touch him. His body formed a zigzag mound down the middle of the bed. Lifting the sheet that partially covered him she slid in beside him, carefully placing the sheet back over them both. Moving up closer to him, her knees tucked in tightly behind his, their legs like jigsaw pieces slotting into place. He stirred and moved up to her but did not wake. His bottom sat neatly in her lap and she relished the vast skin contact made when her chest and stomach met his back. She wrapped an arm around him and nuzzled her face into the back of his neck. Sometimes she feels as if she can't get close enough and wants to unzip his skin and step right in. She hugged him gently, taking in his own special smell, but just a minute of close contact seemed too long in the heat; her lips formed a kiss in the back of his hair and she slowly moved away so as not to disturb him.

14
2002, DAY 4 – The Villa, Lindos

The following morning Anna had woken up ridiculously early again. Hamish, having won his battle to sleep on 'his little bed in the air' in the main 'sala', left Anna sleeping on the converted wooden sofa on the Lindian platform. This was in actual fact very comfortable, but although they had closed the shutters out in the courtyard, the tiny windows high up near the ceiling had no curtains and the sun shone through! Anna, naturally a morning person, had no problem with this. The last six years with Hamish had been good training for early rising. In fact Anna hated to lie in; it felt like such a waste of a day. This was probably due to the fact that her parents had had a small village shop; for as long as she could remember, they had always got up early to prepare the morning papers for delivery and to re-stock the shelves.

The small wooden steps creaked too loudly as Anna climbed up to look at Hamish. She could not believe that he was still asleep, especially when the room was so bright. She decided that it was best not to disturb him. When she stood still on the bottom step she could hear him breathing steadily; it was enough to convince her that he was asleep and not standing at the front gate looking out for donkeys. *He must have worn himself out this last couple of days*, she thought, smiling to herself, knowing how much Hamish was enjoying the holiday. After being unwell for a couple of days, Anna was feeling much better, so after half an hour of tiptoeing about in the room she decided to nip into the village and get some freshly baked bread rolls and yoghurt.

Sally appeared very soon after Anna had been in the bathroom. Anna joked about it being early in the morning for Sally, but she did not seem to find it funny. She was quiet and snappy, but said she wanted to go down to the shop too.

Hamish was dozing when he heard the gate bang shut. His eyes sprang open. He scanned the room, without moving his head. He remembered where he was and abruptly sat up in bed. Crawling to the end of the bed in a nifty kind of way, he could see his mother had gone; he knew this because her bed had been made. In a flash he was down the wooden steps and into his shorts and T-shirt. He made his way across the courtyard – he did this awkwardly, as he had forgotten to slip on his shoes. By the time he'd got the gate open, Sally and his mother were nowhere to be seen. The rest of the shutters were closed so he knew that the others were most probably still in bed. He helped himself to juice in the kitchen and the one remaining yoghurt in the fridge, which he preceded to stand and eat just by the drawer where he had got out his spoon. He heard the donkeys whilst he was scraping out the last little bit in the bottom of the yoghurt pot. Hurling the yoghurt pot and the spoon into the kitchen bin, he ran, just as awkwardly as the first time but faster, to the gate. He caught the end of the train of donkeys, shouted his usual greetings to all his favourites, calling them by name. Yes, Big Belly Bunter and Mr. Stick legs were there, bringing up the rear. The young men accompanying the donkeys waved to Hamish, smiling and shouting 'mera'! After they had gone, Hamish noticed that one of the donkeys had left a deposit on the pavement *'as usual'* he thought. He looked about for the Donkey Man, but could not see him anywhere. Pacing up and down outside the villa Hamish was unsure what to do. He went back up the steps into the courtyard to check the shutters. No, they were still asleep. He put on his shoes and sauntered down the narrow street, a little bit further than he knew he should; peering down each street and into every doorway as he went, he saw it as his job to inform the donkey man of what was on the pavement. He explored a number of the small roads, each time returning to the house before he set off again. There! He spotted him down the street in his stripy shirt. Hamish ran to catch him up; but he'd nipped around a couple of corners before he managed to catch up to him. When the man turned around to see who it was shouting out behind him, Hamish realised that it was not the donkey man. He was taken aback by this and stood for a minute watching the man in the stripy shirt. His face looked thoughtful and serious, eyebrows knitted in a puzzled expression and his cheeks were rosy with the heat and running. Once convinced he set off back, but when he turned around he was not sure which direction he had come from – it was suddenly very busy and he struggled to see past all the legs and bags. Hamish panicked, darting backwards and forwards, tears springing into his eyes. It was at this point that he realised that he had also forgotten his hat – he was really going to be in trouble now!

His panic was short-lived. Once he found the ice-cream parlour he knew where he was. *'Strawberry or chocolate today?'* he thought, his recent worries melted. Nudging through the people queuing to look at the array of flavours in the glass case, he got in everybody's way. Hamish pointed at the one's he had already tried, and then considered which flavour he would choose later on in the day – he had already worked out that his mother would let him have an ice-cream every day, but only one. Flashing a smile to the ice-cream man he ran back up towards the villa.

Close to the villa he spotted the real donkey man through an archway which opened out into a leafy courtyard. Hamish went in.

*

Sally could feel her mood lifting. It had got worse, before it got better. The streets were very busy even though it was early and it was warm already. Heat and bustle always made her ratty. Considering this she wondered why she liked the place so much. Anna was always bubbly in the morning which got on Sally's nerves. Sally laughed to herself thinking about this. When she first began working in her early twenties, after leaving university, she had to get up at 6 o'clock each morning. Her and her sister had developed a routine whereby one used the bathroom upstairs whilst the other got breakfast downstairs. Then they would pass on the stairs as they swapped over. Sally would cheerily say 'morning' and her sister would grunt. They met ten minutes later by the back door, to walk down for the train. As the months went by, their routine became finely tuned to minimise contact. Sally used to find her sister's grumpiness quite funny. They would be half way to Leeds on the train before her sister 'came round' enough to make reasonable conversation.

Here in Lindos Sally laughed at her own grumpiness; that in itself helped her to snap out of it and Anna's high spirits soon made her smile. As they came out of the shop, a familiar face passed by. Anna nudged Sally and pointed. "Yorgos."

"He hasn't changed a bit!" Sally whispered. "No actually, he's better looking than he used to be."

"Do you remember that night, Sal – you and Yorgos?" Sally looked slightly puzzled. "It was the first night Vasilis and I got together. I'll never forget you in that bed the following morning!" Anna started laughing, stamping her foot as she laughed in a manner that Sally had not seen her do in ages – *that's where Hamish gets it from!* Sally was surprised by Anna's mention of Vasilis but her face did not reflect that. She remembered the night; it was the night that Vasilis played his little joke on them in the restaurant.

"When I said I would make up the foursome, I didn't expect to end up in bed with him!"

"You never could handle your booze though, could you Sal?"

"'Ey you, I wasn't that bad! I think someone spiked my drink that night. I remember we had a lot to drink in the restaurant – thanks to Vasilis! But it suddenly seemed to hit me when we got outside. Then that bizarre incident in the bar."

"What was that?"

"I remember feeling very happy and really drunk. I couldn't stop smiling or talking. I was attracting a lot of attention and I was quite enjoying that. I remember dancing – you know I never dance! There was that tall blonde English bloke who was really good looking – until you got close up to him – Paul, I think he was called. He kissed me, but he had big, podgy, soft lips; it was like kissing a half blown up balloon, I thought I was going to suffocate! I think he thought it was some kind of 'tongue skills' competition, because when he'd finished kissing me, I half expected that he had transformed my tongue into one of those dogs you make by tying together long thin balloons!

Then I couldn't get rid of him. He started to make me feel sick and I decided that I might just throw up if I didn't get some fresh air. I managed to give him the slip and went outside and sat at the top of some steps round the back of the bar. Then just when I was beginning to feel okay again, he appeared. His hands were everywhere! I began to get a bit angry when he wouldn't leave me alone, then he turned nasty and tried to drag me down the steps. He was holding my hand really tightly and all I could think was *'just hang on to the door frame and don't let go'*. I remember feeling my hand slipping and imagining him dragging me into some basement room. I have never sobered up as quickly in my life. Then my hand slipped, but it slipped out of his, and I managed to get away. It was as we were leaving there, in a hurry that we bumped into Lou."

"So, if we bumped into Lou, how come you were so happy to go off with Yorgos?"

"I wasn't 'so happy' but I was flustered from the incident in the bar – Lou was with someone else – I put two and two together and made seventeen, and then decided that I would go along with the Yorgos and Vasilis foursome, to help you out."

"Which I am very grateful for – well, I was at the time anyway." The smile dropped from Anna's face momentarily.

"Yorgos was very sweet but my god I felt terrible in the morning!"

*

Hamish

I saw him in the doorway, so I went in to tell him. He was watering the flowers in a garden that Mummy would like. It had lots of flowers and pots. I showed him what the donkey did. The house looked big but dark, mummy would like it – she says ours is too small. Then a man came out. He called the donkey man Zak. He took me up the steps and pointed to his boat. The donkey man called him Captain. He must be the captain of that boat. It was the big Yacht in the sea. The Captain said he would take me on the boat. I heard the donkeys again and ran out to see them. Everybody knows Zak. All the donkey boys shouted to Zak. The Captain didn't come out to see the donkeys. I sat on the steps outside the villa and Zak pooper-scooped the poo. When I went inside the others were just getting up. Then Mummy and Sally came back. I found my hat just in time.

15
1986, DAY 3 – Apartment in Lindos

Sally could not open her eyes, it was too bright and for a moment she panicked thinking that she had slept in her contact lenses. She screwed her eyes up tightly, trying to peep out; no, it was too bright. Her head hurt and her mouth felt disgusting. Had someone removed her saliva ducts in the night and replaced her taste buds with an old piece of leather? She had a real sinking feeling; her heart giving out a slow, strong thud in her chest and blood pounded the inside of her skull and the backs of her eyes. Anna was humming incessantly.

"Has he gone?" Sally whispered.

"They've both gone. Who do you mean?"

"Both?" Sally shuffled, trying to sit up in bed.

"Yorgos went ages ago, Vasilis's just gone."

"Anna, I can't move."

Anna sat up in bed and looked at her friend. "My goodness Sally, what has he done to you!"

"You and Vasilis were getting on alright weren't you?" Sally grinned.

"He – is – gorgeous!"

"And you're in love."

"Maybe."

"Nothing new there then."

"Sally, I mean it, this one is different; you know how you can just tell?"

"So people say. I'm not convinced."

"What, you're not convinced about Vasilis?" Anna looked hurt.

"No! About, just knowing when you meet Mr. Right – silly!" Sally hesitated for a moment. "Or just knowing when you meet Mr. Vasilis, righty?"

"Sally, are you still drunk?" Anna laughed at her friend. "You're very 'on the ball' for someone who looks so rough."

"You liked him then?"

"He was a real gent. He was kind and sexy and funny and intelligent and interesting . . ."

". . . and everything you could possibly want him to be!"

"Exactly. What about Yorgos?"

"My gos?"

"Sally, you're not funny."

"Oh, he was okay. He is quite a sweet bloke really, but not my type."

"He's rather taken with Eva, but she's not interested."

"Now you tell me! How do you know that I wasn't about to tell you that I'd fallen madly in love with him?"

"Intuition, or maybe the state you're in?"

"Anyway, he treated me fine; and I drank too much. That's about it."

"I don't think so. How did you get like that?"

"If you get me a bottle of water, I'll tell you."

"Sally!"

"I'm dehydrating here." Anna moved to get the water. "He is a really sweet bloke, we had a bit of a chat – although, his English isn't brilliant and he's not really my type."

"You said."

"When we all came back here, we'd sort of run out of things to say. Then, when you two went into the shower, to wreck it with your mad passion, he got big ideas. I turned over to go to sleep and his hand crept on to my arm – I panicked a bit realising that there was only a sheet between us."

"And all your clothes, by the look of things!"

"Well you can't be too careful, can you? I found that if I kept turning over I could wrap myself in the sheet so that he couldn't get to me."

"And you haven't been able to move since."

"Eventually I fell asleep. I just woke up now."

"Oh Sal, you do make me laugh. Did you have any sex education lessons when you were younger?"

"I don't remember, maybe. Why?"

"Well, when they said sheath, you didn't think they said sheet, did you?"

"No, I didn't . . . mind you, it worked!"

*

Once Sally had managed to unravelled herself from the sheet and get breakfast, she found that she was not feeling too bad after all; she certainly wasn't going to miss out on a day of sunbathing because of a mild hangover. Anna was being a total pain because she would not stop talking about Vasilis. But Sally supposed that maybe she was just a teeny bit jealous; not that she was after a Greek bloke – Anna could have them all to herself and Sally thought that she probably would, given the chance! No, that was unfair, because Anna was very faithful usually, once she'd captured the man of the moment. Sally was the one that really needed some romance in her life. She tended to be very choosy about who she went out with, she always set her heart on someone who wasn't interested – then hung on in there until she knew for certain that she had no chance and usually made a fool of herself chasing them. Sally was not one for 'one night stands' either – it was so far removed from what she really wanted. She did not understand the sex-for-sex-sake thing; she only ever slept with people that she loved and certainly only one at a time! How people managed to juggle two and three people at once she had no idea.

They made it down to the beach by mid-day. Sally spent the remainder of the day listening to her heart pounding the sand through her beach towel; it was a big, slow kind of a pounding; she half expected that her heart might just pack in under the strain. When she wasn't listening to that, she was half listening to Anna who was still going on about Vasilis. The rest of the time she was trying to keep cool, but every time she decided to go in the water, Lou and his mates were already in and she didn't want them to think that she was chasing him.

"For goodness sake Sally, go in the sea!" Anna urged her friend. "You'll be getting heat stroke."

"Well, will you come with me, so that he doesn't think I'm after him?"

"Oh, we wouldn't want him thinking that, would we?" Anna said sarcastically. "Good grief woman. Get after him! In fact, he's been looking over for most of the afternoon."

"You're making that up." Anna was making it up, but she had caught him looking over once.

"Well you just try it. Wait for a few minutes, then go into the sea and I bet he'll be out there in no time." Anna suggested. Sally did not really believe it but decided to give it a go, insisting that Anna came with her for a game of bat and ball.

The theory worked. No sooner had they got into the water then Lou and his mates were there disrupting the game. They tried to intercept the ball with the Frisbee and generally got in the way, finally resorting to rude comments and jokes, when their attempts to spoil the game failed. Sally was pleased with the attention but for some reason got it into her head that it was Anna that Lou was after. That was until he spoke to her.

"You've not been on your lilo today." Lou said.

"No, I'm suffering from lilo strain." She kept a straight face; he looked puzzled then smiled as he remembered. "Actually, the lilo has gone down and I couldn't be bothered to blow it up."

"Bad hangover day for Sally." Anna chipped in.

"Oh, you were drunk last night and I thought you were just ignoring me!" Lou said. Sally raised her eyebrows in surprise. "Sorry I couldn't stop, but we had a bit of an emergency – one of the lads ended up in hospital in Rhodes Town, when we eventually managed to get him there."

"And we thought you were on a hot date." Anna said. Sally sneakily stood on her foot under the water.

"No, I turned them all down to take him to the hospital!"

"Is he okay?" Sally enquired.

"He will be. I think he'll be spending the remaining few days of our holiday in the hospital though."

"Not long left then."

"No." He looked thoughtful. Then after a moment "Are you out tonight?"

"We should be, if I can muster up some energy. Actually, we'll be out even if I don't have the energy – Anna will have to carry me."

"Can we meet up later? Nikos at ten?"

"Fine," was all Sally managed to say, she was so excited.

*

"Only trying four outfits tonight, Sal?" Anna commented when Sally suggested she was happy with what she had on. She was wearing a pair of exceptionally small, black silky shorts, with a black and white sleeveless stripy top and a wide, black hipster belt.

"Do you think I dare wear these shorts, my bottom's hanging out?" Sally was standing balancing on the edge of the bath, trying to look at her bottom in the bathroom mirror; it was the only mirror in the apartment.

"You look great!" For once Sally believed her; she felt confident tonight and knew that she had to look good, as she was running out of time. Lou would be going home soon and she would never see him again. Anna combed her hair through. She slipped on her purple cropped trousers and a mauve sleeveless cotton shirt that buttoned down the front. Sally put on her black suede court shoes.

"No! You can't put them on!" Anna shouted in mock annoyance.

"Why not?" Sally rolled her eyes.

Anna thought before she spoke. "They're dusty."

"Yes, I'll brush them."

"Errm, you won't be able to walk far, again." Anna said trying another approach.

"I won't need to."

Giving in Anna said "but they make you look t . . . .er"

"What? . . . . Tarty? Were you going to say tarty?"

"Just a bit." Anna scrunched her face apologetically.

"Well if it's a choice between looking tarty, or accentuating my short stubby legs, I'm afraid I'm going to have to go with tarty." Sally was adamant. "Anyway, I think I have the confidence to carry it off tonight."

"You mean – 'you know you have the confidence to carry it off tonight'."

"Yep."

"Good for you – let's go!"

16
1986, DAY 3 – Lindos

They chose not to eat at Manolis' restaurant that night, but Anna called in to arrange meeting up with Vasilis later. "Come back at eleven," he'd said sneaking a kiss, "I should be able to finish early tonight." It was as hot and sticky as any evening, so they ate at a rooftop restaurant close to the main square. 'Ate' is probably the wrong word as far as Sally was concerned because she was so nervous and excited that she could not eat; Anna stuffed herself. The customary fizzy water was followed by beer after beer. Even though Sally knew it was not a good idea to drink on an empty stomach, the beers slipped down easily and the thought of eating the food made her feel queasy. By the time they were leaving the restaurant Sally was beginning to slur her words, but she was feeling far less apprehensive. The confidence the girls exuded worked like honey to a bee – Men flocked around them everywhere they went; the more the men flocked around them, the more confident they felt. Lindos was working its magic! The fact that neither girl was interested in any of the men, as they had set their sights on Lou and Vasilis, made them all the more attractive.

When they walked into Nikos as 9.45pm, Sally suddenly became like a gibbering idiot. Her mouth went dry, so she drank the first drink quickly. Anna told her to slow down, but it was too late, that drink had gone. As the long hand on the clock moved nearer to the twelve Sally had to go to the loo. Her nerves were definitely getting the better of her. She shook uncontrollably. She decided that she must look a bit like her Labrador who managed to wag every bit of her body when greeting those returning home. Sitting on the loo she managed to control the shaking, but then her teeth began to chatter. She did not understand what was happening to her, it had never happened before. She hoped that Lou liked Labradors with chattering teeth. The mental picture made her laugh and she managed to relax a little. If she did not calm down she wasn't even going to be able to make sensible conversation. And with that realisation, she felt sad. She hesitated for a moment collecting her thoughts. Her mother's words came to mind – *'Muck or nettles'* she thought. "Whatever that means!" she said out loud as she left the toilet, much to the amusement of the girls waiting. Smoothing the black and white striped top into her belt and adjusting her shorts in the corridor, she overheard conversation from the bar.

"So what do you do for a living, Anna?" Beany asked.

"I'm a pharmacist." Anna's Yorkshire accent was evident, but fairly subtle.

"We thought you sounded like a farmer," they said laughing.

"No – I work in Boots." Anna informed them.

"Yes, wellies I bet!" Beany shouted, laughing and snorting like a pig.

"No – you don't understand!"

"Eee bye gum. We understand alright." They said, still laughing.

"I give in."

"Ignore them." Lou said. "Where's your friend?" he asked Anna. "She hasn't done a runner, has she?" On hearing this, Sally stepped out into the room. "Here she is!" He said grinning broadly. Lou waved. Sally walked sedately towards him, trying to hide her drunkenness; she couldn't help but smile.

"Hi" she managed.

"Sorry, I've just realised that I don't even know your name!" Lou said.

"I'm Sally . . . Sally Bailey." The Bailey came out like Vailey.

"I'm Lou," he said, and rather formally, he took her hand.

"Is that Louis?" Sally asked.

"Aloysius, actually."

"Aloysius Actually? You're making that up!"

"Aloysius Reeve is my name. But please call me Lou." He was still holding her hand. "You have beautiful hands."

"Thank you."

"You could be a model . . . for gloves." Sally looked at him, and they both laughed.

"What do you do for a living, anyway?" Anna asked Beany.

"I am a fireman."

"What about you, Lou?"

"I'm a fireman, too. We all are." Lou replied to Anna.

"How many of you are there?"

"Six – all from the Oxford Station."

"Well, I hope that's not leaving Oxford vulnerable!"

"I think they will have us covered."

"Are all six in here now?"

"Yes, I'm Lou and this is Beany. That is Mac over there; he thinks he's a comedian." They all looked at Mac who was doing Spiderman impressions, darting in a crab-like fashion across the room. The girls recognised the man with the dead cat – he had a big mop of brown hair.

"Zippy is the bleached blonde." Beany took over introductions. "He is the man of the moment, the one the ladies can't resist."

"I'm resisting, I'm resisting!" Anna put him straight.

"Shammy is the little one – yes, a real life miniature fireman Shammy! . . . and the last one is . . . er . . . oh yes, Dane . . . who is actually English, the fireman that's not so hot, the man who is more like a woman . . . the . . ."

"Piss off, Beany!" Dane shouted across.

"Well, I'm Anna and this is Sally."

"We know Anna's a farmer. What do you do Sally?" Beany took over again.

"If Anna's a farmer, then I'm a librarian."

"What do you really do?" Lou whispered in her ear.

"I'm a designer."

"Of what?

"Fabrics."

"Sounds interesting."

"It is."

Mac, Zippy, Shammy and Dane moved on to another bar after Mac's Spiderman activities had dislodged a large vase which smashed spectacularly, throwing the bar into a momentary silence. Loud jeering followed the silence. They picked up the pieces, offered ridiculous sums of money and then disappeared.

The hour went quickly, suddenly it was eleven.

"I'm going to have to go." Anna announced.

"Why are you dashing off, the night is young?" Beany sidled up to Anna.

"Hot date Beany, never mind." Lou said.

They decided to walk down to Manolis restaurant with Anna, but Beany looked a little dejected. "I'll talk to you,

I'll even buy you a drink, but that's as far as it goes" he said. Anna tried not to laugh out loud. The conversation became stilted and when Lou took Sally's hand as they walked down the street, Beany disappeared.

*

The twisting Olive tree grew up through the stone built raised-bed. Strange, was it inside or outside? It was difficult to tell. Pots lined the courtyard, not one like another, the plants in them well tended. Lou told Sally about the Captains Houses that were built in the 17th century by rich merchant seamen to demonstrate their wealth and success. Although some of the early ones had been damaged in an earthquake, some had been rebuilt or built since the earthquake. All the floors in the building were koklaki. Beautiful patterns carved in stone, framed doors and windows, and the largest room was divided by a grand sweeping arch, the full height of the room. Lou led Sally around the majority of the ancient Captain's House, now called Tito's Bar. As they walked he imparted his new found historical knowledge. Eventually they settled under the Olive tree, in what they decided was definitely the courtyard. Rectangular, piped cushions covered the stone benches and more cushions of all shapes, sizes and colours lay against the wall behind. Sally was in her element, surrounded by these colours and textures – the organic flowing shapes of trailing plants, dark traditional wooden Lindian furniture contrasting with the stark white washed walls, flowers, simple vibrant plates hanging in festoons on the wall. She soaked it all in, half hoping to burn them into her memory, wishing she had her sketchbook, or a camera. People walking through wafted traces of cigarette smoke, then the perfume of the flowers, olive tree, Lou's aftershave, chicken and lemon. 'Just an Illusion' played in the background.

Sally and Lou got on well. She found him easy to talk to, although they struggled with accents for a while. This was exacerbated by noise in the bars, his deep low voice and Sally's inability to get her words out properly. She decided it was time to go back on to the soft drinks for a while.

Sally hadn't quite made her mind up about Lou, although she suspected that she had fallen for him 'big time'. His eyes were large, dark and soulful. Almost too dark, Sally could not decide on the colour. She felt as if he could read her mind when she looked into them. He had lovely teeth, his two front teeth crossed over a little at the front; his gorgeous smile lifted her. The thread of the conversation escaped her as she lost herself in his facial features. His nose was larger than average and had probably been broken at some time as it curved slightly to one side. He had his ear pierced, but there was no earring Sally was relieved to see. He had beautiful hands. His fingers were square, but long, with tidy nails. His broad shoulders were covered by a sleeveless T-shirt, quite high at the front, but not high enough to hide the hint of a hairy chest. Shorts and beach sandals completed his outfit.

"We are outside, look Sal – the stars are really bright." Lou pointed through the leaves of the Olive tree. Together they lay back on to the cushions and looked at the sky. As they did this the music changed to 'Wishing on a star'.

"How spooky is that!" said Sally. "Do you think the DJ can see us?"

"Romantic I'd say."

"Well . . . well yes, and romantic." Lou put his arm around her. Sally found him to be quite tactile; not all over her in a leery, obvious way; it was very subtle. Although, he did give her a big hug at one point when he'd made a joke at her expense. They felt very comfortable in each other's company.

*

It was like coming home; Vasilis Estathio stepped into the tiny old boat. He loved that boat, like a child loves a battered old teddy bear that is worn with parts missing, but comfortable and familiar. It would not be offended by his recent lack of attention, and in fact would welcome his attention on any terms. His neglect of this old friend was precipitated by a new acquisition – a larger, passenger carrying boat that fuelled his ambitions by taking him one step closer to where he wanted to be.

He'd never taken any girl back to his little old boat and had not planned to take Anna. Most of the girls he'd met recently were only interested in going to the clubs, drinking and getting whatever they could out of him in the restaurant. He had not figured out exactly why, but Anna seemed different. Earlier, as they had strolled away from the bars, Vasilis found himself heading towards St. Paul's Bay. He'd got it into his head that he needed to make an impromptu visit, just to make sure that the boat was still where it should be, and that all was well.

Unrolling the blanket he'd stuffed carelessly under the seat, Vasilis laid it with great precision over the bottom of the boat, sitting back on to the seat at one end of the boat when he'd finished. Anna sat just above him on the jetty to which the boat was tied. Swinging her legs over the edge, the tips of her toes just broke the surface of the water below. They sat in silence facing the water; Anna surveying the Bay and its backdrop; Vasilis, initially inspecting his surroundings to make sure that everything was as it should be, before losing himself in the rhythm of the waves, at last beginning to wind down after a busy night in the restaurant. Anna stretched her legs out over the boat and hooked her feet on to Vasilis shoulders; he did not seem to notice the water dripping off her toes on to his T-shirt – or did not mind. He took hold of her feet and used them to pull himself, and the boat, back close up to the jetty, thus allowing him to bring her legs further over his shoulders so that he could admire her feet. She had pretty toes, not spoiled by gaudy red varnish; they were neat, clean and natural. He turned around, the boat wavering in the water as he did. He kissed her feet gently; then, in one swift motion, he bit her big toe and pushed himself and the boat away from the jetty so that she could not get him.

"I had no idea there were piranhas in these waters." Anna said, smiling.

"Oh, you have to be very, very careful, you know. One woman, last seen heading towards St. Paul's Bay, was never seen again." Vasilis replied, using an oar to bring himself closer again. "They found her purple trousers hanging on the jetty." As he said this, he pulled the boat close in to the jetty by grabbing hold of the belt loops on her purple pants. He began to unzip them. Once undone, he helped her into the boat with him; the trousers dropped on to the blanket. Sitting her on to the low seat he kneeled in front of her, then threw the trousers back over on to the jetty. Still on his knees he slid between her long lean legs, moving them wide so that her feet almost touched both sides of the boat. He marvelled at her soft silkiness, stroking her legs, half feeling for flaws, but knowing he wouldn't find any having already explored every inch of her body the previous night. Anna was perfect, he was convinced. He could hardly contain himself. What was it about her that could do this to him? Tenderly he took her face in his hands; kissing her lips gently, but nibbling her bottom lip, desperate for more.

"I could eat you!" he whispered.

"And I thought it was only the piranhas I had to worry about!" Somehow, a picture of his mother sprang into his head and he couldn't shake it. His mother had taught him to savour his favourite meals, just because she was always so offended if he wolfed his food down. *'How is it you can taste this food, I prepare for you with love? You eat like a dog!'* He could hear her now. Of course no one placed restrictions on him, least of all Anna, but something told him that was how he should treat her. His hands moved down, circling her neck, and then slid under the mane of hair, lifting it briefly away from her shoulders. Noticing how the intensity of the moonlight accentuated her flawless skin and picked out the blondest streaks in her hair, he realized how conspicuous the pair of them must look to anyone walking into the bay, so he pulled her bottom off the seat bringing her down on to the floor of the boat. He loosened a rope and then used the oar to push them away from the jetty, before lying down by her side and folding the blanket back over them both.

Midnight feasts are always better in secret.

*

"You ready for a boogie?" Lou asked Sally. They were still sitting in Tito's Bar. The track 'Boogie Nights' came through from the bar area.

"Oh my God! What's going on?" Sally said looking surprised. Lou started laughing. "What?" she said again. Lou continued to laugh. "Did you ask them to put it on?"

"No!" Lou doubled over, holding his stomach as he laughed.

"It's scaring me now."

"No need to be scared – I recognised the intro! It gave me the idea."

"Oh!" Sally thumped his arm playfully. She felt a bit stupid.

"But do you fancy a boogie? Should we go down to one of the discos?"

"Which one do you want to go to? Anna and I like Paradise or Kamiros?"

"We can do them all if you want to. Should we get going?"

"Yeah." Sally replied. She was thinking that she may well need another drink or two before she did much dancing.

Lou took Sally's hand and pulled her up from the seat. He led her out into the narrow street. The air seemed cooler and the streets were darker in that area of Lindos. Sally thought it felt a little creepy, but realised it was probably just that she was feeling vulnerable. She linked Lou's arm and they walked quite briskly towards the Main Square. When they got to the Main Square Lou stopped.

"What's the matter?" he asked.

"Nothing, why?" Sally said.

"You seem to be struggling to walk."

"No, I always walk slowly – well . . . yes . . . actually it's these stupid shoes, they're killing me."

"Do you want a lift?" He smiled.

"I'd love a lift, but we might just cause a stir if you give me a fireman's lift through the village."

"What about a piggyback?" he enquired.

"A piggyback to Paradise?" Sally asked, thinking how good it sounded. Her feet were not feeling too bad really, but she fancied the lift.

"Come on then." He turned around and squatted down slightly so that Sally could get on his back; climbing up, she wrapped her legs around him; as she struggled to get on properly he grabbed her legs, thrusting her up into position. She put her arms around his neck, enjoying being so close to him. His body was warm and glistened with perspiration encouraging his hair to fall into waves in the nape of his neck. Her nostrils filled with the smell of Aramis, well, Aramis avec perspiration. Sally realised that because he was so tall it had disguised how broad his shoulders and back were – *Hunky!* The final scene in 'Officer and a Gentleman' sprang into Sally's mind except she knew that in the film the girl's bottom wasn't hanging out of her shorts.

"Don't you think we'll be frightening the people behind, Lou?"

"What do you mean?"

"These shorts."

"I'll have to get someone to take over, so that I can take a look!"

"Cheeky!" Sally said gripping his body harder with her knees.

"Yes, but not as cheeky as you are tonight!"

Her dusty shoes dangled from her feet, clinging for dear life to the tips of her big toes. After a while she started to lose her grip and began slowly sliding down his back. Shorts wedged between large buttocks are not comfortable and certainly not pretty, so she decided it was time to get down.

"I think I'll be okay now." Sally said and he duly put her down. As he turned around Sally thought he was going to kiss her – but he did not.

*

Anna and Vasilis lay cocooned in the boat rocking peacefully for what seemed like hours, talking. When they faced away from the lights of the village Anna was amazed to see how many stars there were, the sky was clear, the more she looked the more she saw. Vasilis teased her, suggesting that there were probably just about as many in England.

"I'm not totally stupid you know! I suppose it's just that I've never laid on my back looking at the stars before." Anna retaliated. Vasilis was astounded by this. He remembered as a very small child wandering down to the beach and climbing into his Uncle's boat. There he would lie for hours, looking at the sky and the Acropolis towering above him, going over the stories his Uncle had told him of the sea and times long ago in Lindos. The first time he did it the whole village had been out looking for him. It became a regular occurrence – but they always knew where to find him after that.

"My uncle always told me stories about an old Captain who lived in a big house in the village – I used to think he was talking about himself, but as I grew older I realised that it could not be him, otherwise he would have been about three hundred years old!"

"Why's this boat so special?"
"Who said it was special?"
"You don't need to say Vasilis, it's obvious."
"Michalis my father's brother made this boat a long time ago. He wasn't a fisherman or a sailor, he just loved the water. It always amazed him that boats could float, so he built one just to make sure that there was no magic trick to it. It was so exciting when he'd made it; we went out to

test it together. He didn't get it right first time but when he did it was unbelievable. We never went far, we didn't need to, he just had to be on the water. I learned to love that feeling. I listened to his stories and loved them all, but then I also learnt to love the silence and tranquillity too. Sometimes we didn't speak for hours and then we'd both speak at once!" Anna and Vasilis lay quietly for a while.

"I can just imagine you as a little lad sitting here with the old man."

"He wasn't old."

"No?"

"He never had the chance to get old; he died last year."

"Oh, I'm sorry." Anna was kicking herself; she should have sensed from the way he was talking that something was wrong. Vasilis said nothing. Anna looked over to the horizon where a vague flicker of morning was evident. *'Time flies'*, she thought – she didn't want to go back yet. She cuddled up to him. As she looked at him it wasn't difficult to see that little boy he'd been talking about. His beautiful brown eyes looked so sad; his shoulder length brown curly hair shone a rich warm colour in the moonlight. Anna looked up at the Acropolis towering above them and wondered how long it had been perched on the top of the rock. She was just about to ask Vasilis if he had ever seen photos of it in its original glory when she realised her mistake. She wanted to laugh, but now wasn't the time to be laughing.

"Do you know how long the Acropolis has been up there?" Vasilis broke the silence, he'd been watching her. Anna was amazed.

"Can you read minds?" she replied.

"Maybe. Why what were you thinking?"

"Oh, nothing."

"You have to tell me."

"I can't."

"You must."

"I was going to ask if you'd seen any old photos of the Acropolis when it was first built – but I realised . . ." Vasilis started laughing. ". . . but I realised what I'd said straight away, I'm just tired . . . Vasilis stop it . . . You think I'm stupid, don't you?"

"I think you're lovely . . . and funny." He kissed her. Then after a moment "I'll never forget all the things Michalis taught me, you know. I'm going to make him proud of me one day. He gave me his boat."

"So this is yours now!"

"This one's been mine for a long time. He left me his other boat."

"What's that like?"

"It's a lot bigger. I can carry about 20 people."

"Will you take me in it?"

"I'm thinking of running my first tourist trip."

"Brilliant idea!"

"That will just be the beginning. You know – he never left this island!"

"Wow."

"One day I will show the famous and wealthy people of the world this wonderful country, in the best way possible – by sea." Vasilis talked on, confiding in Anna about his plans and how he was going to get to where he wanted to be. It became clear to Anna that he was fiercely ambitious. He talked about his family – how they were too wrapped up in the restaurant. They never understood Michalis, he knew they would not understand him but it was clear that he would always support them; they meant the world to him. Vasilis made her laugh one minute and cry the next and every now and then there was a word he just could not put into English and suddenly it was like a game of charades. Anna was fascinated.

*

Paradise was quiet, but Sally managed to get topped up with a couple of drinks. They chatted to people in the bar and the barman told them about the film that was being made in Lindos. The actors were staying locally. Various people had spotted different actors and each had their own story to tell. A famous footballer came in with a dazzling woman, ordered champagne and sat in the corner.

They eventually bumped into Lou's mates in the Kamiros Disco. The lads jeered as Lou and Sally walked in; ignoring them they went to dance.

"Come on, I'd better walk you back." Lou said surprised to find that the nightclub was closing. As they sauntered back Mac caught up to them and entertained them with a string of impressions for a few minutes then ran off towards the beach.

"He's comical" Sally said, especially his 1970s hair!"

"You shouldn't laugh, he has cancer."

"Oh god, I'm sorry! How stupid am I? I should have guessed. The w . . ." she just managed to stop before she said 'wig'. Lou did not seem to notice.

"Well you weren't to know. It's actually a wig; he has no hair at all at the moment. His hair is naturally quite big and curly, but not as big as that. We booked the holiday as soon as he had the Doctor's permission, after his chemo."

"I'm surprised that they let you all take holiday at the same time, it must be a very big fire station."

"We're not firemen. We lied because we thought – you know men in uniform – women love it don't they!"

"Well I fell for it anyway!"

"Have I put you off now?" Lou grinned.

"Maybe," Sally said straight faced. "Well what do you really do for a living?"

"I'm a Chef. Look at these hands; do they look like the hands of a fire-fighter?"

"I noticed your hands before. You have nice hands. You could be a model . . . for gloves."

"Ha ha ha." Lou said sarcastically.

"That explains the piggyback too – bet you couldn't manage a fireman's lift!"

"You may live to regret that comment young lady!" Lou said, his face serious now. He turned to face her and before she had time to do anything he had thrown her over his shoulder. Sally squawked. Lou would not put her down until she was quiet.

They chatted all the way back; Sally had sobered up but still felt the same about him. He was gorgeous. As they neared the apartment the village lights petered out.

"It's just here on the left, this doorway. Thanks for walking me back." Sally said.

"My pleasure" he replied, grinning. He stopped Sally just after the last lamp before her apartment gate. It was very dark in the shadows; the moon seemed to have deserted them. Suddenly it crossed Sally's mind that her apartment was empty and what that might lead to – her mind was racing. Lou thanked her for a nice evening and gave her a peck on the cheek, a bit like you would to your grandma. *'A nice evening? I've just had possibly the best evening of my life, so far, and he thinks it was 'nice'!'* She must have hesitated, as he was looking at her with questioning eyebrows. Sally went blank. The silence shouted to her – *'Do something! Say something!'* *'OK, OK'* she shouted back!

"See you later," she muttered, turning towards the gate, her confidence getting the better of her.

"Hey! You don't get away that easily – don't I get a kiss?" He smiled and grabbed her back from the gate. When she looked up to him, his eyes repeated the question, but they whispered softly, so that she had to move nearer to make sure they meant what they'd said. As she moved closer something was pulling her in, as if she was hooked onto his clothes. He kissed her – long, slow, tender; then held her in a big warm hug. But she wanted more – he knew she wanted more. Sally lowered her eyes so that he couldn't see how much she wanted him. He kissed her again. His hand slipped downwards over her shorts, resting on her bottom. He pulled away from the kiss briefly, smacking his lips he whispered "nice bottom – I've been wanting to get my hands on your arse all night." Sally guessed that he had no idea what he was doing to her when he fiddled with the hem of her shorts. Against her better judgment, she considered inviting him in – the empty apartment beckoned. Carefully, he moved her against the wall, his feet straddling hers, his pelvis leaning into Sally's. She could feel him through her shorts.

"I want you" he said "but I have to go. We're up early tomorrow morning on a trip. I'll never get up if I don't go now."

"Ok." Sally said, disappointed. *'Fucking hell!'* she screamed inside. He kissed her again and said goodnight. For a moment it seemed as if the hook had disappeared. But as he stopped higher up the street and turned to wave, she realised that the hook was still there.

Sally watched him move out of sight, then she walked through the gate into the courtyard; the other apartments were quiet. The room felt hot, but she dared not leave the door open when she was on her own. She lay awake for a long time, partly due to the heat, partly due to the frustration, but mainly because her mind was buzzing. *Had she lost control for a moment back there?* She was horrified to think that if he had not gone, she could quite possibly be having sex with him right now – having sex, with someone that she had only really met today. *How could she even consider it? But then again, how could she let him walk away? Surely that's not the end?*

*

As the dawn broke an orangey-pink light filled St. Paul's Bay. Anna marvelled at how the boat naturally seemed to drift into the centre of the bay. She'd been worrying that the boat would drift out of the bay or on to the rocks before they noticed, so every now and then she would sit up to get her bearings, until eventually Vasilis could stifle his laughter no longer.

"Anna, the boat is tied up."

"It's not, I saw you undo the rope."

"That's just a small rope that I use to keep it tight up to the jetty while I get in and out. It's anchored in the bay." Anna pounded his chest, "Why didn't you tell me! I've been worrying about that for hours."

"I suppose I thought you might work it out."

"Vasilis! You must be absolutely convinced now that I'm not very bright. Anyway, I've had my mind on other things."

"Not just your mind." He said with a twinkle in his eye. The rapport between them was electric. They moved about each other comfortably and naturally, their thoughts in tune. For a while Anna had been lying on top of him in the boat. She sat up, straddling him. Vasilis, marvelling at her naked body, was understandably disappointed when she slipped on his white t-shirt. Having come out from under the blanket Anna had only just noticed that the breezes had picked up. Her nipples stood out through the thick white cotton and he traced the shape of her breast almost subconsciously as part of his admiration – no, the t-shirt did not do them justice. He slid his hands down her body where they rested briefly in the indentation of her waist, then slowly round to her buttocks. Enjoying the roundness in his hands, he lifted her bottom up carefully and entered her.

As they began to rock the boat, the rhythmic ripples radiated out in ever widening circles; they touched every part of the bay before reflecting back to the centre and the boat. Some of the waves slipped through the small gap in the bay moving on and on, out into the Mediterranean and beyond. The repercussions of these being felt for years to come, in many places, but eventually coming back to that same little bay.

It was like coming home.

17
1986, DAY 4 – Lindos

Sally was not aware of the blast of light that came through the door as Anna came back into the apartment after spending the night in the little rowing boat with Vasilis; but it was probably that light that disturbed her. She first became aware of someone fumbling their way across the room.

Anna tripped over the half empty suitcases pushed against the wall at the back of the room. She fell against one of the beds, nudging it across the floor; it moved with a sound that resembled fingernails on blackboard. Mumbling curses, she managed to get around the end of both beds but then started to sneeze; tiny little sneezes – mouse sneezes – over and over again, at least five every time. When she reached the window she opened the shutters a little.

"Anna, what are you doing? I am trying to sleep." Sally moaned.

"Well I need to see where I'm going, without falling over all this stuff on the floor."

"Can't you just put a lamp on?"

"The lamp on my side isn't working and anyway that would be a waste of electricity on a day like today. It wouldn't be a problem if there wasn't all this stuff on the floor."

"Are you insinuating that it's my stuff?"

"Well some of it is."

"And some of it isn't."

"Well if you would just shut your case there'd be half as much space on the floor."

"Or even twice as much."

"Whatever. There would be more room Sally."

"Ok."

"Well, you know I'm right."

"But if you just think about it for a minute, Anna, you'll realise that the suitcase is there, like that, because you borrowed my clothes. It was you who left it like that!" she sighed. "You come in here at God knows what time, screeching and banging about, and now you're accusing me of all sorts."

"Sally, it's after eleven o'clock in the morning."

"Maybe it is, but I'm tired."

"Oh yes, it's a different story now, isn't it? When I came in tired, you got up early, singing and clattering around . . ." Sally did not respond, so Anna carried on. "I hate wasting my holidays lazing in bed all day." Still no response. Eventually Anna shut up.

Sally dozed for a while, but woke up feeling really rough. She dragged her hand out from under the sheet and squinted at her watch – it was midday. Anna was nowhere to be seen. The chair outside the window creaked, and then there was a small trumpeting sound which ricocheted around the courtyard. Sally realised that it must be Anna and couldn't help but chuckle to herself – Anna never farts!

Sally smiled when she remembered her evening with Lou. She struggled to remember his name – *'Lou what? Begins with R . . . Lou R . . .'* No, her mind was blank. She started to panic a little. *'What if I never see him again? We made no arrangement'*.

Anna was sitting on her bed when Sally got up to go to the loo. They didn't speak. When Sally came out of the bathroom she tripped over the suitcase.

"I told you it was in the way." Anna said without looking up from her book.

"Yes. And if you'd closed it like I suggested I wouldn't have fallen over it." Sally retaliated.

"I don't see why I should tidy it up."

"Are we going to have to go over this stupid argument again?"

Anna did not reply.

"What should we do today?" Sally tried to sound cheerful.

"I don't know, beach I guess."

"Ok."

"You don't sound very enthusiastic."

"I don't feel very enthusiastic. I'm a bit tired, not feeling too good. Feeling a bit down, too."

"Again?"

"What?"

"It's always the same when you meet someone Sally, big high – big low!"

"Well you're one to talk. Just because you haven't hit the bottom yet."

"I don't know what you're talking about. I'm fed up of you being miserable, I'm going out." Anna said. She grabbed her beach bag and off she went.

Sally could not hold back the tears once she heard the courtyard gate close and she was sure that Anna had gone. *What a great holiday this is turning out to be!* She considered the prospect of spending the rest of the holiday on her own, eating out in restaurants on her own, sitting on the beach on her own. Sally guessed that Anna would be spending it with Vasilis.

*

Once out on to the street, Anna forgot all about Sally. The sun was shining, she was feeling good. She set off towards St Paul's Bay. She wanted to see it properly in daylight. A lone donkey stood in the field. *'How cute'* Anna thought. She could have sworn that it smiled at her!

At the water's edge she stood glancing around; the bay seemed smaller today. Looking up the steep rock sides towards the castellation of the Acropolis, she could see countless tiny faces peering down to St Paul's Bay and out across the village. Maybe the Acropolis would be worth a visit after all.

She sauntered across the beach hardly noticing the sunbathers, past the tiny church and on to the jetty. She sat down on the wooden planks, exactly where she had been hours earlier. The little boat was still there. She dipped her toes into the water – it was certainly warmer than last night. She thought about Vasilis for a while, but the argument with Sally niggled away at her. *There is someone for everyone,* she thought, *Sally will meet someone one of these days – I wish she would hurry up.*

*

Sally was in quite a state. The palpitations had started – a racing heartbeat that brought her to her senses. She realised that it was not worth worrying about having to spend the holiday on her own. She used the breathing technique that she had been taught and managed to slow down her pulse.

It wasn't just the argument with Anna that was bothering her; she could not help thinking about Lou. Half worried that she had in fact met the man of her dreams and he was just about to slip away from her, half worried that she was making a fool of herself, that it was all in her head and he did not feel the same way about her.

Not wanting to go to the beach on her own, Sally grabbed some lunch in the village and sat out in the courtyard reading a book.

*

The gate swung open and Anna walked in with her head down and shoulders uncharacteristically hunched. Sally glanced up, but Anna did not look sideways, walking straight into the apartment. Sally felt uncomfortable, but also annoyed with Anna. She heard sobbing coming from the room and so after a moment went in to see her friend.

"Don't worry Anna, we can sort it out." Sally said but Anna cried even more. "I know you didn't mean any harm. It doesn't matter," Sally rambled on. Anna howled, trying to get her words out.

"No . . ." she managed to say between sobs.

"No really it doesn't matter, let's just forget about it" Sally was not sure what to do or say.

"No, it's not that." Anna said eventually.

"Well what's the matter?"

"I've just been . . ." again the sobs took over.

"Where? Where've you been?"

"No! I've just been bitten by a donkey!"

"You what?" Sally scrunched her face. Anna showed her the marks on her torso.

"The donkey was out in the field on its own. I thought it looked really cute – in fact it smiled at me as I walked up there." Sally gave Anna a look. "No really!" She sobbed as she spoke, holding her side. "When I walked back it was nearer the road, so I went over to see it. My sandal strap came undone and I bent down to fasten it. Then the stupid thing butted me, I nearly fell flat on my face. As I struggled to get up, it bit me. It really hurts." Sally couldn't help but giggle. "It's not funny Sal."

"I know; I'm sorry. I can't help it – only you could be bitten by a donkey." Her face crumbled into hysterics and the great big horsy grin appeared.

"Oh, God . . . no . . . Sally . . . your scaring me!" Both girls laughed and cried at the same time.

18
1986, DAY 4 – Lindos

Anna and Sally were still laughing about the horsey grin and the biting donkey when they came out of the restaurant that evening. Things between them seemed to have settled down, but there were still little niggles. Anna kept going on about Vasilis. Sally liked him and thought they made a good couple, but he was Greek – *international relationships hardly ever work, do they?* Neither had been drinking after the heavy night before. They called in to the Kamiros disco, doing their usual – sitting in a corner out of the way, people watching. Sally got up to get them both a drink. Making her way around the edges of what seemed to be the dance floor, she weaved in and out. The music slowed and morphed into 'Live to Tell'. The people dancing merged into pairs. Someone took Sally by the hand, leading her into the mass of swaying couples. He embraced her, wrapping her up in his arms and whispered "I missed you today." As they moved to the music Lou told Sally that Anna was waving goodbye to her from near the exit. Sally let her go.

"I'll walk you back." Lou whispered.

"Haven't you just got here?"

"Yes, but I was only looking for you."

Sally was pleased but slightly nervous as she was stone cold sober. In the past, a drink or two had given her a little confidence and helped her to get rid of her self-consciousness. She checked and was surprised to find herself feeling calm and comfortable. Lou took her hand as they walked back; he seemed much more serious than the previous night, though he peppered the conversation with funny anecdotes from the day's trip. He talked about his girlfriend from home; they'd been together, on and off, for a long time but had split up a while ago.

Nearing the apartment she thought he might stop her at the gate, but he didn't, asking if he could come in instead. Sally hesitated a minute remembering that Anna would be in the apartment. She suggested that they should sit in the courtyard. He took the rickety chair out from under the table, pulling her on to his knee and they talked for a long time.

A Tom cat walked along the high wall surrounding the courtyard, if a cat ever had a swagger, this one did. He stopped, turning his head towards them; he was very vocal. He said his piece then went on his way.

"Go for it Tiger, there are plenty of ladies about for you." Lou said, laughing.

"Shhush" said Sally. The cat continued its strut along the wall and up on to the roof out of their view. Progressing along the roof and around the back he jumped down to join his lady and their litter; he fed the mother.

"What?" Lou said loudly.

"You'll wake the neighbours!" Sally said covering his mouth with her hand.

"Who?" Lou asked from under her fingers.

"The neighbours. There are three people staying in the apartment on that side and two in this one. And Anna of course, she'll kill me if I disturb her! No that's wrong, these two left on Saturday and no one arrived today so that one is still empty."

"Still empty?"

"Yes, look they've left the key in the door for the next people." Lou raised one eyebrow looking at Sally with a cheeky grin. His eyes invited her to go into the room.

"We can't do that!"

"Why not?"

"I wouldn't dare – what if someone arrives on a late flight?"

"If someone turns up, they won't be able to get in, will they?" Lou said jumping up from the chair taking the key from the door. He locked the door behind Sally, who against her better judgement had followed him inside.

Lou went straight to a bed at the far end of the room, switching on the lamp at the side of the bed. Sally was amazed how big the room was, much larger than theirs. The bed was clean and newly made, with just a single sheet folded at the bottom. Lou held her at arm's length; his look of appreciation and the warmth in his smile put Sally at ease. She battled to keep a lid on her negativity but the hook was firmly in place, she wasn't going anywhere.

"I can't believe I'm doing this, especially when I am absolutely sober." Sally said.

"That's nice." He replied, cradling her as he laid her carefully backwards down on to the bed. Lou began to peel off her clothes; Sally's initial reaction was an awkward one, she was not one to be taking her clothes off in front of people. He did not seem to pick up on that and eventually she began to relax. *'I may never see him again, what do I have to lose? He is gorgeous.'* By this time he had also taken off most of his own clothes. Sally had seen it all before (well most of it) on the beach, but she was still impressed. Before she knew it she was lying on her back on the bed completely naked. Lou lay on his side, by her. He traced the outline of the small white triangles where her bikini had been.

"How come you only went topless for twenty minutes?"

"I chickened out – I can't believe you saw that!" Sally said embarrassed.

"I don't understand you, you have a lovely body." Something about the way he treated her made her feel very special. Moving his leg over her body he sat up, straddling her, and as she moved to touch him he took hold of her wrists, pinning her to the bed, blocking any attempts by Sally to return his attention. Leaning forward he kissed her again. Sally smiled as she gave herself up to the moment wallowing in his admiration. She just lay there; she did not have to worry about doing the right thing because he would not let her do anything. The pleasure he gave her was marred only by the realisation that he was obviously very experienced. Adeptly he moved over her, nothing was awkward; there were no uncomfortable nudges, no limbs in the way. His lips traced the curve of her belly and nestled between her legs. "I'm gonna make you come." He glanced up at Sally. *'That will be a first'*, she thought, hoping there was no indication of the thought on her face. After some time she considered faking it – but surely someone so experienced would recognise her as a fake! She moaned. It seemed to work.

She knew his focus had changed when he began to manoeuvre her into a number of different positions; effortlessly they flowed from one position to the next. When he took her to the centre of the room, held her in his arms, lifting her so that she could rise and fall on to him, she wanted to laugh. The words *'Piggyback to paradise'* again sprang into her mind. In no time at all and much to her astonishment she found herself perched on the edge of a waterfall and within seconds she dangled like never before, facing the fall of her life. Lost in the accelerating rhythm, she let go, dropping downwards – it caught her by surprise. He didn't stop; she wanted to scream. Unable to contain her pleasure the moans turned into laughter as he thrust his final thrusts, then overcome, her laughter turned to tears. He put her gently back down to stand on the cool tile floor. As they stood together in the centre of the room in each other's arms Sally noticed that the sun was beginning to rise.

Within seconds Sally heard the courtyard gate.

"Ohmygod!" Sally whispered. Lou smiled. "The new people are here." Her face full of fear. She was moving frantically, picking her clothes up, trying to put them on.

"Oh I see!" Lou laughed silently. He grabbed his clothes and quickly switched off the lamp. Already they could hear voices outside the door.

"It's gonna have to be the window, Sal – I'll lift you up." Speedily they got in position under the window.

"Have you got the key?" Sally asked. It was an over pronounced mouthing of the words, rather than a whisper.

"Yes. Come on!" he said signalling her into his arms. He heaved her up on to the windowsill. It was a long drop, so Sally had to manoeuvre herself around so that she was sitting on the windowsill and then immediately before she jumped she remembered her shoes. "Just jump!" Lou said, his hands motioning as if to push her out of the window. After picking up the shoes Lou jumped too, just managing not to land on her. They ran up the street, dusting themselves off, laughing as they went.

"Wait! We need to go back in now and somehow give them the key."

"Leave that to me." Lou said, heading back. They went into the courtyard. After initial hellos, the new people explained that they had just arrived. They said that they had been told that the key would be in the door, but it was not there.

"It was certainly there earlier today." Sally said.

"I saw it too" said Lou, moving over to the door. He looked around the door checking the key hole and the door step.

"They haven't hidden it under anything have they?" Lou said pointing at a plant pot. As they looked at the pot he bent down near the door. "Look it's here, it must have dropped out!" He gave them the key.

"I can't believe we didn't see it there!" One of them said.

"I think we are just a little tired . . . thank you. Hopefully we can get to bed now, it has been a long day." They went in.

"Good work!" Sally whispered once the door was shut.

"I suppose we had better get to bed." Lou held Sally in a long embrace. "I've enjoyed tonight. See you soon" he said as he went out of the gate. Sally's eyes lingered on the gate that he had left ajar. Moments later he popped his head back around the gate. "By the way, your top is on inside out."

19
1986, DAY 5 – Lindos

Sally heard Anna humming as she came through the courtyard door. The shutters in the room were closed. When Anna opened the door the bright sunshine and the heat flooded in.

"Wakey wakey, lazy bones!"

"What time is it Anna?" Sally grunted.

"Oooo, heavy night was it? You must be poorly; you weren't even drinking last night. I think it's time you were getting up."

"What time is it?" Sally repeated.

"It's lunch time – twelve thirty to be precise; I've got some stuff to eat." Sally grunted again. "Good night last night, was it . . . where did you get to . . . back to Lou's?"

"I did go out, didn't I? It seems like I dreamt it."

"In a good way? . . . Oh, before I forget, we're going on a boat trip today and by the way, we've got new neighbours."

"Yes, I met the new neighbours, late last night."

"Apparently they're going to complain."

"Why?"

"Well, they reckon that the room wasn't ready? Bed not changed etc."

"That's terrible." Sally smiled. Anna looked slightly puzzled. "Which trip are we going on, we can't really afford it can we?"

"Vasilis is taking his big boat out; we're going to be his first customers. I invited Lou and his mates as well, this morning."

"Well that was a bit risky! What if things had not gone very well with Lou last night?"

"I asked him and he winked, so I presumed things went OK."

"Maybe he had something in his eye."

"Not judging by the smile on his face!"

*

It was too hot to be sitting on the jetty; at two o'clock the sun was at its hottest. Lou and his friends had arrived and were keeping cool in the sea. Sally was not quite sure how to be with Lou. He waved to her when she arrived and as usual his mates jeered.

Anna and Sally rolled their towels out on to the jetty. They were hoping to snatch a few minutes of sunbathing before the boat arrived, but it was not long before they started to burn. Anna applied more sun-cream and turned over. Sally rolled on to her stomach and peered between the wooden boards. The water beneath her lapped against the rocks, just the sound made her feel cooler. She was not sure that this trip was a good idea. She longed to slide her feet round and drop down into the water, but Lou and his mates were there; she could not face a possible rejection from Lou. She went over the previous evening in her mind, it made her smile. Everything had gone so smoothly, they were good together, they laughed at the same things. What could be wrong? She wished that she could spend time on her own with Lou. The lads were too close – Beany as usual, the instigator of yet another kind of game to find the fastest, the strongest, the loudest and invariable discovering the stupidest, the one prepared to go the furthest to prove their masculinity. Sally jolted out of her thoughts.

"Sal . . . Sally! Are you asleep?"

"No." She lifted her head and turned to face Anna.

"So, what do you think then?"

"Erm . . ." Sally didn't have a clue what Anna was talking about. "Sorry Anna, I didn't hear what you said."

"Never mind." Anna said coldly.

Their wait had stretched to thirty minutes and was just about becoming unbearable when Vasilis came around the corner in his 'big' boat – just in time. "Thank goodness for that!" Sally stood up straightening her hat and pulling her skirt back down to a respectable length.

Vasilis Estathio looked cheerful and totally in control as he manoeuvred his 'big boat' into a position that would enable his passengers to board. He was clearly excited, but his enthusiasm did not distract him from the job in hand. Everything had been thought through in detail, there was nothing he had overlooked. He spoke briefly to his passengers about timings for the day and safety information. Within minutes his passengers had embarked – he loved it when they called him 'Captain' even though he knew there was an element of jest. He stood proudly at the helm with Anna by his side, as the boat swung around the end of the jetty and pulled out of Lindos Bay – his dream was beginning to take shape – his first ever passenger boat trip. Today Captain Vasilis is aided by his crew of three: Yorgos, long-time friend of Vasilis, one night friend of Sally and worshipper of Eva; Dimitris, one of the boys who works with the donkeys and Yannis a waiter in a restaurant close to the Estathio's restaurant. Eva, Vasilis' sister and her friend Veronik are there for the ride and to make up the numbers. Eva has also been involved with preparing the food.

Sally joined Vasilis and Anna, she felt a bit of a spare part – uncomfortable talking to Lou and his friends, still mildly uncomfortable speaking to Yorgos and unhappy to approach the others with whom she had not spoken.

They moved around the corner, the mouth of the bay narrowed and was beginning to open out again. Vasilis talked animatedly about the Captain's Houses and briefly outlined the history, as he understood it, from the building of the Acropolis. Anna was just about to tell Sally about her request for photos of the Acropolis when suddenly Vasilis pulled back on the throttle and was out of the door – "Hold her steady!" he shouted.

"Of course, Vasilis." Anna said. She smiled to herself, pleased that he trusted her with such an important job. Then she realised that there was actually an emergency – he flew down the stairs, around the seating area and was at the side of the boat in no time, waving his index finger and shouting at the top of his voice to Dane who had just jumped overboard.

"Stupid! Stupid! Stupid! Get back in here, here is not the moment!" Anna didn't recognise the gruff voice coming from his mouth. He disappeared below deck momentarily before appearing with a ladder which he hung over the side. "How dare you break the rules of my boat?"

"Bloody tourists!" Yannis muttered and the rest of the crew and passengers watched in silence as Vasilis dragged Dane back on board.

"I don't think he'll do that again!" Sally failed to stifle a smile.

"Well, he should know not to jump off here; I knew he wasn't listening when Vasilis went through everything at the beginning."

When he got back to Anna at the wheel, he stopped the engine and went back out to speak to everyone. Unbelievably calm after such an outburst, he spoke slowly and clearly as he re-iterated the rules:

"For you to be having a trip with me, we must stick like glue to the correct times. Because my boat is extraordinary I cannot be letting you jump off just when a hat drops – plainly because it takes too long to be getting out the ladder again and again to be helping you back. Plenty, plenty more of opportunities will arise to jump into the water but I will tell you of the best times to be doing this."

Sally and Anna burst out laughing – amazed at Vasilis' bad English and by the confidence and diction with which it was spoken. Vasilis glanced across to the two standing at the heart of his ship, his eyes wide with surprise. Unsure as to how he might react, the smiles dropped from their faces. Then after a momentary silence the crew and passengers cheered and clapped. Vasilis bowed, warily.

"They want to swim Vasilis; they all got too hot waiting for the boat." Anna shouted back to him. Vasilis motioned with his arms to silence the cheering group, like a conductor quietens his orchestra.

"OK, OK! I drop the anchor; you can swim if you like. One moment please." He dashed down to lower the anchor and then fumbled in a picnic hamper, pulling out a bottle of Champagne. He waved the bottle at the crowd. "Later you can dive for champagne – but here is too shallow for the best champagne, I will find somewhere very, very deep for that. You have just five minutes. Lucky diving!" he shouted, at the same time throwing a small bottle of sparkling wine over the side. Again the crowd cheered and one by one they jumped ship, hurling themselves off as if it was sinking.

The challenge to dive for the bottle proved to be too much for any of them as the bay was too deep at that point. The boat became like a fairground ride, with people queuing to get back up the ladder so that they could dive back in again. Anna made an attempt to go for it. Sally paddled her way across the slimy wet floor and got herself settled so that she could sunbathe on the deck – although it was difficult to find a seat that was not soaking wet. She was still bothered by comments from Lou's friends which were not actually directed at her but she knew that they intended her to hear. She felt tired and slightly emotional. It was getting close to the end of Lou's holiday, she really hoped that they would have chance to spend a little more time on their own, but that was looking less and less likely.

Sally felt the sun move behind a cloud, then lifted her hat to find that the cloud was actually Lou standing between her and the sun. "Get that top off!" he whispered to her, then walked away smiling.

"It's against my religion," she replied, before pulling the hat back over her face. But she didn't pull it right back down. She peeped from under it, watching him walk gingerly on the slippery deck to the edge of the boat.

"Get ready for a celebration!" he shouted back to her as he stepped up on to the bench that ran along the edge of the boat. But as he lurched forward to jump, his back leg slipped backwards on the wet seat. His other leg went forwards, over the edge of the boat. The metal rim of the boat had sprung away from the wood, waiting like a mantrap to break his fall. It was a slow motion moment for Sally. There was nothing she could do as the knife edge of metal ripped through his calf. She jumped to her feet with legs like jelly and screamed for Vasilis and Anna. Eva came running with Vasilis – Anna was still in the water. Eva was calm and appeared to be giving clear instructions to Vasilis in Greek. Sally stood at the top of the ladder trying to get everyone back onto the boat, realising that he may be needing hospital treatment fairly quickly. Yannis and Dimitris took over the running of the boat. Yorgos and Veronik helped Sally to get everyone back on board. Within minutes the leg was wrapped tightly and the boat was manoeuvring sharply back around into the bay. The mood was sombre. Sally wanted to go to Lou but felt like she could not with everyone there. Yorgos swam to the jetty and quickly ran along the wooden pathway to get to the taverna on Pallas beach to phone for a doctor.

Eva sat close to Vasilis. In a voice, low and almost bitter, she spoke scornfully of Lou's behaviour and that of his friends. Her gentle face shattered by her harsh mood. Lou remained quiet, listening and watching. He reached out and touched her hand as she adjusted the bandage on his leg – "sorry" he said softly. She briefly glanced up at him and nodded sharply. Beany and Mac's continued attempts to lift the mood with humorous banter petered out. Anna fussed. Sally wallowed in self-pity. She knew now, that these would be her final moments with Lou. She must forget her wished for private goodbye.

Medical assistance arrived and assessed the damage – he would need to go to the hospital in Rhodes Town. Lou aided by two of his friends hobbled across towards the back of the beach. He waved and said a fleeting 'bye'. Sally's heart sank, her eyes filled with tears and the hook ripped through her as he walked away. She could not remember ever having to say goodbye to anybody knowing it to be the last time she would see them.

The remaining party members picked up their things.

"What is Lou's surname?" Sally blurted out to Beany, she felt stupid, but her desire to know drove out the question. Beany glanced at the others. "Lou Reed is his name" he said seriously, but the smile that followed said otherwise. The others were laughing as they made their way off the beach. Sally knew that he was lying but decided to let it drop. It really didn't matter now; she would never see Lou again.

"He's only got himself to blame." Anna piped up again.

"Who?"

"Lou. It was rather a silly thing to do."

"Shut up Anna!" Sally said in an uncharacteristically harsh retort. She lay face down on the sun bed and buried her head in her hands.

"He'll be fine Sal, don't worry." Anna said, finally realising that her friend was upset.

"Maybe he will, but I'll never see him again."

"I thought they were going tomorrow?"

"They are, but he's going to be at the hospital for a while, and if he gets back there's some big 20S group do tonight."

"Oh."

They lay in silence, each lost in their personal thoughts of the injustices of life.

"Maybe you'll see him tomorrow." Anna said after a while.

"Maybe. I hope so, but I think he's going fairly early."

"Maybe he'll get in touch with you when you get home."

"How?"

"Ring."

"He doesn't know my number."

"He could find it out."

"He won't remember my name and he doesn't know my address anyway."

"Can't you get in touch with him?"

"I only know his name and the town he lives in."

"Well that should be enough."

"Actually I think he lied about his name."

"What did he say?"

"Well Beany said he was called 'Lou Reed'."

"You know 'Lou Reed' is a rock star."

"Oh great!" Sally said sarcastically. "I thought I recognised the name when I heard it, can things get any worse?"

"It's not that bad, he only lied about his name."

"No, he swept me off my feet, had unprotected sex with me and then lied about his name. I must be such a crap judge of character. I'm probably pregnant or I've got AIDS."

"Don't be so hard on yourself Sal. It was an unfortunate time to say goodbye, he was clearly embarrassed about the whole accident thing."

"Yep, but I stupidly believed that he felt something for me."

"He probably does . . ." she stopped for a moment unable to think of something positive to say. "I noticed that Eva was being pretty harsh, she must have felt very disappointed for Vasilis."

"I suppose." Sally looked serious. "I have to say I felt sorry for Vasilis, he had obviously put so much effort into preparing his trip." Then she smiled briefly. "He was funny – his English is normally so good. I think we should help him with his next trip as there are one or two things he has overlooked."

20
1986, DAY 6 – Lindos

Sally slept very little the following night. Her mind went over and over the events of the previous few days and she could not shift her mood. She got up early and dressed quickly so that she did not wake Anna, then wandered down to the village. After calling in at one of the supermarkets for breakfast supplies, she perused the postcard racks in a number of shops, deciding to try on sunglasses that she had seen a day or so earlier. She had just about decided, one last try on. Standing on tip-toe she stretched to see herself in the mirror at the top of the rack. Yes they look fine. But as she took them off she noticed that someone else was looking at them in the mirror too, peering over her shoulder. She swung around to find Lou standing there.

"Hi" he said.

"I thought you'd gone!" Sally said.

"Any minute now!" he replied. His smile warm, his eyes looking at her tenderly. "I got my leg fixed."

"That's good" said Sally "What's the prognosis? Will it be ok?"

"It'll be fine!" Lou said. "It's a shame it had to end like that!" Sally wasn't quite sure which 'shame' he meant, but presumed that he meant the trip.

"Come on Lou, we've got to go." Mac called his friend from outside the shop.

"Looks like we're going, Sal . . . take care." He touched her arm and kissed her gently on the cheek. Sally managed a smile. *'This is the bit where you say something,'* she thought, *'don't let him get away.'*

"Bye" was all she managed to say through the tightening in her throat.

21
2002, DAY 4 – The Villa, Lindos

The two families congregated around a long table in the courtyard. Algie was quiet and a bit dopey, he'd already spent two minutes trying to put a pair of sandals on before he realised that they were Will's and two sizes small for him; then proceeded to pour milk into his bowl before he'd got the cereal in. The others had watched him covertly, laughing to each other. "He's not too good in the mornings, are you Alge." Will said affectionately, in the usual family manner of over shortening names. He managed an 'uh?' in reply, without looking up.

Hamish was re-arranging the small pots of flowers placed randomly along the bottom of the low wall that ran alongside the table. "Hamish you're going to have to go and wash your hands again now. Why don't you just get your breakfast, then you can play?"

"I've had mine."

"You mean you've had a yoghurt. I spotted the empty pot and spoon that you'd thrown into the bin; I thought you'd grown out of that trick. Come and finish your breakfast."

"In a minute, Mum!"

"Have you seen that fantastic garden just down the road, Will?" Sally asked her husband.

"Which one's that?"

"The Captain's house on the corner – as you walk back up from the shops it's facing you?"

"Do you know the Captain?" Hamish asked, butting in; he looked surprised.

"That's just what they call that type of house Hamish, there's no Captain." Anna laughed.

"There is, I've seen him!"

"Oh, right." Anna humoured him.

"He's pretty old then, Hamish, this captain you've seen?" Will asked. "They built the houses for the Captains hundreds of years ago."

"He's not that old."

"Do you think he's staying in the house on holiday, Hamish?" Sally tried to placate him.

"No, he lives there."

The others smile. "Well did he have a big beard?" Will continued, "Don't all Captains have big beards?"

"No." Hamish was confident in his reply. He moved a few stones near the bottom of the crumbling garden wall – he remembered that he had never found the lizard.

Sally had spotted the garden at the Captain's house the first time this morning as she and Anna had walked back from the centre of the village. She could not understand how she had not noticed it before. Sally knew nothing of plants and flowers; it was Anna who was the garden genius. Sally could paint flowers, making them look as if they were growing out of the paper, but had no idea of their names, the seasons and soils, or the animals that lived amongst them. The garden on the corner had almost enticed her in with its heavy perfume, its colours and textures, and the promise of cool shady areas.

Jo appeared at the doorway to her room. She had on a large yellow t-shirt of Sally's – she was wearing it like a dress. "Is it okay if I borrow this Sal?"

"I suppose so, Jo. I thought you had shorts on today?"

"I did have, but I changed my mind." She sat down at the table next to Anna who was wearing a yellow strappy sundress.

"If you keep changing your clothes at this rate Jo you'll run out ages before we go home and I for one won't be washing them for you!"

"Leave her, she's alright." Will jumped to her defence.

"I can't understand why she needs to change them so oft . . ."

"Leave her!" Will mouthed the words to Sally, clearly annoyed. Sally shut up.

Anna knew why Jo had changed her clothes; she'd noticed that every time she changed her clothes, Jo had disappeared and come back wearing something similar. She was always slow to get dressed in the mornings, waiting to see what Anna was going to be wearing. She had become like a little shadow, choosing to sit by Anna at the table, offering to help with washing up whenever it was Anna's turn. Sally did not seem to be giving Jo much of her attention. She seemed rather distant at the moment, Anna thought, preoccupied maybe; the appearance of Lou certainly seemed to be having an effect on her and tensions seemed to be developing between Sal and Will. Anna hoped it wasn't due to her and Hamish staying in the villa; she was really enjoying feeling part of the MacFaddyan family, they were definitely beginning to lift her spirits and she knew Hamish was loving it.

Hamish cajoled Jo into hunting for the lizard. After their alfresco breakfast, the adults had disappeared inside to clear away pots, tidy beds and make plans for the day. Algie reclined on his bed; the sound of his guitar seeped through the open door into the courtyard.

"The Captain owns that big boat in the bay. They think I'm making it up, but he does." Hamish told Jo.

"Oh" she replied.

"Everyone knows Zak."

"Who is Zak? Is he the captain?" Jo asked.

"Zak is the donkey man; he thinks the Captain's silly."

"Right!" Jo could not work out what he was talking about and was losing interest.

"Zak waters the Captain's plants."

"How do you know all this, Hamish?"

"I went to see the donkey man and he was watering the plants."

Jo decided that Hamish was making it up. "You'll be frightening the lizard if you talk so much, then it'll never come out."

"Mornings are best to catch them – Sally said."

"Is that lizards, Captains or Donkey men?" Jo asked. Hamish looked at her as if she was stupid.

In the kitchen, pots clattered. Anna, back to her bubbly self, had her arms buried in the sink up to her elbows; the front of her dress was soaking wet, but she did not notice. Will had noticed. He was quieter than sometimes. He dried the pots that Anna washed, wiping away the bits of food that she'd failed to wash properly. Occasionally he bit his tongue so as not to offend her, aware that he would not have put up with such sloppy washing up from Sal. When they were particularly bad and he thought he could get away with it he sneaked the odd pot back around to the other side to be washed again. Politely he answered Anna's questions about their trip to Rhodes town the previous day. Sally put the pots away; she had not spoken for a while. Anna had made various attempts to bring Sally into the conversation, but she remained miles away.

Sally turned to put the last pots away. "I think I'll do some post cards before it gets too late to send them."

"That's a good idea Sal. I'll do mine too." Anna added.

"I'm going to walk into the village if that's okay. I'll see if Algie wants to come." Will said.

"Fine. Aren't you taking the other kids?" Sally was hoping for a bit of peace and quiet.

"They're happy enough playing here."

"Okay."

"Oh, look what I've done!" Anna exclaimed. She waved her sleeves at them both. "I always do that – dip my sleeves in the washing up water without realising I'm doing it. If it's not the washing up water it's my soup, or jam that I've spilt on the worktop!"

"Life's a bit like that." Will said.

"It is, is it?" Anna said.

"You know it's like the extra things you gain in life, unexpectedly, when you're concentrating on something else."

"She's just a sloppy bugger if you ask me." Sally added.

*

Hamish peeped around the door. Both Sally and Anna had their heads down, busy writing. He did not go in but headed straight back to the gate. He was getting better at opening it and managed to stop it before it banged shut. Leaving it off the latch, he walked quickly back to the Captain's house.

When Jo nipped into the bathroom, Hamish had just gone up into the main 'sala' where Sally and Anna were.

So when he wasn't there when she got back, she thought nothing of it.

Hamish

Zak was in the garden. He was digging up a plant. He made a mess dropping soil on the path. The captain came in and told him off, so I started to sweep up the soil for him. Zak was really grumpy; he shouted at me and told me to go home, he tried to sweep me out of the gate. The Captain did not mind; he smiled and waved when I had to go home. Jo didn't hear me open the big gate back at our villa; she was listening to mum and Sal at the main 'sala' door. She shouted at me for sneaking up on her.

22
2002, DAY 4 – Lindos Beach

It was a sound they both recognised, but neither could work out what it was. An insect getting nearer and nearer? Pat – pat – pat – pat – pat, rhythmic and regular, not the bat and ball, but a similar sound. Something was different, not quite right. The pat – pat – pat intermingling with a pitter – pitter – pitter. Anna worked it out just before Sally and pushed herself upright in the sun bed.

"I don't believe it Sal, he's still here!" Anna pointed down the beach.

"Fillipen-Floppos! And it looks like he's been busy!" Sally replied. Following closely behind Fillipos was a small boy – same strut, same flip-flops, same tan, same hair and the same money bag – a mini replica, about a quarter of the size. Anna and Sally were beside themselves with laughter. Hamish heard them laughing and worked out who they were laughing at. He paraded past the sun beds, puffing out his chest, flapping his sandals and completed his impersonation with a frog-like strut. Being a similar size, with curly blond hair and pale skin, he was a vision of the boy – in negative! Will managed to grab Hamish, swinging him into the air, before he flicked too much sand accidentally at the surrounding sunbathers who were by now chuckling at the young entertainer.

"Hey, you'll be getting us thrown off the beach, young man!"

"It's not your old boyfriend is it Anna?" Jo enquired.

"Who do you mean Jo?"

"That man down the beach. He's not your old boyfriend is he, the one you had here years ago?"

"Where've you got that from Jo?" Anna asked slightly defensively.

"Oh, I don't know." Jo lied. "Didn't you have a boyfriend here a long time ago?"

"Well, yes I did, but . . ."

"Is he still here?" Jo butted in.

"I don't think so, Jo." Anna sounded weary.

"Do you remember that evening on Fillipos's bike?" Sally jumped in to save Anna.

"You mean when everyone was on the bike?"

"Yes, how many was it?"

"Well, Fillipos was driving. I was sitting on one knee and you were on the other. Vasilis was on the back. So four of us." Anna laughed.

"Fun times! He was wiggling all over the main square. It was a bit dangerous though."

"We didn't think about that at the time, did we?"

"So were you with Fillipos, Sally?" Jo asked.

"No." Sally said vehemently. "I was not."

"We were walking back up from the nightclub. Our judgement was probably a little blurred. Fillipos stopped to talk to Vasilis and ended up giving us a lift up the hill to the main square. No one was wearing helmets and we were all in shorts or similar."

"Yes, we must have been doing at least 4 miles an hour – that's why we nearly fell over."

"So, was Vasilis your boyfriend Anna?"

Anna smiled eventually, giving in to Jo's questioning. "Yes Jo, Vasilis was my boyfriend."

"Just think Anna, you could have married him and then you could have lived out here!"

"How do you know that I didn't?" Anna said. Sally and Anna exchanged glances, then giggled. Jo didn't ask any more questions.

*

At the end of another long day on the beach Sally, Anna and Jo saunter back to the villa. Hamish, who was also supposed to be going, was adamant that he wasn't tired and that he would not be grumpy tonight when they went out to eat late.

Jo was dawdling behind. Sally only realised that Jo was missing when she turned around on the steps of the villa whilst Anna was opening the door.

"Jo" Sally shouted, walking back to the corner. "Jo!" She spotted her hovering on the corner inspecting her camera. "Come on!"

"Coming," Jo muttered without taking her eyes off the camera. After hearing the door bang shut she looked up to check that Sally wasn't standing waiting for her and then furtively walked to the gate of the Captain's house. The gate was open partially. She pointed her camera between the gate and the gatepost and quickly glanced around her before pressing the button. She filmed for as long as she dare, pressed stop and then ran back to the villa.

*

Down on the beach the usual female football supporters were already in their positions on the sidelines. Algie's mind was in a spin. *'How am I going to get talking to her? How can I even get over to that side so I can speak to her? Maybe Hamish could help. If I can get him to run over there, then I could chase him. No, maybe I'll just walk around that way to the kiosk.'* Algie set off; it was obvious to anyone on the beach, including Will, that Algie was interested in the girls. As he approached them he became more self-conscious again, his legs becoming awkward and his feet sticking in the sand. "Hi" he muttered, but she didn't hear him. Coughing, he repeated it again. "Hi." She glanced up and half smiled but looked embarrassed, returning her attention to the game that was just starting. Algie hovered by the kiosk whilst he drank his drink, joining in the game as he made his way back.

Will recognised the newcomer that was playing tonight; it was Fillipos the sun bed man from earlier. Fillipos' son kept trying to get in on the game but kept getting sent away by his dad. It was obvious that Hamish had spotted him as he began to impersonate him again. Initially this was just for Wills benefit. But spurred on by Wills amusement he strutted across the edge of the pitch; he was careful not to let the Greek spot him, but some of the other players laughed too. Each time Fillipos turned around Hamish stopped, beginning again the second he looked away. Algie's little Greek girl began to laugh. Playing to the crowd Hamish made his way to the side where the girls sat. Watching him like a hawk, Will was at the ready. The girl laughed so much, pointing at Hamish and telling her friends, that Hamish ended up strutting up and down right in front of her – until he tripped! Will was on his feet immediately, but the girl was there first.

"You OK?" she asked him. Hamish lay face down in the sand. He pushed himself up shaking the sand out of his curly hair.

"Yes" he said with a cheeky grin. To the girl's surprise Hamish sat by her side.

"What is your name?" she asked.

"Hamish. What's your name?"

"Tatiani".

"Mummy would like that name."

Will arrived. "Is he bothering you?"

"No, he is very funny, he is a clown!" she smiled.

"He certainly is!"

"Is this what the donkey boys do when they aren't working?" Hamish asked Tatiani having recognised some of the players.

"Yes."

"Where do the donkeys go at night?" he asked.

"You like the donkeys?" she replied and he nodded. "Donkeys sleep at night; they are very tired with walking." She cocked her head to one side placing it on to her hands suggesting a pillow. Will noticed how different she was with Hamish, talking easily; she was clearly taken with him. Not wanting to drag him away too quickly from his new friend Will waited a moment before reaching forward to take Hamish's hand.

"Come on, I think it's time we were going." Hamish shuffled up close to Tatiani, reaching out for her hand instead.

"Not yet!" he protested. Will didn't push it.

"Let's go Algie!" Will shouted. Algie was there in a shot.

"Come on Hamish we'll have to go." Will repeated. Algie stretched out his arm to take Hamish's hand. Hamish took it.

"Bye Hamish." Tatiani smiled at her little friend.

"Bye bye Tatti" Hamish said as he got up.

As they left the beach Algie was quiet and looked thoughtful for a while. Eventually he aired his feelings. "I don't believe it dad, where did I go wrong? How come

Hamish got to sit with her and she even told him her name? She barely smiled at me."

"Hamish has an unfair advantage – he's cute."

"So am I."

"Well maybe, but he also poses no threat to her."

"Neither do I – I like her!" Algie protested.

"You know what I mean. Anyway, Hamish is on your side, thanks to him you know her name now."

Hamish had been listening. "She's too little for you Algie, she's more my size and she knows the donkey boys."

"He has a point." Will added with a wicked smile.

23
2002, DAY 4 – Manolis' restaurant, Lindos

The restaurant seemed to be basically the same, although memories had become a little frayed. The air conditioning was much better and the lighting too. Manolis sat on a chair to the left of the steps outside at the front of the restaurant, Anna could have sworn that was just where she'd left him – as she'd said her goodbyes to walk with Vasilis to catch the coach, sixteen years earlier. The emotions of that moment fought their way through the barricade she'd pushed them behind, washing over her, sprinkling tears in her eyes. She had never felt as happy to be with anybody. Anna ridiculed herself – *'nobody came close, did they? And you let him ruin every other relationship. You fool.'* Jo spotted the tears, asked awkward questions and clearly dissatisfied by the answers realised that she had better leave Anna alone – *it wasn't even dusty, for goodness sake!*

Manolis was busy with some other customers when they arrived. They were shown to a large table just inside the door, the waiters quickly altering the settings to accommodate everyone. Sally had noticed that Anna was nervous – she knew that Anna would be wondering if Vasilis was going to appear at any moment. When they both caught a glimpse of Eva at the kitchen door Anna became more visibly anxious. So to put her mind at rest Sally asked one of the waiters if Vasilis was there. He said he did not know anyone called Vasilis in the restaurant. "Vasilis Estathio?" Sally said. The boy looked puzzled –

'Vasilis?' he muttered with a flicker of recollection in his eyes, then nothing. 'No' he shrugged his shoulders. Jo made a mental note.

"Hamish!" Tatiani appeared from the kitchen door then dashed across the restaurant, patting the Ash white curls. Anna was quick to respond to the stranger. "Well Hamish, I think you'd better introduce us!"

"Oh, Mummy this is Tatti."

"Tatiani" she quickly corrected him.

"Yes – Tatiani, I bet you like that name don't you Mummy?" Hamish looked proudly at his new friend.

"Very pretty name Hamish. How do you know Tatiani?" Anna said.

Will chipped in. "We all met up at the football on the beach, didn't we Algie?" he attempted to bring his son into the conversation thinking he was doing him a favour. Algie's brain was definitely in gear, you could see it in his eyes, but he'd slipped the clutch – nothing came out of his mouth! Everyone looked at Algie who was getting pinker by the second. "W... Ye..." Then nothing! Again Will jumped in. "Hamish was entertaining the girls on the beach."

"What is he going to be like in a year or two?" Anna said in mock despair. Algie remained quiet for a while; once the attention had moved away from him, he began to relax again. Tatiani was taking someone's order towards the back of the restaurant, a little too far for Algie to really scrutinize her but it was good to get a look at her from a distance. *'God, she's cute!'* He found himself wanting to pick her up – physically pick her up and take her home. *'Yes, pick her up, carry her home and put her in a box! – Put her in a box? What are you thinking?'* He panicked; *'why would anyone want to put anybody in a box? I must be sick.'* He over analysed his thoughts, deciding eventually that, he wasn't some kind of murderer or someone with a strange fetish, it was just that he wanted to put her in a box like you would a doll, because she was so cute. Then he started to think about what else he could do with her if he took her home.

They all decided that they would have to have a Hamish 'rota'; he was as high as a kite, giggling, shouting out and dashing around the room if he was given the chance; if no one was watching him he would sneak down from the table out to the doorway looking up the street for the donkeys – he was a donkey expert by now and knew that they would be past just one more time this evening. Will had the job of watching the children at that moment. Sally and Anna were reminiscing again – it was starting to get on his nerves – Jo surreptitiously listened in to Sally and Anna's conversation and Algie was watching Tatiani. *'Oh God, she's coming over'*, Algie thought. He could feel himself going red, but had worried unnecessarily, as Tatiani walked straight passed him on her way to the door. Tatiani looked for Hamish, but he was one step ahead of her. Together they stood just outside the doorway. Will had followed Hamish to the door.

"It's the donkeys Tatti!" Hamish shouted.

As the donkeys reached the restaurant, she called out to the boys that were leading them and they stopped right outside. One of the donkeys had no rider, so Tatiani took Hamish's hand and walked him down the steps to meet them.

"You want to sit on the donkey, Hamish?"

"Yyyeeeaahhh" he squealed. Tatiani looked at Will as she picked him up, waving him in the air. He nodded. "I'm on a donkey, I'm on a donkey! Look Mummy!"

His ride was short lived as the donkeys needed to get on their way. "Do I have to get off Tatti?" he moaned.

"For now" she said. "Do you want to go up to the top on the donkey in the morning, Hamish?"

"Yeah!" He squealed again.

"Is that OK?" she asked Will. Will checked with Anna who was mid conversation and wasn't listening properly.

"Fine" she said waving them away with her hand.

"If you bring him down to the donkey station at ten thirty in the morning, I will walk up with him. We will be about an hour. Okay?" Tatiani made the arrangements with Will.

Whilst the women continued their constant chatting, Will hatched a plan to allow Algie to spend some time with Tatiani. When there was finally a break in the conversation he outlined his plan to Anna.

"You are okay with Hamish going up to the Acropolis with Tatiani tomorrow aren't you?"

"What do you mean?" Anna said, looking puzzled.

"We've arranged for Hamish to go up to the Acropolis on a donkey with Tatiani tomorrow. She seems to have taken quite a shine to him."

"Is that what you were talking about earlier?" Anna asked and Will nodded. "Oh dear, I wasn't really listening, sorry. What do you think Will, I'm not too sure about this?"

Will took Anna aside. "If we do this right, Algie will hopefully offer to escort Hamish, that way he gets to spent time with Tatiani, you'll feel happier about letting Hamish go and Hamish will be chuffed to bits because he gets Tatiani and the donkeys."

"You're so clever Will MacFaddyan," she spoke to him in a flirty manner. "You sit there looking like you haven't a clue, or a care in the world and all the time you are watching and listening, weighing everybody up. So what's the prognosis for me then Will?" Will thought for a while; he looked Anna up and down, pulled concerned and then finally lustful faces, making Anna laugh. He then replied in his best hospital consultant's voice.

"You have been giving us some concern in recent days Ms. Howard." Anna raised her eyebrows. "However, in my opinion you are beginning to relax at last. You worry too much about your son, who is quite clearly fine and a real credit to you. You don't give blokes half a chance – there's very little likelihood of you ever batting them to death with those eyelashes, simply because you've usually scared them off with your grouchiness before they've even got up the street . . . and in my opinion you could probably do with a good shag!" Anna's eyes widen and left her looking totally gob smacked. "Not that I'm offering!" Will added quickly.

"You are wicked!" Anna said, throwing back her head and stamping her foot as she laughed.

When Algie came back from the toilet, they initiated their plan by repeating their previous conversation, exaggerating the problem for Algie's benefit. They stressed how much Hamish wanted to go and how they did not want to offend one of the locals when she was being so kind. Will offered to take him. Anna pooh-poohed this, suggesting that Will would not want to be trundling up there. Algie seemed to fall for it and offered to take him. Will joked about the chances of Algie getting up on time to take him, but he was adamant and the deal was done.

24
2002, DAY 5 – The Villa, Lindos

Will stood in the kitchen. He had been watching Hamish for the last ten minutes. The six year old sat on the steps in the courtyard. He shuffled along the step to the row of plants and poked a stick between the pots shouting 'got you'. There was nothing there. He shuffled back, looking through to Algie's room, straining his neck to see if he was on his way, ready to go to see Tatti and the donkeys. Will had told Hamish to stop shouting Algie, that he wouldn't be long.

He rooted through the drawers in the kitchen whilst he waited and pulled out an unfamiliar object. Two lollipop shaped loops of metal protruding from a small box. The implement had no cable, but Will found a switch. He pressed it. The loops of metal began to spin around each other. It must be a whisk.

"What time is it Will?" Hamish asked as he walked into the kitchen.
"You tell me. What time does the clock say?"
"Is it ten o'clock?"
"That's right!"
"But it was nearly ten o'clock last time."
"Don't worry; he's nearly ready, I think."
"What's that?" Hamish asked, pointing.
"It's a whisk."
"Do you use it to make Whisky?"

"Not usually." Will smiled. "Watch this!" he pressed the switch and it buzzed as it whizzed around.

"Cool. Can I have a go?" Hamish whisked the air, making high pitched whisking noises. "What can I whisk?"

Will pointed to the sink. Hamish dipped it into the washing up water and drenched the front of Will's shirt when he switched it on. After a short intake of breath he burst out laughing. Will dabbed his shirt. "We could make a windmill." Will poked a small piece of paper into the whisk. It made a louder buzzing noise and crumpled up the paper. Hamish giggled. "Let's try this." Will said pulling one of the lollipop loops out. This time the paper stayed in longer, before flying out. "Hold this a minute." This time Will put a biro into the whisk and was surprised to find that it worked, albeit at a much slower speed. The motor strained, the whisk slowed down and stopped, and the biro dropped on to the floor.

"That was rubbish" said Hamish. "Try something else Will, this is like experimenting isn't it? We are like scientists." Will looked around them for ideas. Something caught his eye – he noticed a line on Hamish's forehead. He wiped it with his thumb, but it didn't move. It was very strange. Then he noticed the line on the wall, and the sink, and the tea towel. He looked again at Hamish and noticed a line on his shirt too. He started laughing. "What?" asked Hamish. "What you laughing at?"

"Go and look in the mirror." Hamish ran out of the kitchen towards the bathroom and bumped into Algie.

"Are you ready Hamish? What's that on your face?" Algie grabbed Hamish, picking him up to look closer. He started laughing too. "What have you been doing?" Will joined them in the courtyard, but every time he tried to explain to Algie what had happened, he could not say it for laughing. Tears ran down his face. Algie and Hamish joined in. All Will could do was to show Algie the whisk & the remains of the biro which was on the kitchen floor battered, bruised and half empty.

*

Sally and Anna sat in the same seats at Yolanda's Bar as they had on the first day. Their sun tans were beginning to give them a healthy glow. They chatted easily – not that they ever had a problem chatting, but when they hadn't seen each other for a while there was always a period of adjustment before they got back to their old comfortable ways.

They were amazed to see that Emelda was in again with three young children.

"Are you sure she's called Emelda?" Anna said, screwing up her nose. "I thought it began with a 'V'. Lou's done pretty well for himself really hasn't he, pulling a sassy young chick like that? She must have been very young when she had the two older boys."

"Maybe they aren't hers?" Sally said, then after a moment of contemplation "I'm not sure whether she's sassy or tacky."

"The only thing that is tacky about her is all the pink she's wearing, particularly the pink shoes."

"But then again with long dark hair and an olive complexion she really suits pink."

"So she's not really tacky then?"

"I suppose not."

"Well just look who there is! It's Algie and Hamish on their way down to the donkeys. He is so good with Hamish isn't he?" Anna said.

"Yes, he is." Sally agreed, she had just been thinking a similar thought. "I wonder how he'll get on with Tatti today. His nerves always seem to get the better of him where women are concerned."

Ironically Algie sauntered down the street and went up to Emelda. Sally and Anna watched in amazement as the young man, oblivious to their presence, nonchalantly folded his arms and chatted to her. He looked every bit a confident and flirtatious hunk. Was this really the Algie they knew and loved?

"Well!" Anna exclaimed "I wonder where he's hiding his nerves now!"

"I wonder why he's talking to her anyway. I must admit he looks very confident and smug. Slightly defensive though – he's got his arms crossed." Sally replied, bewildered by what she saw.

"No that's his tough masculine stance; he's chatting her up, puffing out his chest to try and impress her. I must admit I hadn't noticed how hunky he's getting. Ha! Hamish must be getting impatient he's pulling Algie away. He'll be worrying that they're going to miss Tatti."

"Do you think that maybe he's been dipping his cuffs in the washing up bowl of life?"

*

Algie was pleased to see Mel sitting in front of him as he walked down with Hamish. He'd been looking out for her ever since their swimming challenge, but hadn't actually seen her since then. He was slightly shocked to see that she had three small children with her and was just considering whether to stop to speak to her when she called him over.

"Algeeee" she said, over pronouncing his name as before.

"Kalamari!" Algie said. He stopped in front of her, grabbing Hamish before he disappeared up the street.

"Kalimera," Mel replied laughing. "How is the Lindos Loser today?"

"I presume you're referring to our little race? I'm no loser, I came second – that would be a silver medal at the Olympics!"

"I like the way you think." She flashed Algie a beautiful smile. "How would you like to meet for a drink tonight? Are you free?"

'God she really fancies me' Algie thought to himself. "Erm, yes, erm I might be able to. When?" He tried to be cool, but was struggling.

"I'll get off babysitting duty by ten; I could meet you at ten thirty," she suggested.

"OK. Where?"

"Niko's." Hamish tugged at Algie's shirt.

"Right, see you later! – These aren't all yours are they?" he added as he turned to walk away, hoping that none of them were actually hers.

"No. See you at ten thirty!" Algie sauntered off to be dragged through the crowds by Hamish. He felt quite excited, but also slightly apprehensive about the fact that Mel might have children, or in fact be married. He visualised her getting her husband to look after the kids whilst she went out for a drink with him. Then laughed to himself thinking how ridiculous that would be. Anyway, he was going to spend the morning with his number one girl – he would see how things went with Tatti before he made any decisions about meeting up with Mel.

*

As Anna and Sally made their way from Yolanda's Bar they bumped into Lou coming down to meet Emelda.

"Will we get chance to catch up on old times?" Lou asked. He had the same twinkle in his eye, Sally thought.

"We could do." Sally said slowly, thinking quickly.

"Meet me for a coffee at Yolanda's tomorrow Sal?"

"What time? Can you do early?"

"Is nine thirty early enough for you? We could make it breakfast."

"See you then."

25

September 1986, Northern England

Anna was busy when the young girl who works on the till near the door stuffed the small folded piece of paper into her hand. She did not get chance to look at it until the queue of people she was serving had gone.

"Cover for me!" she gave her colleague a pleading look. "Please!" He made her wait. He was enjoying having a little bit of power over Anna – those occasions didn't happen often, he would make the most of it. "No, really Chris, please?" Giving in he waved her away, laughing.

"Catherine, where did you get this from?" she thrust the paper at the young girl by the door. "Has he gone?" Anna asked impatiently. The girl always annoyed her, she was so dozy.

"Who?"

"The bloke that gave you this – has he gone?"

"What bloke? Erm . . . a woman gave me it." Anna always made her nervous.

"Oh, I see. Well has she gone?"

"Yes, she walked straight out again."

"What did she say?"

"Erm . . . I can't remem . . ." she noted the look on Anna's face. "Oh, yes . . . erm . . . she said 'could you give this to Anna for Sarah, no er for Sally' yes, that's right." She corrected herself, speaking slowly and properly in her best Queen's English. "Could you give this to Anna for Sally" presumably imitating the woman. Anna wanted to laugh at her.

"What was she like?"
"Quite old."
"Forty, fifty, sixty?"
"Fifty or more."
"Ok, thank you."

The paper was folded. On the outside it said 'Sally'. Anna opened the paper again. Inside it just said 'Lou Reeve' and there was an address.

26
2002, DAY 5 – Lindos

Algie considered how right he had been to be apprehensive. *'It's not like I was scared'* he thought, *'just apprehensive'*. He'd tackled the situation head on – he wasn't going to let her know how he felt. He had managed to get a smile from Tatti with his natural charm, when they arrived at the donkey station, but she was so different with Hamish – so warm and demonstrative. She had been all over him, cuddling him and picking him up, patting his hair and showing him the donkeys, letting him choose which one he wanted to go on – it had to be Mr. Chocolate Brown apparently! Algie had tried to make conversation with her but she just smiled and shrugged her shoulders most of the time, as if she did not understand him.

He could feel his skin burning now and realised that he'd forgotten the sun cream. His T-shirt looked as if someone had thrown a bucket of water over him. It was unbelievably hot for eleven o'clock in the morning but a shiver slipped up Algie's spine when he thought about the atmosphere developing between Tatti and himself. He had been trying to chat to her for the first half of the climb up to the Acropolis and was sure that she understood him – especially when he'd heard the English she had spoken to Hamish – but she hardly responded to him at all and now his confidence had begun to wane. Deciding he'd given it his best shot he fell silent and followed dutifully behind them.

It had been slow going up the latter reaches of the hill to the Acropolis. The pathway was busy with people coming down as well as those going up and they began to get on his nerves. Algie could not understand why they would all want to go traipsing up to some broken down old building. His attention drifted away from the Acropolis when he realised that he had been watching Tatti's bottom oscillating before him for – well, for how long he didn't know! *'Maybe she'll change her mind on the way down, what do I have to lose?'* Algie thought. As they neared the top, the pathway got very steep. Algie dashed forward so that he could speak to Tatti.

"Are you tired?" He spoke confidently and beamed an enormous smile.

"A little." she smiled at him – it was working!

"Do you want a lift?" she looked puzzled so he said it again pointing at his back and doing the actions. She put her hand on to his soaking wet t-shirt and pulled a face.

"Ah, maybe not!" *'shit'* he thought. "You like children?" he said quickly before the conversation evaporated. She looked slightly shocked. "You seem to like Hamish, you are very good with children?"

"Yes!" realisation dawned. "I want to be a teacher one day."

"Little ones or older ones?" Algie indicated the height difference with his hand. He was pleased he was managing to keep this conversation going.

"I don't like the big ones, only little."

"They'll have to be very little to be smaller than you!" Algie could not help sneaking in a 'little' joke. She looked annoyed and turned away from him. *'Shit'* he thought.

When they reached the top Tatti stopped and turned to speak to him. "Do you want to go inside?"

"I don't think we'll have time today. Do we just walk back down the same way?"

"No, I have arranged for Hamish to go back down on the donkey as well, I hope that is okay."

"That's fine" said Algie. "Do you mind if we quickly get a drink?"

"No, that is okay."

"Do you want one?"

"Yes please, but just a little one." She emphasised the word little. Algie smiled, but she did not.

Every time he opened his mouth on the way down he put his foot in it.

"Poor little donkeys" he had said at one point.

"They are not very little." She replied, again she did not smile.

"It's only a small island isn't it? I bet you could sail around it in a day." Algie said later.

"It is not one of the really little islands" she replied sharply. Algie's confidence was going again. Half way down they passed a large building that looked out over the bay. *'Large building with playground, must be a school.'* Algie thought.

"So is this the local school?" he asked.

"Yes" she replied "and before you ask, it is for the little children." Algie laughed loudly, but when he looked at Tatiani she still wasn't laughing.

"Anyway" he said after a moment, his face serious and sulky "they can't be that little, otherwise they'd never be able to reach the basketball nets in the playground."

"They just have to be very good at basketball" she said and smiled. After which she turned her attention to Hamish until they got back down into the village.

As they neared the donkey station Algie decided to have one last try – what did he have to lose? He caught up with Mister Chocolate Brown. "How's it going folks?" he said, putting an arm around Tatti's shoulder as he spoke. Her reaction he thought was extreme – she looked horrified!

"Fine, fine" she said pulling her shoulder away. But it was too late. Algie had timed this affectionate gesture to be just as they were walking past the restaurant where Tatti worked. Her boss was sitting outside where he always sits and surprisingly he jumped up and ran down the street after them. Algie's initial reaction was to run, but he stopped himself as he knew he had done nothing wrong. The angry gentleman bombarded both Tatti and Algie with Greek. *'He's even spitting'* Algie thought. There was little he could do as he did not understand a word; extreme arm waving, finger pointing, raised voices and now a small crowd. *'I don't believe this!'* Algie thought and stood shaking his head. The conversation was clearly about him and Hamish seemed to be getting a mention – Tatti guarded Hamish, protecting him with an arm around his shoulders. Tatti tried to walk off, but he forced her back pointing out the distance between her and Algie.

"Algie, please will you go on ahead to the donkey station" she whispered "I will meet you there with Hamish."

"But . . ."

"Just go please." she said, her face looked serious.

"See you in a minute little man, it'll be ok". Algie said, squeezing Hamish's knee. Then he ran on ahead wondering what the hell was going on. He could still hear them shouting as he turned the corner at the end of the street. He peeped round the corner after a minute or two to make sure that they had not absconded with Hamish.

She was pleasant enough when they said goodbye. "See you later, my friend," she smiled and hugged Hamish. But then didn't smile at all as she said "Bye Algie, I hope you enjoyed your little walk."

"What was that all about?" he asked.

"Oh it is nothing." Tatti made light of the whole thing. "Nothing!"

"He is a little mad."

"You don't say!" He said sarcastically, astounded that she seemed to just accept the verbal abuse from this old man.

"But . . ." Again she cut him short.

"I must go. Bye Hamish." She flashed Hamish a cute smile and seemed to disappear into thin air. They both stood for a moment, gormless, looking for her, then without saying a word turned to walk back to the villa.

Tatti watched them until they went out of sight. *'He really is quite cute'* she thought – in Greek of course – and this time she did not mean the little one.

27
2002, DAY 5 – Lindos

'Ironic' Algie thought, *'since I've just spent the last fifteen minutes dashing around the villa looking for a hairdryer – without any success!'* A strong, hot wind quickly dried any moisture remaining in Algie's hair and bullied it out of its newly sculpted shape. The wax that he had used on his hair could not compete with the wind, but when Algie checked his hair in the bakery window, he decided that it gave him a trendy tousled style. *'Mel is going to love me'* he thought. *'She is going to love me'* he repeated it to himself, out loud, under his breath. He knew he would have to convince himself if he was to have any chance of convincing her. He swayed slightly. His plan had been to bolster his confidence with alcohol. Earlier, during the meal with the family, he had been topping up his glass with wine when no one was looking. Then on his way round to meet Mel he had popped into one of the supermarkets to pick up a bottle of Ouzo – it was cheap and he quite liked it with water.

Nobody knew who he was meeting; they seemed to think it was Tatti. For a minute Algie wished that it was Tatti he was meeting – *'at least I know where I stand with her'* he thought. Then he thought about Mel and her breasts. He took a large swig of Ouzo, swiftly followed by another. *'What am I going to do if she comes on to me? As long as she doesn't know it's my first time I should be okay – I suppose I'll just have to shag her.'* He finished the Ouzo and walked into Niko's Bar.

She looked like a movie star sitting at the bar on a high stool, long legs wrapped around each other, high stiletto heels hooked on to the cross bar of the stool. He tried to be cool when he spotted her at the bar, but it was like a dream.

"Algeee" she shouted and beamed a massive smile. "I've bought us a cocktail to start with – I'm making up for lost time."

"Did you deliberately choose the drink to go with your dress?" Algie asked, holding the glass that she handed him close to the skirt of her dress. Both the drink and the dress were graduating tones of lime green. The dress complimented both her figure and complexion; a simple style, buttoning the full length of the front. There were just enough buttons fastened to keep her breasts inside the dress. 'Oh God, she's not wearing a bra.' His eyes lingered just a little too long.

"Stop looking at the dessert! You haven't even had an aperitif yet!" she said laughing. He jolted to attention and decided to concentrate on the large emerald eyes gazing up at him, too petrified to look anywhere else.

After the third cocktail he began to relax a little. She was all over him. He didn't even have to worry too much about the conversation – he'd been afraid that he would give away his age by what he said – cheerfully she chatted away. He watched her speaking, without listening. *'This could be my big night!'* he thought, his mind wandered. Mel noticed that he wasn't listening and so she fondled him in the groin to surprise him.

"Just checking it's not your hanky!" She said smiling seductively. "Good to see I'm keeping your attention – Save it for me!"

Algie now doubted that he could actually 'save it for her'. She was driving him wild. He could not risk looking at her breasts anymore. He tried to concentrate on what she was saying, but closely watching her mouth as she spoke, he was captivated by her tongue as it slipped over sharp white teeth. He ran his tongue along his own front teeth as he contemplated their sharpness. He wet his lips.

"Let's move on Algie."

"I'll just nip to the loo," he replied getting up.

"Need a hand?"

"I think I can manage, thank you" he smiled wryly.

She took his hand to stop him walking away, pulling him towards her for a kiss. It was a playful kiss. Mischievously Algie bit her tongue and said "You will have to wait" before disappearing off to the toilet.

Falling out into the street from the bar, Algie and Mel looked like any other drunken couple on holiday. Algie could hardly walk. Mel was not much better. They stumbled along together, wrapped around each other, occasionally bouncing off the white walls. Arriving at Mel's apartment she unlocked the door and took him in. Again, just for a second, Algie pictured Mel's husband, this time waiting behind the door. He could not stop himself glancing behind the door as he walked in.

The apartment was not as traditional as the MacFaddyan's villa. It was more spacious with minimalist furniture. *'Great kit – very luxurious.'* Algie thought.

"How many people are staying here? This is massive!"

"Just me, my Dad and the three boys."

"Your Dad!"

"Yup, he is so good to me. Mum couldn't make it so he asked us . . . I mean me along. Anyway, enough about me." She grabbed his hand and led him into the bedroom.

". . . but what will your Dad think?"

"He'll be fine. This room is separate from the others . . . and it locks. You make yourself comfortable and I'll get you a drink."

Algie's stomach turned at the thought of another drink. He spent a minute or so hovering near the toilet, just in case. Mel breezed in, glasses in hand and nearly tripped over Algie who was bent over, trying to undo his shoes. She looked around for somewhere to put the drinks down, but noticed Algie falling forwards on to his head. Without spilling a drop of the drinks she managed to stop him with her foot. Instead, he fell backwards on to the bed. She giggled.

They lay fully clothed on the bed together. Mel had had a long wait whilst Algie took off his shoes – he had insisted on this after remembering stories of men 'doing it' with just their socks on – even though he was not wearing any on this occasion. Once settled on the bed, Algie lay with his head resting on her breast, her nipple stood tantalisingly close to his mouth. She chatted, telling him about her holiday, a story about her best friend, and then straight into a story about what she was hoping to buy before she went home. Algie half listened, but he was finding the breast too much of a distraction. Without thinking he licked her breast through the thin green dress, his tongue exploring until it found the small hard mound.

"Do you eat sweets with the wrappers on as well?" Mel asked.

Fundamentally Algie had made the first move, but it was like finding the 'on' switch. Mel went into overdrive. Within seconds the dress was off and she knelt over him in just a pair of tiny G-string knickers. She bossed him about, ordering him here or there, do this now, do that now, faster, slower. "Use your initiative" she said at one point – Algie was positive he didn't have any. He just wanted to play with her breasts.

Her enthusiasm and fervour reached such intensity that Algie began to feel distant from the whole situation. It was all going on without him and he worried that he was out of his depth. In an attempt to get his attention she unzipped his jeans. Her slim hand slipped inside, but groped about for just a little too long. Feeling slightly crushed to find very little that she could get her hand around her initial reaction was to pull her hand away. She began to wonder if she had misread the signs – maybe he didn't fancy her after all, this had never happened to her before. Algie was devastated when he realised, the more he thought about it the worse it got. For a moment Mel took it as a challenge, but very quickly the mood changed, the ardour of the moment evaporating almost instantly. They both went quiet, smiles dropped from faces. Conversation became awkward.

Mel put her dress back on. Algie finished his drink as quickly as he could without making it too obvious; he could not get out of the door fast enough. Hugging in the doorway they muttered 'sorry's' and 'me too's'. Crestfallen, Algie made his way back to the villa.

28

September 1986, Northern England

'Papa Don't Preach' roared out of the ghetto blaster. The aerial slipped off the central heating pipe as Sally slammed the power switch with her left hand. The signal fizzled before stopping abruptly. She put the leaflets from the doctors into an envelope and slid the envelope into a book, it was a 1950's book 'A Ladies Guide to Needlework' – *no one will be reading that in the foreseeable future*, she thought.

*

Mist like drizzle, or was it drizzle like mist, mizzle? – Whatever it was, Anna found herself getting a lot wetter than she expected. The world looked grey. A monochrome mixture of mizzle and misery. The end of summer 'going back to school' feeling, had continued well into her twenties for Anna. Maybe a life in the Mediterranean would not be such a bad idea.

Making her way home from work Anna nipped down an alleyway from the Main Street and dropped down the steps on to the canal bank. She clutched the note from Lou. Her initial reaction had been excitement; she knew what it would mean to Sally that Lou had wanted to see her so much that he had sent his address in a note. She went over in her mind the last couple of weeks of her own life. The month that she had spent with Vasilis when she returned to Lindos had been idyllic. She smiled to herself.

But something had unnerved her, something was wrong. Anna had found Vasilis distant in the last few days before she had left. At the time she had presumed that it was because he was sad to see her go. He had promised her that he would be over to see her as soon as the tourist season was over, but when she had spoken to him on the phone last night the conversation had been stilted. There were problems to do with the family, he was not going to be able to come and see her just yet. Anna had feared that it was his way of ending the relationship, even though he had reassured her that he would come and find her . . . 'when things calm down' . . . 'what things?' She had asked. 'Don't worry I will come for you' he had said. 'But if you're always going to put your family before me, what's the point!' she had said, her disappointment getting the better of her. 'Our love is strong' he had said.

Anna could not bear to lose Vasilis – not now . . . and if Sally and Lou got together, that would be too much to bear! She scrunched the paper in her pocket and before she could change her mind dropped it into the canal.

29
2002, DAY 6 – Lindos

Zak walked with a spring in his step. In the narrow Lindian street he overtook Manolis who was passing the time of day with another local.

"Stupid fool," shouted Manolis when he spotted him down the street.

"A little slow this morning, are we?" Zak replied.

*

In the courtyard Jo and Hamish were convinced that they had cornered a lizard.

"What can we catch it in?" Jo pondered.

"I've got a tub we can put it in." Hamish said.

"Where is it?"

"In the room, just ask Mummy. Quick!"

Jo ran to the door of the main 'sala'. The door was ajar so she went in. Anna was standing throwing something high up in to the middle of the room, as if checking out the height. The object dropped back down and she caught it and carefully threw it up in the air again, over and over. Jo did not dare to speak, she stood in the doorway. On the fourth throw Anna struggled to catch it, and as she tried she turned towards the door. Startled by the intruder, she missed the catch altogether and the item dropped to the floor.

"What!" Anna said.

"Have you got a tub to put the lizard in? Sorry Anna, I should have knocked." Jo moved to pick the things off the floor.

"Leave that, it doesn't matter . . ." she rooted around the sink. "Will this do?" she said handing Jo an empty ice cream tub.

"Thanks." Jo said and ran out.

Anna picked up the two pieces of stone from the floor. The mauve stone had a white stripe through it and it had cracked along the white line. The pieces slotted back together to form a simple heart shape. '*How apt*' she thought, before putting them back into her pocket. The beautiful endless tactile surface was lost, the broken edges jarred in her hand and the pieces clanked together as she walked.

*

Walking the short distance down to Yolanda's Bar to meet Lou, Sally wrestled with any reasons as to why she might not have told Will. It was easier. But then as it was turning out it wasn't easier, she had never lied to Will before; only little white lies anyway. '*Why don't I just tell him if I have nothing to hide? Is it really easier to say nothing? But I don't want to hurt him or worry him unnecessarily. Although just thinking that suggests that there is a chance I might hurt him! What am I thinking? I know that I have no intention of taking this relationship any further, it's just a curiosity satisfying exercise.*' Sally pushed the discussion to the back of her mind – it was getting out of hand.

30

September 1986, Northern England

In the Park by the canal Anna sat on a swing in the children's playground area. She did not mind the fact that her bottom would get wet. The mizzle had turned out to be rain, which quickly soaked through her summer dress, chosen to show off maximum golden tan. Overcome with guilt she wept uncontrollably. *'How could I be so cruel to Sally? She didn't deserve that. It would make such a difference to Sally, just to know that Lou had tried to contact her.'* Anna knew that there was no way to get around the problem, even if she jumped into the canal, the note would be impossible to read now. She wondered when she had become so selfish. Maybe jumping into the canal wasn't such a bad idea. Without rushing anywhere, she considered her options.

"We have a bell you know!" Sally managed to laugh as she opened the front door that Anna was thumping continuously. "What's the matter?"

"Can . . . I . . . come . . . in?" Anna's words came out hoarse with heaving great breaths between them.

"Of course, come in. Are you ok?"

"Oh Sal, I'm so sorry!"

"What do you mean? Sorry for what?"

"You won't believe me – but it's true." Anna glanced up at Sally, her face serious suddenly.

"Go on. Tell me!"

"Someone brought Lou's address into the shop today. But . . ."

"You are joking!" Sally butted in, her smile wider than ever.

"No, but Sal listen! I . . . I . . ."

"Who brought it?"

"A middle aged woman called in the shop today and left a piece of paper with one of the girls. By the time I got it she had gone. The paper said 'Sally' on the outside and inside was Lou's address." Sally opened her mouth to speak. "But," she held her hand up to stop Sally speaking. "I dropped it on the way home."

"What do you mean you dropped it?" She emphasised the word 'dropped'.

"Well I . . . I had it in my pocket and when I took my hand out, it flew away.

"We can go back and look for it!"

"It floated into the canal . . . I couldn't reach it . . . the ink started to run and then it sank." Sally looked sad. "I'm really sorry."

"I can't believe it."

"But it's true – it just flew into the canal. I couldn't bring myself to jump in and get it."

"I mean, I can't believe he sent his address, maybe he did like me after all." Sally managed a smile. "Can you remember what it said?"

"I can't remember the address, but I can remember that it said Oxford."

"Yes I knew he lived in Oxford. Can you remember his surname?"

"It began with an R."

"Yes, it's not Reed though."

31
2002, DAY 6 – Lindos

Of course there were lines, quite deep lines radiating out from the outer edges of Lou's eyes, laugh lines around his mouth and small furrows down his forehead, between his eyebrows. His face seemed fuller, with jowls forming. His eyes, dark green pools – as deep as you like, lit up when he smiled. Sally remembered a time when she wondered how anyone could find older people attractive. She found the face before her very attractive – every line tells a story. He had kept his figure well, a middle-aged version of the one she had known, still toned and reasonably lean.

They sat at a table towards the back, outside the front of Yolanda's Bar. The early conversation belied the history between them; they could have been any couple meeting for the first time on holiday. The weather, accommodation, trips, flight over – we've heard it all before.

"I noticed you're on holiday with Anna. Have you been coming back every year?"

"No, I haven't been back since 1986. I must admit that I wondered if maybe you'd been coming back regularly."

"No, this is the first time I've been here since 1986 – which makes it all the more amazing that we've bumped into each other. In fact that's a bit spooky! It must be fate Sal!"

"It must be! I wonder why now?"

"I presume you're here with your husband and children?"

"He is my husband, but they're not my children. If you think about it, if Algie was mine I would have been pregnant in 1986."

"For a minute there I thought you were going to say that he was mine?" Lou chuckled.

"No" she laughed. "He's not yours or mine. I have two step children, Algie is sixteen and Jo is twelve. Are you here with your wife and children?"

"Just the kids." Sally looked surprised, Lou continued. "I am married – to Jane – and have three children, but my wife is not on holiday with us. She's just started a new job and they were getting awkward about her taking time off, so rather than the kids missing out on the holiday she suggested that Emelda came with us.

"So Emelda's not your wife?"

"No, she's my daughter."

"Oh!" Sally was shocked, but tried not to show it. "She looks about twenty five! We were thinking maybe Sugar Daddy."

Lou laughed. "No sugar, just Daddy. She's only nineteen though."

"Oh."

They sat for a moment. Neither spoke. Eventually Sally's face changed. "So that means . . ."

"Yes" Lou interrupted, "that means she was three when I met you here, she was born in 1983.

"You never mentioned her."

"It's a long story."

"Four words – I have a child! – Not actually that long." Sally was feeling slightly annoyed.

"It isn't quite that simple."

"Is she the child of the girlfriend you had about that time?"

175

"Yes, we eventually married and had two boys as well, Robert and Stevie." Sally opened her mouth to speak. "The other one is Jack, he's Mel's."

"Mel's?"

"Emelda's – yes, I am a grandad!"

"Well I don't know what to say."

"I don't look that bad for a grandad do I?"

"No!" Sally laughed. "I don't mean that. I guess I didn't get to know you that well, though I am surprised that you didn't tell me you had a daughter. Mind you, I suppose you did lie about your name. A minor point I know!"

"I never lied; that was just the lads messing about."

"Funnily enough I didn't quite see it like that!" Sally pulled a face. "Have you got time to tell me that long story?"

"Sally you look hurt." Lou said seriously.

"That's just me being silly." she laughed.

"No, apart from that."

"I suppose I've been thinking about that day when you hobbled off the beach and I knew that there was no way that I'd ever see you again, we hadn't exchanged addresses; I didn't even know your real name."

"I intended to catch you before I left, then when I saw you in the morning in the shop I forgot to give you my address."

"Anyway, we met up eventually. What's sixteen years between friends?" Sally laughed.

"I did try to contact you. Did you get the note I had delivered to the chemists? I always wondered if you did get it and just decided not to contact me."

"No, quite the opposite. I wanted to contact you but Anna dropped the note into the canal on the way home and she could not remember what the note said. How on earth did you manage to find us and deliver it anyway?"

"I remembered that Anna worked at the chemists. A woman that I worked with at the time was visiting someone in your home town so I asked her to take my address to you – well Anna. She handed the note to someone at the chemists to give to Anna."

"Good work. Who knows what might have been, eh?"

"I'm a great believer in fate."

"I am touched that you tried to find me. I guess it just wasn't meant to be."

"Yes it is funny how things turn out in the end. I suppose in a way it was because of you that I found out about Emelda."

Sally laughed again "Presumably you knew about Emelda. It was me that didn't know."

"Well not exactly." Lou sighed.

"Tell me your long story."

"Jane and I had been going out a long time. I suppose you could say we were childhood sweethearts. Things got very rocky in the '80s, the relationship became on/off and eventually messy and bitter when other people got involved. Jane went off with someone else for a while; I had a number of flings."

"Me included?"

"No this was way before I met you."

"We had been separated a while when I met you in Lindos."

"So you were married then?"

"No, but we had been living together. Emelda was born in the middle of the rocky patch. Jane always led me to believe that she wasn't mine," Sally looked shocked. "I think she actually believed that Emelda wasn't mine. We stayed friends, but went our separate ways."

"Right."

"By some ridiculous string of coincidences, the woman who took the note for you, just happened to know someone who knew someone who told Jane. It turned out that Jane had kind of been taking me for granted a little, always believed I would be there. Then when she heard about the note she came to see me. She told me that she wanted to come back. We did a paternity test and found out for sure that Emelda was mine. Things just slotted together, we got married and never really looked back."

"It sounds like it was a good job I never got that note – I was heading for heartache!"

"I suppose we will never know." Lou looked fondly at Sally. "And I know it might seem as if Jane and I got together because of Emelda, but we didn't, I do love Jane – always have. We have a very steady relationship really, we grew up together, and she knows me inside out." Sally eyes began to fill with tears. "Sal, I'm sorry, I never meant to hurt you."

"No, it's not that." She wiped the tears away with the back of her head. "Imagine not knowing that Emelda was yours, missing being her dad when she was a baby." Lou touched Sally's hand affectionately.

"Fortunately I didn't miss out totally; I was around a lot of the time." They sat in silence for a moment.

"Well, not quite the ending to the book I was expecting!"

"What book, Sal?"

"The other day when you first came over to speak to me on the beach, I was thinking it's a bit like when you find the missing pages of a book you never finished."

"Ah, and now the book is finished."

"I suppose so."

"Maybe there's a sequel."

"I presume this is the sequel."

"Does it have a happy ending?"

"I think so, don't you?"

"Happy enough for me."

"Happy enough for me, too." Lou patted her hand on the table.

32

2002, DAY 6 – Lindos Beach

Noisily, the bubbling, foamy water gushed out from the back of the pedalo. Intermittently the boat was propelled forward when the top of each wave caught in the paddles. In vain, Will shouted to his daughter to stop pedalling. He was so effective in pushing the boat out of the shallow water, that he fuelled her drive to pedal faster and harder – *'this is easy!'* she thought, unaware that her father was now drenched and struggling to run through the knee high water. He banged his fist on the boat as he made his way around the side. She glanced round.

"Come on Dad!"

"Don't you 'come on Dad' me, I'm soaked here. Stop pedalling!" he shouted, but once she had stopped and seen how wet he was, they both laughed.

It had not been as easy as Jo had thought, once they were up to full speed. But it wasn't long before she worked out that she could keep her feet on the pedals and let her father do most of the work. Far out in the bay the pedalo rocked gently. They had stopped the boat to rest for a while. Will was feeling tired, he had not slept well; an afternoon nap seemed like a good idea. They sat together with their feet up, enjoying the sun, Will very still, Jo fidgeting as she tried to find the best position for getting a suntan.

Jo coughed and Will jolted out of his nap, making that snorting noise he always makes when he is woken abruptly.

"Sorry Dad" Jo said, "oh, but now you're awake, why does the sea wave?"

"I don't know, why does the sea wave?"

"No, it's not a joke. Why does the sea have waves in it?"

"Why do you think, Jo?"

"Erm" she thought for a while. "Is it something like when you're in the bath and you move forward and all the water nearly flows over and then it goes back the other way and then forward again, then back and forward until it stops?"

"Wouldn't the waves stop if that was the case?"

"Well maybe something keeps moving, to set it off again."

"So what might keep it moving?"

"Is it the earth spinning?"

"It's actually the wind."

"What about in Blackpool when the sea goes right out? That's not the wind, is it?"

"No, not exactly. That is the tide and it's caused by the moon."

"Yeah right." Jo said.

"It is to do with the moon – the moon pulls." Will took her hand off the rudder and nipped the skin on the back of her hand. "It sucks the sea up like this, then lets it go again" The skin fell flat on her hand again. Jo laughed.

"Let me try, on your hand," Jo said. But when she did it, she noticed that the skin on Will's hand took much longer to return to how it was. "Looks like the tides out for a while!" she laughed again. "The moon can't really pull the sea though, can it?"

"It can. It's the gravitational pull between the earth and the moon . . . and also because the earth spins around."

"So I was a bit right. But I thought there was no gravity on the moon, that's why astronauts float about when they're up there."

"There is gravity on the moon, it's just much weaker because the moon is smaller. There is a gravitational pull between any masses."

"Masses?"

"Things – between any two things. We'll look it up on the internet when we get home. Anyway, I think we need to start pedalling again."

"I've just realised that I've not thought about home all holiday!"

"Are you enjoying it, my little Chuckie?"

"Yeah, are you?"

"Mostly." Will said. Jo didn't dare say anything, but she knew her Dad was not happy. She tried various ways of asking him in her head, but could not find the right words.

Eventually Jo spoke. "What do you think of Sally's old boyfriend Dad?"

"I can't really comment, because I haven't met him."

"I saw him this morning with Sally at Yolanda's Bar."

"Oh." Will looked puzzled, but did not ask any more questions.

"They looked like they were holding hands when I walked past." Jo could not resist telling him.

"Oh" Will said.

*

Flat out, face down and snoring; Algie looked like he had fallen asleep the second his body hit the towel. Jo videoed anything and everything on the walk back up the beach, until she glimpsed Algie in the viewfinder.

"Dad look!" she whispered, grinning.

"No, you look where you're going!" he replied, grabbing her before she walked into an unsuspecting sunbather.

"Guide me Dad, I'm making a film."

"I don't think your leading man is looking particularly charismatic."

Jo zoomed close up to his face. "No, he's 'down and out' at the moment. He'll never get the girl looking like that."

"I have a feeling maybe he already has."

"What do you mean? He hasn't even met her yet. She's just about to walk into his life." Lifting the camera slightly she framed the first woman walking towards them, in the viewfinder. "Look here she is now." The woman was very large; her body falling out of her bikini.

Jo continued, whispering. "The gravitational pull between them was so strong he couldn't help himself. But really she's not the one; she's just trying to tempt him away from his true love."

"Who is his true love?"

"Shh. You'll disturb them!"

Algie wasn't going to move. The threat of sunburn merely drove him to move under a parasol in the heat of the day. Will and Jo made their way back to the villa. Jo had become irritable; she needed her lunch and the batteries on the video camera had gone flat, curtailing her movie making. Will was apprehensive, unsure as to how he felt about his wife's secret rendezvous. He knew Jo had a habit of exaggerating, but that generally she did not make things up. Even if they weren't holding hands, why didn't she tell him she was meeting him? He supposed she may well have bumped into him, but then again it was odd that she had gone out so early this morning. Should he mention it, or wait to see what she said? He bought Jo a sandwich on the way back through the village.

*

An atmosphere developed very quickly once they arrived back in the villa. Hamish played happily in the yard. Sally was in the kitchen preparing lunch for the two of them, Anna and Hamish had already eaten. The conversation between Sally and Will was stilted. Anna decided to go for a walk to give them chance to talk, she also wanted some time on her own. Jo spotted Anna going through the gate. Sticking her head out of the door she noted the direction Anna was going, then nipped into the kitchen to Will and Sally.

"I'm going with Anna, see you in a bit."

"Wait, I'm coming too!" Hamish shouted. But Jo whispered "No, you stay here." She looked and sounded mean. Hamish went back to his lizard game. Once out of the gate, Jo dashed up the road to see where Anna had gone. At first she thought she had missed her, then Anna stepped out of a shop within inches of Jo. Jo held her breath and stood very still, hoping she would not be spotted. Anna was in a dream, totally oblivious, she sauntered off in the other direction. Jo scurried after her, hiding in shop doorways and behind people when necessary. In actual fact, she didn't need to bother, Anna's mind wandered to another time in her life in a place not far away. She made her way out of the village towards St. Paul's Bay. As the buildings petered out and the landscape opened out, there was nowhere for Jo to hide, so she waited until Anna was almost out of view, and then set off again.

Tatti and her brother Alekos do not often venture on to the beach during the day. But they were waiting to be picked up by their Uncle, so it was a special occasion. They hovered in the shade at the back of the beach and considered the likelihood of their Uncle not turning up. As soon as he was five minutes late Alekos doubted his Uncle and quickly got bored. Tatti reassured him that he would not let them down. She was happy watching what was going on. She spotted Algie asleep in a ball. Against her better judgement she decided to go and speak to him, she knew that she had been a little harsh with him on their trip to the Acropolis. He looked so sweet and harmless asleep like that.

She crouched down by his side and spoke softly. "Hi, Algie."

Algie opened his eyes and then blinked big, long blinks. "Hi" he said, as he wiped a dribble from the side of his mouth.

"Thank you for coming to Acropolis with me yesterday. I think Hamish enjoyed it."

"Me too . . . er . . . I mean I think Hamish enjoyed it too." Algie said.

"Are you playing tonight?"

"What?"

"Are you playing football tonight?"

"Er . . . no, I am not very . . . er . . . not very well, today.

"Oh, that is a sorry."

"That is a shame. But I think I am just very tired."

"My brother and I are going to see my Uncle; he is going to show us his new yacht" Tatiani said, the excitement was evident in her voice. She swung her arm around to point to the Bay. "That is my uncle's yacht." Algie sprang to life, momentarily. Tatiani pointed to her thirteen year old brother by the trees. "That is Alekos. Oh and this is my Uncle just arriving. I must go, we are late. Bye Algie."

Alekos and Tatiani greeted their uncle with hugs and kisses and Algie quickly drifted back to his own little dream world. Their Uncle was interested to know who Tatiani had been speaking to and before she knew it he had talked her into inviting Algie along. Woken by Tatti a second time, Algie was convinced he was in some kind of deep sleep that he could not get himself out of – especially after his escapades with Mel the night before.

*

Sally was in a good mood. She felt like she could finally close the book, that loose ends had been tied up. It had been lovely to see Lou, but now she could put that all behind her and concentrate on her family. Will was tense, waiting for Sally to say something; as yet she had not done. Sally talked chirpily, asking Will about his boat trip with Jo. He said very little. She pressed on, chatting about what she'd bought in the village that morning. She did not mention Lou. Will kept quiet giving her time to tell him everything. She asked about Algie. They had both heard him come in late the night before, stumbling his way into his room, but had had nothing but grunts out of him all day. Neither of them seemed to know how his date had gone or who his date had been. For a moment Will forgot about his own worries.

*

Picking at the large rock she hid behind, Jo's attention wandered to a trail of ants. She laughed to herself thinking she had tricked one of the ants into carrying a tiny piece of the rock she picked at. *'He'll crack his teeth when he gets that home!'* she thought. She tried various ways of breaking the chain of ants; digging a hole, but they just walked into the hole and out again. When she put a stone on to one of the ants she thought she had killed it, but it dug its way out from underneath, the rest of the ants just walked around the outside. Her final attempt involved dribbling water that she had carried in the palm of her hand from a nearby pool, over the ants; this seemed to cause them some problem, but only until the water seeped away. She filmed the ants, in her head there was a story that went with the film.

Jo had got bored watching Anna – she did not seem to be doing anything. She couldn't believe that anyone could stand still for so long, doing nothing. She glanced up to the beach where Anna had been standing. Panicked by the realisation that Anna was no longer on the beach and could be anywhere, she hid further behind the rock. Peering out again, she located her on the jetty.

The Jetty was more substantial than Anna remembered. She stood on the jetty looking over the water and up to the Acropolis towering over her. Nothing had changed and Anna felt just the same. She reflected on the fact that it is cruel to make us feel twenty four when we are forty. *'Gosh, I'm nearly forty'.* For a moment she was bowled over by the realisation that those sixteen years had gone so fast. *'Anyway, I'm sure I don't look forty'.* She sat on the jetty; memories of that night with Vasilis were so clear in her mind it seemed like yesterday. She dipped her toes in the water and glanced down for the little old boat. *'That can't be it!'* A battered old rowing boat nudged its way out from under the jetty. Anna grabbed the rope – no ropes – *surely not!* When she pulled the ropes, the little boat swung out in front of her. She looked behind her, feeling eyes watching her. No one. Stretching her feet out into the boat she half expected to touch a fleecy blanket tucked beneath the seat.

*

Sally knew Will wasn't happy, but had no idea why. They sat at the kitchen table. Will picked at his lunch. Sally thought he looked old.

"What's wrong Will?"

"You tell me."

"I don't know what you mean."

"I could ask you the same question. What's wrong?"

"Nothing, I'm fine."

"Right."

"What do you mean 'right'. I don't know what's wrong, I'm fine."

Will sucked on his cigar, gazing out of the window. They sat in silence for a while until eventually he spoke again. "Jo said she saw you in the village his morning with Lou." Will tried to sound 'matter of fact' but it came out quite bitter.

"I was in the village with Lou this morning."

"And when were you going to tell me."

"I don't know. It sounds silly now you've said it, but you seemed unhappy and I didn't want to make things worse."

"Oh, so it makes things worse does it. Do you fancy telling me what is going on?"

"Nothing is going on." She reached out for her husband's hand. He did not move his hand away, but did not return any of the affection Sally gave him. "There isn't really anything to tell you. We were just catching up on what had happened since the last time I saw him."

"And when was that?"

"Years ago."

"Yeh?"

"Of course!" Sally felt annoyed now. "I can't believe you're saying this! I know I should have told you, but there just didn't seem to be the right time."

"But if nothing was . . . is . . . going on"

"Will!" Sally shrieked.

". . . if nothing is going on, surely anytime would be the right time to tell me."

"I know I should have told you. I'm sorry, but it doesn't mean anything."

"What doesn't mean anything? The fact that you didn't tell me, doesn't mean anything, or this relationship you're having with this bloke, doesn't mean anything."

"Will, this is silly, you're twisting my words. Listen." Sally began to panic. "I should have told you I was meeting Lou. I haven't seen him for something like sixteen years. I admit it was nice to see him again, to find out what happened sixteen years ago. But there's nothing going on. We had a coffee. We talked. You know I would not do anything to threaten our relationship."

"You already have."

"What?"

"You lied to me."

"I didn't lie, I just . . ."

"You just didn't see fit to tell me – it's the same thing."

Sally didn't know what to say, she seemed to be making it worse every time she opened her mouth. She wanted to shout at him.

Will was surprised at how quickly she gave in. He decided her silence meant she had no defence. Neither of them moved. Sally eyes filled with tears.

*

The afternoon sun raced towards the horizon. Out on the deck Algie sat with his new friends feeling very much at home. *'This is the life'.*

"I presume you have not told your Mama about Algie." The captain of the ship said with a twinkle in his eye.

In Greek Tatti explained that actually there was nothing to tell, certainly not as yet. She told her uncle about this English boy who played a very mediocre game of football and had a very cute, six year old blonde friend whom they had jointly escorted to the Acropolis the previous day. Her uncle tried to ascertain whether she really liked Algie. Algie looked at them both trying to pick up a hint of what they were saying, he knew they were talking about him but had no idea what they were saying. When Algie began to look hurt Tatti gave in and spoke in English "He meet Grandfather yesterday!"

"He was your Grandfather!" Algie exclaimed.

"And was he as grumpy as usual, Tatiani?"

"More than grumpy, he was an ogre. I think Algie fear for his life!"

"He probably has good reason to fear for his life." Tatti's uncle kept his face straight, Algie waited for the smile that didn't arrive.

"Oh God!" Algie said at last, looking anxious. After a cruel silence, the other three burst out laughing.

*

'Is that it – no secret meeting or anything?' Jo had been sitting hiding behind the rock for over three quarters of an hour. Anna had not moved from the jetty. For a while Jo had gone through scenarios in her head, imaging some tall, dark haired stranger pulling into the bay in a fancy boat and sweeping Anna into his arms. Or even a shark

circling the jetty and ending up biting Anna's feet off. Jo tried to work out what she would do if it did; her main concern in the latter scenario was being exposed as a spy when she ran out to help a footless Anna. Ultimately she decided that Hamish's invisible lizards were more exciting than this and that she might as well go back. Just as she was about to leave she spotted a lizard; it was very close to her and so she quickly grabbed her camera to film it, then made her way up from the bay being careful not to let Anna see her.

*

Will sat in Algie's room strumming his guitar. Sally walked in and interrupted him. He hated it when she did that; normally she waited until he finished, but not today.

"Where's Hamish?"

"Isn't he out there playing?"

"No."

"Well didn't he go with Anna and Jo?"

"I'm hoping so. I've just searched the entire villa. He didn't actually tell us he was going with Jo though, did he?"

"Don't panic Sally he'll be fine."

"But I should have been listening. We should have been listening!"

"You're right, but calm down. Have you looked out in the street, you know he's always looking out for the donkeys." Sally dashed across the courtyard and opened the gate. She walked up and down the street keeping close to the villa, and then ran back inside.

"Will, he's not there. What can we do?"

"Nothing really, until the others come back. He's most probably with them. Don't worry."

"I knew I shouldn't have done that drawing of Hamish."

"What! What on earth do you mean?"

"Oh nothing."

"Come on . . . what do you mean?"

"Oh it's just that when I was younger I used to draw people, but then I started to notice that things happen to whoever I drew."

"Like what?" Will looked scathingly at Sally.

"Like my sister and her boyfriend split up after I drew him. I split up with my boyfriend after I drew him. Someone else I drew I never saw again."

"Sally, you cannot be serious, this is a load of twaddle."

"Well, it's just what happened."

"Don't be silly. It's just a string of coincidences. Forget about it. Now come on, let's think, where would he go?"

It wasn't many minutes before Algie walked in. Both Will and Sally bombarded him with questions about Hamish. Algie was no help.

*

"Are you going to come down and see Mama?" Tatti asked her uncle. "I know she wants to see you."

"I will come and see Eva when she invites me and not before." Vasilis hugged his sister's children. "Thanks for a wonderful afternoon. See you soon." The two children ran off down the street waving.

*

Tempers were getting frayed. "I feel like I should be doing something but I don't know what to do." Sally said.

"We'll go out looking again soon, hopefully Hamish will turn up with Anna and Jo in a minute."

"Anyway, you'll never guess where I've been!" Algie said cheerfully. Sally raised her eyebrows enquiringly.

"I've been with Tatti and her uncle! On a yacht in the bay, no less!"

"Fantastic." said Sally.

"So things went well when you went up to the Acropolis with Tatti?"

"I wouldn't say it went well . . . and the worst thing was when we got back into the village, the old guy from the restaurant Tatti works in, came running after us – he was so abusive – he scared me anyway."

"Easily scared." Will laughed.

"Anyway, I found out today that apparently this old bloke is Tatti's grandad, the owner of the restaurant. Her mum works there too." Sally was not concentrating; she heard the catch rattling on the gate.

"I'm back!" Jo shouted as she swung the gate open.

"Hi Jo, have you got Hamish?"

"No."

"Is he with Anna?"

"No, he stayed here."

"We'd better do something. Oh Will, what on earth are we going to do?"

"He'll be fine, Sal don't worry."

"What's the matter?"

"Hamish is missing. We haven't seen him for at least an hour; we thought he went with you and Anna."

"Right, we need to think logically and be methodical. Where would he go? Any ideas?" Will was calm. Sally was close to tears.

"Ice-cream shop." Sally suggested.

"I'll go look down that way." Algie said and off he went.

"He's not on his bed is he?" Will said with a wry smile, dashing through to Anna and Hamish's room. He was soon back. "No, he's not there."

"He could be anywhere the donkeys might be," Jo said.

"Right, I'll do a donkey route check. We need to go both ways along the route, but someone should stay here in case he turns up."

"I'll stay here, if you go down towards the village Will and maybe Jo can wander up towards the Acropolis. But if she bumps into Anna what will she say? Where is Anna, Jo?"

"Oh, she shouldn't be long."

"I'll set off anyway." Will said and was gone.

"I'll go the other way then." Jo said. Sally noted a hint of apprehension.

"Wait Jo. What's the matter?"

"Nothing." There clearly was.

"Come on, spill the beans."

"It's just that I didn't go with Anna." Sally looked surprised. She nodded for Jo to continue. "I followed her. She's going to find out now."

"Why were you . . . oh, that doesn't matter now, we must find Hamish. Think Jo, think! Where would Hamish go, anywhere at all."

"Well, he says he goes to the Captain's House. The one down the street. I videoed it today, look." She handed Sally the camera. "Just press play."

"This is just a bunch of ants, Jo."

"Yes, you can fast forward past the ants and the lizard and then it's the people at the Captains house."

"There's no lizard. Anyway is this relevant, we are losing time? I can see the Captain's House, I know where you mean. When has Hamish been there and what for?"

"I don't know, he said something about Captains and Zak and watering plants and lizards, or something."

"It's the Captains house on the corner on the way back from town. That looks like the donkey man in the video."

"It is." Jo was very quiet.

"Stay here Jo. Don't say anything to Anna until we get back." Sally headed out of the door.

"But what if she asks me!" Jo shouted after her, running to the gate.

"Make something up – you're good at that!"

*

"Where have you two been?" Eva shouted at the children when they walked into the restaurant.

"We jju . . ." Alekos stuttered.

"No lies! I know you've been with your uncle. I saw you on the boat." Eva, stern faced, looked first to one child and then the other. Both stood in silence. "Well?" She asked, waiting for a reply.

"You just said. You know where we've been!" Tatiani replied eventually "We want to see him; he wants to see us – and you! Why won't you see him?"

"Anyway who was the boy? . . . never mind, tell me later." Her voice trailed away as Manolis walked in.

33
2002, DAY 6 – Lindos

It was the garden on the corner that Sally loved. She stood on tip-toe looking over the gate for a moment. Relief forced a smile across her face when she saw Hamish, then she laughed as she watched the scene unfold before her. Hamish had a long garden brush and a watering can. He was following Zak around the beautiful garden. Zak grunted at him in Greek. Hamish twittered away in English, he clearly thought he was helping, but Zak's body language and the tone of his voice said he was in the way. Zak would dig a hole to put in a plant; Hamish would sweep up any fallen soil and then water the plant with the watering can. The only thing was, he would not put the watering can down because he knew that Zak would take it off him and so was struggling to sweep up with a watering can in his hand as well as a brush. Zak would chase after him, but Hamish was too quick, he would run around the garden and get back to water the plant before Zak could catch him. "OK, ok" Zak muttered. For a moment Sally just watched.

The Captain appeared on the stairs down to the courtyard; Sally watched him walk sedately down the stone steps, he was also engrossed with the Hamish and Zak double act. He looks Italian she thought, there's something about the way Italians wear their clothes, the pale linen suit, the hat and sun-glasses. She was nervous, embarrassed to be caught trespassing in his yard. Worried that Hamish had been a real problem for them. As he moved out into the courtyard the sunlight caught his face. *'Attractive as well,'* Sally thought.

"Hello?" He said when he spotted Sally near the gate. "Is he yours?" He spoke perfect English. *'His clothes are a disguise!'* Sally thought.

"We'd lost him. Has he been here long?" Hamish stopped his game when he heard Sally's voice. He looked sheepish.

"Thirty minutes or so, according to Zak. I've just got in."

"I hope he hasn't been too much bother."

"No, we've become used to his visits. He's very entertaining."

"So he's been here before? We had no idea! Sorry – we should have kept a closer eye on him." Hamish had skirted around the yard to the gate. "Yes, maybe you had better run home before your Mum finds out that you've been missing, or we'll all be in trouble." Hamish ran off shouting "Bye Captain Silly".

"Hamish! You need to . . ." Sally shouted, but he had gone . . . "tidy up I was going to say. I had better help you with that."

"No, it is fine." The old man answered this time. "He has been no trouble, he make me smile." He displayed brown teeth as he grinned.

The Captain approached Sally, took off his hat and held out his hand. "Hi, I'm Vasilis. Are you on holiday?"

Alarm bells were ringing; ringing so loud in Sally's head that she missed the question – *'what was Algie saying before'* she thought *'I've been with Tatti and her uncle. – the old man from the restaurant is Tatti's grandad, her mum works there too.'* "Hi, I'm Sally, pleased to meet you." They shook hands. Sally looked beyond the deep sun tan, the smart clothes – it was Vasilis!

He repeated his question. "Are you on holiday?"

"Yes, yes, we are on holiday". She hesitated "Vasilis, I think we may have met before."

"Yes?"

"A long time ago. I came here on holiday sixteen years ago with Anna and . . ." Vasilis looked shocked. Sally stopped speaking, unsure whether to go on. He was silent for a moment, almost as if he was composing himself, Sally thought.

When he finally spoke, he was very quiet. "Sally . . . of course, how could I forget? I remember it like it was yesterday. I am sorry I didn't recognise you immediately."

"It's not surprising, sixteen years is a long time."

Vasilis looked sad. "Can I ask about Anna?"

"What do you want to know? She is alive and well and at this moment in time just around the corner."

Vasilis could not help but smile. "That's good." He nodded as he spoke.

"In fact – Hamish your little visitor is Anna's son."

"No!" Vasilis laughed. Then his smile dropped.

"Sally this is unbelievable! If you knew . . ." he hesitated "if you knew the years I . . ." again he hesitated, "I suppose, like you say, it is a long time ago."

"You should come and say hello."

"I would like that, but maybe not just now."

The silence grew loudly between them.

"Do you still have your boat, Vasilis?"

"Come and look! I pointed this out to Hamish the other day." He guided Sally up the small stone steps onto the roof. My yacht!" He said this proudly. "You must come and take a proper look – we could dive for champagne!" he laughed.

"Because my boat is extraordinary I cannot be letting you jump off just when a hat drops. Plenty, plenty more of opportunities will arise to jump into the water." Sally imitated Vasilis, then looked at him embarrassed, wondering if she had gone too far. But they both laughed loudly.

"My English was so bad!"

"No your English was good, until the moment you walked out to speak to us. And now you could almost pass as an Englishman, or maybe American." She scrutinised the yacht. "Your new yacht is fantastic. I would love to come and see it close up and I am sure that Anna would."

"My latest guests left this morning. I will get it cleaned up and we will have a party. You're not leaving soon are you?"

"No not yet. I must be getting back, they will be wondering what I'm doing." She stumbled, rushing on the small stone steps. "We will sort something out with Anna. It's her birthday soon; maybe we could have a party for her 40th! Great to see you, Vasilis." She shouted from the gate. He waved from the roof.

34
2002, DAY 6 – Lindos

Sally had tried to stop Anna from going to see the Captain. She'd tried to find the right point in the conversation to break it to her gently. Anna was having none of it! "I must go and thank the man. It sounds like Hamish has some tidying to do, as well. Come on Hamish, let's go and see your friend." Anna checked her face and straightened her dress. She took her son's hand and led him out of the gate. He immediately broke free and ran on ahead.

Sally thought she was going to throw up. It was too late to warn her now. *Would Anna go in to shock?* Sally realised how little she knew about what had happened between Anna and Vasilis. *Could things get any worse this holiday?*

"Can I have another look at your video Jo?" Sally asked.

"It's on the table. I don't understand what I've done, I can't find the lizard on there but I definitely filmed it."

"I'll have a look." Sally watched the ant video first. She smiled as she watched it because Jo had added a whispered voice over and it was very entertaining. There was a bit of a gap and then it went to the Captains house. "There's definitely no lizard. Maybe you were imagining it."

"I definitely filmed it."

"Well the lizard is not here." Sally looked closely at the video – it was Vasilis and Zak sitting talking in the courtyard. When she zoomed in she could see Vasilis clearly. "What made you take this video anyway?" Jo looked worried. She said nothing. "You're going to have to tell me Jo, it's an odd thing to do."

"I was looking for Anna's old boyfriend. I thought it might make her happy. She's too lovely to be on her own."

"Well that's very thoughtful of you Jo."

"I overheard them talking through the gate as I walked back up and the little old donkey guy called him Vasilis, so I filmed him. I was going to ask Anna if that was him but then . . ."

"Then Hamish went missing and luckily because of you we've got him back safe and sound." Sally gave Jo a big hug. "Do you think this guy would be alright for Anna then?" She played the video so that they could both see it.

"Oh yes, he's gorgeous, just right for Anna and I think he's rich."

"Is that the most important thing?" Will asked his daughter.

"Erm . . . probably yes. Is it him?"

"Er . . . it's difficult to tell, it was a long time ago. He used to have long dark curly hair." Sally felt uncomfortable and hoped it did not show.

"Let me have a look at the video." Will said. He laughed his way through the ants, but couldn't see the lizard either. "Maybe the lizard is there but is just moving so fast that you can't see it. We could try slowing it down."

"Or maybe this is the second time this holiday that Jo has seen something that didn't actually happen." Sally didn't look up when she said this and her face was serious.

It was ten minutes before Anna and Hamish got back. Anxiety had drained the colour from Sally's face. "What on earth's the matter Sal?" Anna asked her friend.

"What on earth's the matter Sally?" Hamish repeated.

"Shush Hamish!" Anna commanded.

"What do you mean – I'm fine! How did you get on?" Sally needed to know.

"The gate was locked, there was no one there. Gorgeous house though! We went for an ice-cream."

Sally tried to hide the relief. She was pretty sure that she had got away with it – for now. But she was going to have to speak to Anna soon.

35
2002, DAY 7 – Lindos

"Come on you stragglers." Anna shouted back to the others.

"What's Anna saying about stranglers, Dad? Is she trying to frighten me?"

"Stragglers, Jo, stragglers – the people hanging around at the back. She means 'hurry up you lot!'"

"Will" Sally grabbed her husband's hand from behind him. "Would you mind if I took Anna out for a drink tonight? What I mean is – do you mind babysitting for an hour?"

"Not at all! You can go now if you like, I will put these monkeys to bed, if need be."

"What do you think Anna, fancy a drink?" Sally asked her friend.

"Actually, that sounds brilliant – come on Sal, let's be off. Be good for Will, Hamish."

"Bye Mum." Hamish said, he never had a problem spending time with Will.

"Can I come?" Jo asked in a whining voice.

"Not this time Jo." Will said as he took them away. "See you in a bit ladies – there's no rush."

"Well that was easy Sal, we should do that more often!"

"Where do you fancy?"

"Should we try Yolanda's for a start?"

They headed there.

*

Sitting on high stools at the bar, chatting like old times. Anna nodded towards a skinny middle-aged lady wearing tapered mustard trousers.

"Have you seen Mrs Mustard over there? People shouldn't wear pants like that!"

"That's a bit harsh!"

"Maybe it is harsh, but people who look like that, shouldn't wear pants like that!"

". . . or not go out!"

"Oh Sally" Anna laughed, slapping her thigh. "When did we get to be so opinionated?"

"We always were."

"But we mean well, don't we?"

"We do Anna, we do."

"We should try and get out on our own again before we go home."

"It's weird how I feel so at home here. I only came here for two weeks and that was sixteen years ago, but I do feel quite at home."

"I do too. But I did stay here longer than you."

"Did you? I know you came back to England with me at the end of the holiday, because I remember getting the bus and wondering if I would ever drag you and Vasilis away from each other."

"Yes, but remember I came back, almost straight back, in fact. I was here for most of August that same year."

"I don't remember you coming back."

"But you remember the note. I had literally just got back to England. I had only been back at work a day or two."

"You mean the note I never got?" Sally said.

"Yes, the note from Lou. Anyway, that's why I always thought it was meant to be, you two, that is – if I had stayed away any longer you would probably never have got that note."

"But I never did get that note, it went in the canal remember . . . it wasn't meant to be."

"Well yes, we know that now. Unless there's something you're not telling me." Anna gave Sally a sideways glance.

"There is something I'm not telling you, but that's a whole other story. I want to know what happened to you and Vasilis when you came back."

"Well you tell me, then I'll tell you."

"No, you tell me, then I'll tell you."

"We could be here all night. I'm thinking we should be getting back. But if you just tell me and then we'll go." They both laughed.

"But, what you tell me, might affect what I tell you."

"Oh! . . . . So it's about Vasilis – maybe we should leave it for now."

"Don't you want to know what happened to him?"

"Yes, of course! Do you know?"

"Not exactly but . . ."

Anna butted in. "Just tell me what you know."

"I saw Vasilis today." Sally waited for Anna to react but she said nothing. "In fact I spoke to him."

Anna was slow to respond. "Is he ok? Why didn't you say earlier?"

"He seems fine. He wants to see you." Anna's face still gave nothing away and urged Sally to continue. "I didn't say earlier because I don't know what the score is between you two." There was still no reaction from Anna. "You know the house where Hamish has been going? . . . The Captain's house."

"Yes."

"That's where he lives." Anna looked surprised. "He is the captain." Sally continued, but when she looked at Anna, her face crumbled and she began to cry. Sally hugged her. "Come on, let's walk back up."

When they got to Vasilis' the gate was open. Sally could see him sitting at the table in the courtyard. She led her friend towards the gate. "No, I'm not ready!" Anna cried.

Vasilis heard them and looked up. "Hello" he said, getting out of his seat. Anna and Sally stood perfectly still at the gate, unsure what to do or say. When he got close to them, the light near the gate lit up his face. He smiled like a grinning cat.

36

2002, DAY 7 – The Villa, Lindos

Sally could hear the guitar as she approached the villa. Once inside the gate she sat down at the table near Will waiting patiently for him to finish the track. "Has she pulled? That was quick!" Will said.

"She is just around the corner at the house that I found Hamish in."

"What, with Captain No beard!"

"Captain Vasilis, no less."

"Who?"

"Vasilis, the bloke she met here years ago."

"Are you sure this isn't some kind of planned reunion?"

"I am sure. I realised it was Vasilis when I found Hamish there this afternoon. Oh God, I hope things go OK, she seemed a bit shaken, I don't have a clue what went on between them before and now I've just left her there."

"She's a big girl and anyway I'm sure that's the chap Algie's been with today. He has been on a yacht with Tatiani and her brother and their 'Uncle Vasilis'. Algie also saw him on Jo's video."

"That fits. How did you get on with the kids tonight? Where's Algie – gone to bed already?"

"They were no trouble at all. Algie's just gone out. I think he's hoping to see Tatiani."

37

2002, DAY 7 – The Captain's House, Lindos

Anna and Vasilis stood awkwardly in the dimly lit courtyard. Vasilis turned Anna round so that her face was lit by the lamp hanging from the wall of the house. He admired her face, then lent forward and kissed her cheek. He smiled and indicated to her to a sit at the table, offering wine with a shake of the bottle. She nodded and he poured it into a large glass. As they sat in silence, the sounds of music and faint chatter from the village seemed amplified by their focus. Eventually Anna broke the silence. "Is this your house?"

"It is" he hesitated. "It took me a long time to get it, but it is mine now."

"And it's your yacht in the Bay."

"It is."

"So things worked out just as you planned!"

"The business did."

"How did you do it?"

"That's a long story, but basically my second boat did very well for me, once we got her fixed up, of course. Slowly I built up the business, worked hard and gained a good reputation. Then when my business was established I travelled, went all over the world, making good contacts, networking Anna – you know how it works!"

"Just as you planned."

There was an awkward silence.

"What about you?"

"I stayed working as a pharmacist for a number of years. But I finished when I had Hamish. I am just thinking about going back to it – though my heart's not really in it."

"Hamish is lovely. Such good fun! His father . . . is he here?"

"In Lindos?" Vasilis nodded. "No, no!" Anna laughed. "We keep in contact for Hamish, but he is not really part of my life. We are divorced."

"Ah."

"What about you?"

"Me, divorced? No." He looked at Anna, she looked serious for a second. "I never married, Anna."

"Oh, I see" she replied.

The silence returned. A big fat silence that emphasized the time that had passed, the people they had become – what might have been. Anna juggled the questions in her head; she did not know where to begin. A warm smile spread across Vasilis' face. He sighed. "It's good to see you. Should we walk?" Anna nodded. There was no discussion but they both set off towards St Paul's Bay.

The breeze had dropped and it felt muggy, even at the water's edge. The sea lay flat and still.

"I came down here today." Anna said. "I was sitting on the jetty, thinking about that first night we spent here in the little boat."

"You hadn't forgotten me then."

Anna did not manage an immediate reply. "What happened, Vasilis? Why didn't you come to England?"

"I did Anna. Why weren't you there?"

*

Algie was starting to look conspicuous in the street outside Manolis' restaurant. He stood eating a crepe. He had walked up and down four times now, having made the decision not to go inside. Grandfather Manolis was in the doorway, as usual. The last train of donkeys made their way passed and as Manolis came out to speak to them Algie took the opportunity to make his move. Tatiani took the opportunity to make her move and they crashed in the doorway. Simultaneously they jumped backwards, glanced towards Manolis and then turned to face each other, Algie with a wide chocolaty smile, Tatiani looking cross. "Go back" she whispered loudly, motioning with her hands. "Fifteen minutes. I will see you at the crepe shop." Algie stumbled backwards, nodding manically, just managing to get his balance before reaching the steps.

Zak followed closely behind the donkeys. When Manolis saw him, he turned to go back up the steps, grunting at him in Greek. Zak grunted back, half-heartedly. Manolis swung round, shouting raucously down the street at him, before disappearing inside.

*

"So, when did you come to England?" Anna asked.

"It was the following September." Vasilis said.

"You took your time."

"It wasn't easy to get away. But why weren't you there?"

"Well, where did you look?"

"I went to the only address I had. I was told you had moved away."

"And you just believed them and gave up on me?"

"Well, I had no reason not to believe them. But, no, I did not just give up on you. I spent the rest of the two weeks looking for you. I must have been to every pharmacy in Yorkshire."

"Well why didn't you find me?" Anna was close to tears again.

"I think you need to answer that. Where were you?" He sounded dejected, the memories bringing with them the feelings all over again.

"Well, I don't know. When did you say, September?"

"Yes"

"September '86?"

"87."

"Well . . . I had moved away by then." Her voice faded away. "Why did it take you so long? A year is a long time when you're 25."

Vasilis studied the planks of wood nailed together to make the jetty. He picked at the grain of the wood, running his nail along the grooves, pulling at a splinter.

"Didn't you find Sally? There must have been someone there that knew me? Are you lying to me Vasilis?"

He poked the splinter of wood through the open weave of his linen trousers, in and out like a needle. "I don't know what to say Anna. I am not lying to you. I looked for Sally as well, but I had no clues for her, I didn't know where to look. I couldn't believe someone could just disappear like that. I thought you knew that I would come to you when I could."

"But why did you leave it a whole year?"

"If you remember, your last words to me were 'if you're going to put your family before me every time, then there's no point.' I literally had to choose between them and you. I thought I would sort things out, then they would understand and I would go and find you. As it turned out I lost both."

"Both what?"

"You and then my family as well."

"Did they just not like me?"

"When you came back to Lindos in the August of '86 things were fine for a while. Then August 17th 1986 I went home to find all my family screaming and crying. There was a big row."

"Your Mum and Dad?"

"Papa mainly, and Eva. Mama was upset, but quiet. Eventually I found out that Eva was expecting a baby. She wouldn't say who the father was, but apparently he was English. Eva said that it had been a fling; there was no question of them getting together. She was upset, but was unbelievably calm considering the accusations and insults Papa was throwing at her, I feared for her safety. We all did."

"Why did that . . . well, where do I fit into this?"

"You are English."

"Well I didn't get Eva pregnant!"

"No, but you are English. Papa would have nothing to do with anyone English. The restaurant suffered terribly for a long time. I certainly didn't dare to take you to see them."

"Why didn't you tell me at the time?"

"Until we knew what was going to happen to the baby, we had to keep very quiet about it all. The saviour, of course, was Yorgos."

"Yes I suppose he always had a soft spot for Eva."

"I took a risk and told him and he went straight to her and proposed."

"He is so lovely, she is lucky."

"I don't think she sees herself as lucky. At the time she turned him down, said it wouldn't be fair on him, but eventually he convinced her and really they have been very happy, she is lucky, even if she can't see that!"

"So the baby was Tatiani!"

"By the time the wedding was planned and my father had calmed down, you were long gone. I had to cancel going to England originally just because of the wedding."

". . . and then?"

"They went crazy when I said I was going to England to see you. I just thought I would let things calm down and then go and find you . . . and then you rang the restaurant that time and said 'if you're going to put your family before . . ."

"Yes, yes." Anna sighed a long sigh. "I can see how it maybe seemed to you. I was just upset that you weren't coming over. I suppose over the next year I just thought you had given up on me. Oh dear, it's a bit of a mess."

*

Algie had just stuffed the last half of his second chocolate crepe into his mouth when he felt a gentle tap on his shoulder.

"Hi Algie" Mel spoke in a quiet voice which she was surprised to find made him jump. He raised his eyebrows, opening his eyes wide and nodded in greeting. His cheeks bulged and he was unable to manoeuvre the food in his mouth well enough to chew it. He appeared dumbstruck. "Not speaking?" Algie's nodding became faster and more pronounced. He tried to smile, but the chocolate made a run for it – oozing down his chin. "Ah, I see." Mel said. "You out on your own?" Algie nodded 'yes', then panicked thinking she might tag along, he nodded 'no'. She glanced around his back, first one way and then the other, then down the street both ways. Eventually she joined in the miming, shrugging her shoulders and raising the palms of her hands in a questioning manner.

"Must dash," Algie said, forcing out more food than words; he pointed down the street and began to walk away. He was worried now that Tatiani would find him with Mel. She moved to walk with him, but he moved faster and the panic showed in his eyes. He disappeared down the next side street. Mel stood for a minute looking for someone with a moustache.

When Algie peeped back round the corner, she was still there, standing in the queue for a crepe. *'Shit'* he thought. He managed to swallow the food, but the pain that followed left him clutching his chest. He waited nervously, hoping that one would leave before the other arrived.

*

"I found some old photos of the Acropolis when it was first built – I have them on the wall in my house, they remind me of you." Vasilis lay back on to the jetty looking up at the Acropolis. Anna started laughing.

"Oh, Vasilis!"

"I lied a little. They are engravings, old, but probably an artist's impression rather than an accurate documentation of how it looked."

"I look forward to seeing them."

"I have missed you."

"That's a long time to be missing someone."

"Maybe."

"I missed you, too."

*

The next time Algie looked around the corner Mel was waiting with her father and the three little boys. She was just about to be served and the boys were arguing about which crepe was best. Tatiani appeared up the street, then hovered by the crepe shop for a moment, looking around her. Algie watched. She wandered back towards the restaurant. Algie realized that he was going to have to go and get her whether Mel was there or not. He was about to step out only to find that Tatti had vanished into thin air, he panicked, but before he made a move he noticed that Tatti's mother had appeared, walking back up to the restaurant. He waited, realising that this was why she had disappeared. Then smiled as he watched, struck by the resemblance between Tatiani and her mother.

"Hi, Eva. You're still here!" Mel's father greeted Tatti's Mum.

"Sorry?" Eva replied, looking puzzled.

"I saw your father, I didn't realise you were still in Lindos, it's good to see you." His smile was warm and friendly.

"Sorry, you must be mistaken." Eva kept her head down and quickened her step. Lou's smile faded, then he leaped forwards.

"1986, you must remember – the boat trip, the beach." He tried to show her the scar on his leg.

"No sorry" was all she said, without stopping.

Algie was intrigued. As Eva left, Tatiani appeared again.

"Got you!" Algie said, grabbing her arm as she walked by, pulling her into the side street. "I bet you thought I'd let you down."

"No, I knew you would be here." She said this calmly, after the initial shock. "Let's go down to the beach. I am hungry. Do you want to get something to eat on the way down?" Then she spotted the chocolate on his chin. "I see you started without me."

*

"Did you know there's a little boat under this jetty?"

"I know there used to be. It's not my old boat, but I bet I know whose it is."

"Yes?"

"It will belong to Alekos. He knows that I used to keep mine there."

"Who is Alekos?"

"My nephew, Eva's son."

"So Eva and Yorgos had a son after Tatiani."

"Yes, he's thirteen now and just like his Dad."

"You said earlier that you lost both me and your family. What did you mean you lost your family?"

"My father said that if I went to England to find you, that the family would disown me. Even though I waited until Eva was married and the baby was born, he couldn't forgive the 'English'. When I left for England we had a big row – I always thought he would get over it. When I couldn't find you I didn't want to go back to Lindos, so I travelled." Anna listened intently. "I spent a number of years in Italy learning about boats, working in the tourist trade. I kept in touch with Zak . . ."

"The donkey-man, Zak?"

"Yeah, he always encouraged me in my business ventures, we are quite close. He helped me financially too. I used to send money back to Mama and beautiful Italian clothes for her and Eva. Zak tells me she loved them but never dared to wear them, it makes me feel very sad to think about it. Anyway, he got in touch to let me know Mama was ill – I came straight back. She died within days of me getting back."

"I'm sorry."

"Then Papa blamed me, said she was heartbroken when I went away. He won't talk to me. Stubborn old fool."

"But . . . Oh Vasilis that's terrible!"

"Eva still won't talk to me. Maybe she blames me too . . . Yorgos introduced me to my nephew and niece and now I see Tatiani and Alekos regularly – they sneak out to see me."

"Unbelievable."

"She will come round eventually; the kids are working on her."

"This just doesn't make sense."

*

Tatiani and Algie sat at one of the tables outside Dionysus, a small bar on Pallas Beach. Both had ordered and eaten food.

"We very busy tonight. Lot of people have been in the restaurant." Tatti said, Algie smiled. "Mama is drive me mad this week, she is bitch from hell." Algie gasped. "Sorry, is that bad thing to say?"

"'Bitch from hell' is pretty . . . well very bad."

"Oh, maybe she is just 'bitch' . . . No . . . no, really she is bitch from hell!"

"Is she becoming an ogre like your Grandfather?"

"Yes, maybe!"

"Not as big and scary as he is though."

"No. Little and scary!" Tatti said and Algie laughed. "Everybody has bad moods this week, it drives me mad. Mama say she is . . ." she struggled to find the right word then eventually pulled a 'stressed' face . . . "she is so bad today that she said that we will go on holiday – we never go on holiday in the middle of tourist season!"

"That will be nice, where will you go, to England?" he laughed again when he said it.

"No, no, no! We wills not be going to England! My father has a brother in Athens, we may go and see him. Maybe tomorrow."

"Tomorrow?" his face dropped "That's very soon! How long will you go for?"

"Mama say a week or two. I say to her that I don't want to go. She say I must go."

"So, I might not see you again." Algie said this quietly, the disappointment was obvious.

". . . I . . . I don't know. Just when I was beginning to think you are ok."

"Thank you. I think you are ok too." He smiled sweetly. Then after a moment, "maybe you should hide."

"Maybe." They sat in silence for a while.

"I suppose we better be getting back. I will walk you home."

Tatiani thought for a minute then said "I think we should call in to see my uncle, maybe he can help."

"It's a little late, isn't it?"

"Yes, but tomorrow may be too late."

*

"Anna and Vasilis made their way back up from St Paul's Bay. They stood together outside the villa.

"You want to come back to look at my paintings?" Vasilis asked using a heavy Greek accent and his best smile.

"I would love to come and look at your paintings, Vasilis, but I feel I have left Hamish too long."

"We have much to talk about."

"We do have much to talk about, but I must go for now."

"May I kiss you?" He said this a little too loudly for Anna.

"Sshhh! They will hear you. But yes, you may." Anna giggled.

The giggling soon stopped.

*

When Vasilis walked around the corner, he found Tatiani and Algie waiting by the gate, they were just about to give in and go. He took them into the courtyard where together they explained the situation. He was very understanding, but said that as it was so late there was nothing he could do at this time.

"Your Mama would not appreciate me calling to see her this evening."

"So you will come and see her!"

"If you go back home now, I promise I will come to see her in the morning, so long as my father is out of the way. I will suggest that you could stay with me."

"Oh thank you, thank you!" she hugged him.

"I doubt it will work Tatiani, but I will try. Algie could you walk her back home?"

"Sure."

38
2002, DAY 7 – The Villa, Lindos

For a while Will sat in the courtyard just outside the room. From the bed, Sally could see that the door had been left ajar. Intermittently she heard the chair squeak, shuffling noises as he readjusted his position and that familiar sound that he made when he sucked at his cigar. It was a scenario she knew well, a habit from home, but without the television to 'plug into' she wondered what he was thinking about. She fidgeted in the heat, unable to settle, going over the events of the day in her mind. Her mind wandered and she began to doze.

Sally became aware of him as he climbed into the bed; she immediately relaxed a little. He turned away from her and she could feel the heat radiating from his back. She moved up to him but he moved away.

39
August 1986, Lindos

The bike roared as they pulled up the hill out of Lindos Main Square. The rush of cool air was bliss Anna thought, shaking her head to get Vasilis' long curls out of her face. She clung to him, surprised to find how quickly and naturally she picked up cornering on the bike. It was not until they reached the main road at the top of the hill that she considered the implications of being scantily dressed and not wearing a helmet. She felt vulnerable suddenly. As the road levelled out at the bottom of the slope from Lindos, Vasilis pulled away. Anna remembered the state of the road surface and buried her face into the back of his neck. In less than 10 minutes they were on Haraki Beach.

Anna was into her third week on Rhodes in August, having flown back out on the first of the month on her own. The temperature had certainly gone up a notch since she had left in early July, but the Meltemi wind had arrived as it usually does in high season – a natural antidote to the fierce heat.

Hand in hand they walked along the pebble beach. With the lights from the buildings behind them, their only source of light was the moon; large and low in the sky, its broken reflection wriggled rhythmically as each wave approached. In contrast to the gentle sound of the sea, their sandals crunched through the pebbles. Anna had reached the point where she could no longer look at Vasilis' sandals without laughing and because he got annoyed when she laughed, she found that she had to avoid looking at them altogether. This was difficult to do as she had to look carefully to see where she was going. Vasilis stopped suddenly. He pulled Anna towards him, wrapping his arms around her tightly he held their bodies together from top to toe, nuzzling his face into her neck. He lay a row of kisses diagonally up towards her ear, then whispered "I love you."

"I love you too." Anna replied. "But do you know what you are saying?"

"What do you mean? Of course I know what I am saying!"

"Don't the Greeks have lots of different words for 'love'?"

"They do, but I know how I feel Anna. I don't want to let you go, I want you in my life. I love you." He repeated this in Greek. "I never expected to feel like this about anybody, you have taken me by surprise."

Anna didn't know what to say at first, it was so out of the blue. But she knew how she felt. "I love you too Vasilis."

They made love on the beach. A passionate toast to the feelings they now acknowledged.

Later, as they lay in silence, Anna heard something move just in front of her feet. "What was that?" she said panicked.

"What was what?" Vasilis replied.

"That noise."

"I didn't hear anything."

Anna heard it again. "There, you must have heard it that time!"

"What did it sound like?"

"I don't know – like something dropping onto the beach."

"Like footsteps?"

"Animal footsteps maybe."

They listened for a while. Anna drew her feet up towards her body. After a significant length of time it happened again.

"Should we go now?" Anna asked. Vasilis started laughing. "What?"

"It was me."

"No it wasn't, it was over there." Anna said, sounding just a little bit grumpy.

"See." Vasilis picked up pebbles that were by his side and threw them quite accurately to land at Anna's feet. "It goes up, it comes down. It goes up, it comes down." Each time he said this, he threw a stone to demonstrate and then laughed again. Anna remained silent. "Hey, it is a joke."

"You and your jokes, frightening me to death."

"Watch this!" he threw the stone high in the air and eventually it plopped down into the sea. "Gravity does that." Vasilis said.

"I know what gravity does."

"Love is like gravity. It is a force – you can't get away from it. You can't see it, but you know it's there. Sometimes you forget it's there, but then something happens to remind you that it still exists." He threw another stone, higher still. "Love is there, even if you cannot see it."

"You know I have to go back to England at the end of the month." Anna said.

"Don't go. Stay here."

"I wish I could, but I have already left my job too long, I was very lucky to get a month off."

"Well work for a while then you can come back, or I will come and see you."

"We will make it work – there is no rush."

"Just remember that I love you."

40
2002, DAY 8 – Lindos

Vasilis walked across the courtyard, through the gate and out into the street. He did not need to walk past the villa where Anna was staying, but he glanced around the corner at the shutters, he knew they would be closed; he just could not help but look. It was too early for most people; some were just making their way home. He felt tired because he had been unable to sleep. Intending to go to his yacht before summoning the courage to visit Eva, he walked through the centre of the village and down towards Pallas Beach. But looking out across the bay, the empty beach called to him. He needed no persuading. Turning sharply, he went down the steep steps in the rock.

He took off his clothes, leaving them in a pile on a rock at the end of Lindos main beach, then ran into the water. The splashes prepared him for the temperature of the sea. Diving in, he swam in a straight line, on and on and on.

*

The implications of Tatiani's outburst the night before had kept Eva awake. She lay in bed waiting for the sun to rise, preparing to go and speak to her brother for the first time in years. Rising with the sun and too distracted by her thoughts, she found herself at Vasilis' house too early. She wandered down to the beach to kill some time. Walking the length of the long wooden jetty on Pallas Beach, she could not help but smile to herself when she realised that Vasilis' yacht was so big that it had to be anchored away from the jetty. Even from a distance she marvelled at the detail, the unmistakable quality of the yacht and in that moment she knew that she had underestimated her brother. Maybe it was in her blood; the sea, the boats. She felt proud to see her Mother's name on the side of the yacht and sat on the jetty swinging her legs in the sunshine. For a short moment her worries disappeared and she lay back on to the wooden boards.

A gentle splashing sound brought Eva back to the present. It was the delicate splash of an expert swimmer. She sat up, watching the swimmer come back into the Bay, recognising him in the same way a bird watcher knows a bird by the way it moves, it's posture and colouring. She whistled loud and long – the family whistle – a sound they all know. The swimmer slowed, his feet gliding down from the surface of the water. He glanced round, shielding his eyes from the sun. When Eva waved, Vasilis spotted her on the jetty and swam to join her. Eva's worries gripped her stomach and scrunched her face. She considered running home, but knew it was too late.

"I was going to come and see you this morning."

"Yes, Tatiani told me." Eva said curtly.

"AAhhgh, that girl!"

"Don't worry, I dragged it out of her. It's been a long night."

"It's nice to see you." Vasilis smiled, he looked fondly at his sister. "You look tired."

"You mean old. When did you get back?"

"About a month ago . . . and, I mean tired."

"When were you going to come and see me?"

"When were you going to come and see me?" They looked at each other. Eva's eyes dropped to the floor. It was a while before they spoke.

"I've left my clothes on the beach; I'd better go and pick them up before someone else does."

"Armani, no doubt!"

"I didn't realise he was in the vicinity."

"I mean . . ."

"I know what you mean. Do you want a closer look at my new yacht?" Eva's face softened. "Just wait a minute while I save my clothes from Mr Armani."

Eva laughed. "Ok."

"Or better idea, if you will go and grab my clothes, I will get the Tender and I'll pick you up on the beach in a minute."

*

"Wake up, princess." Yorgos shook his daughter gently.

"Erh!" groaned Tatiani.

"Come on, it's late!"

"I don't want to go, Dad. I really don't want to go."

"We're not going anywhere, but you need to be getting up." Tatiani beamed at her father.

"Why did you change your mind?"

"We didn't. We couldn't get fights for a couple of weeks – it would be too late then."

"Oh, I don't mind going in a couple of weeks." Tatiani said. Yorgos looked puzzled, then rolled his eyes in disbelief.

*

Anna, Hamish, Sally, Will and Jo sat having breakfast in the courtyard. Algie was fast asleep in bed.

"What do we all have planned for today?" Will asked.
"Beach." said Hamish.
"Beach" said Jo.
"Beach" said Sally.
Will looked at Anna. "Well?"
"Beach maybe, but hopefully I am going to have a guided tour of Vasilis' yacht."
"Can I come?" Hamish asked.
"I don't see why not."
"Can I come?" asked Jo.
"Ah, not sure Jo, we will have to see."
"Well it looks as if we will be on the beach. If Vasilis decides that we can have a guided tour you know where we'll be. I presume the yacht is still in the Bay."
"It's still there. I will see what I can do."
"Yeah!" they cheered.

*

"Where is Mama?" said Tatiani
"She has gone to see Vasilis."
"Why couldn't she just wait for him to come and see her?"
"I think she thought it was better at his place, to make sure that they wouldn't run into your Grandfather."
"I suppose so."

*

"Your boat is fantastic Vasilis! Michalis would be proud of you.
"Boat!"
"Yacht. Whatever it is, it is very nice. You deserve it."
"Well, it's taken me sixteen years, but it was worth all the hard work."

"Every minute?"

"Yes." Vasilis spoke proudly. "Remember that first boat trip, when it all went wrong?"

Eva did not look up.

"Eva?"

"I . . ." Eva began. Vasilis waited. "I remember." She managed at last. "If it wasn't for that buffoon slashing his leg."

"It was bad news at the time, but really it just made it all the more memorable! I saw L . . ."

"I know." Eva interrupted.

"You saw lions too?" Vasilis smiled.

"You weren't going to say lions." Eva managed a smile.

"What was I going to say, if you can read my mind?"

"I saw Lou." Eva struggled to speak his name.

"I was going to say that." Vasilis acknowledged.

"You did see him?"

"I did. Did you?"

"I did . . . he tried to speak to me."

"Tried to speak to you?"

"Well, he spoke to me. He tried to make conversation. I told him I don't remember."

"Why would you do that Eva?" No reply. "Why would you do that?" Vasilis repeated. "I think you remember him very well."

"No not really."

"In fact I guess there is hardly a day has gone by that you haven't thought about him." Eva suddenly looked very sad. "It's him isn't it?" Again no response. "Don't lie to me Eva. I know it's him."

"No one knows."

"I know."

"Think you know."

"Don't you think Tatiani has a right to know?"

"I must go." Eva turned to go.

"Don't run away."

"You're the one who runs away!" Eva shouted, close to tears.

"That's why you were going to go on holiday, wasn't it, to run away?"

"It would be for the best. When we get back he's gone. Never see him again. No problem."

"So it is him then?"

Vasilis could read Eva's face well enough to know the answer to his question.

41
2002, DAY 8 – Lindos

Sally had found the villa too busy. The joking and music, the spasmodic donkey braying and general chatter were altogether driving her mad.

"I'm off to the shops." She had shouted. The door on to the street banging closed before the frenzy of flapping flip-flops caught up with her. "Stay there I won't be long" she shouted from the street.

The sun had risen with some kind of vendetta that morning. The heat was stifling, now that the wind had dropped and because it was so muggy there was nowhere to get away from it. Tourists, donkeys and locals packed the streets; *'makes me want to walk with vicious elbows'* she thought.

Over the years she had learned to handle stress. *'Surely when you're stressed you know about it, it would be obvious'* she had thought at sixteen. The first signs for Sally were palpitations – no pain, just strange rhythms, irregular thumps and missing heart beats; mistaking them for a heart attack her panic had made them worse. She had not realised that she was stressed, but after considering the Doctor's questions she decided that maybe there had been a lot to deal with: school exams, sixth form lessons had been very different, more responsibility, new friends and routines; learning to drive, she wanted to drive so much, but she failed the first test that she took; boyfriends, everyone had one, except her; numerous events, little in themselves but adding up to more.

Sally learned to deal with the palpitations; she could even physically slow them down using her diaphragm, once she had been taught how to do it. It was not until her late twenties that the panic attacks had started. It was the panic attacks that had led her to a clinical psychologist, Marcus Berry; he had changed her life in six short weeks. He taught her to relax and also to capture her thoughts and write them down where they could be looked at objectively, and managed. She learned about a lifestyle that would help her to manage stress; eating healthily, reducing stimulants like caffeine and alcohol when palpitations appeared; she found out that exercise was a magic ingredient that helped her to sleep and lifted her mood. Marcus Berry taught her to celebrate her achievements and to forget her mistakes; time management skills and reading at bedtime; finally to have realistic expectations, to lose the perfectionist attitude and be kinder to herself because she is, in fact, good enough.

Today was one of those days when she had forgotten everything that she had learned, the stress had crept up on her, sneaking its way in. Holidays are not supposed to be stressful.

Nearing the centre of the village Sally dropped into a small supermarket to pick up supplies. She perused the shelves looking for milk. The words on the carton were in Greek, everything about it said milk and there was even a cow on the front, but something was annoying her. She picked up a pot of yoghurt, this time the words were in English, but she still could not read it. Eventually she realised that there was a blob, like a smudged mark on her glasses, right in the centre of her vision. She tried to remove her glasses, but was not actually wearing any. She left the shop. Now she could not see the facial features of the people approaching her and letters were missing from the centre of words above the shops and restaurants. Her heart sank with the realisation that they were the signs of a migraine and she knew she had about ten minutes before her vision would be so bad that she would not be able to continue in the street very easily. She needed to sit down on her own somewhere.

Although there were a few tourists, the church looked quiet. She stepped up into the entrance area.

As she made her way into the church a lady grabbed her arm and pointed to the basket of garments, Sally picked one out and wrapped it around her skirt and legs. She walked in, waiting for the waft of cool air. The sudden darkness left her disorientated and the smell . . . What was that smell? As soon as her eyes became accustomed to the darkness she sank into the nearest seat.

The cool air never arrived. The floating blob of blind spot grew bigger each minute and developed flashing zigzagged lights around it. The lights would not leave her, it did not matter whether her eyes were open or closed. She had no option but to stay put. The smell, whatever it was, irritated her. She slipped rapidly into the depths of despair, burying her head in her hands she sobbed silently. Images began to flicker across her mind, it was her father, or was it someone else in there? Standing, leaning on the doorframe wanting to go in, but feet rooted to the spot, unable to walk the tiny step into the room. The step that took her somewhere she had never expected to be, surprised to find that step physically difficult to do. At one point deciding she could never do it, turning to move away, but ultimately pulled over the step by the desire to say a final goodbye. To see for herself that he had gone, that it was just the body he had used all these years.

42
2002, DAY 8 – Lindos

His portly frame and confident swagger were unmistakable as Manolis made his way to the restaurant. It was the same route to work that he had taken every morning for the last thirty-eight years and as usual he passed Zak on the way. No eye contact was made and no words were exchanged until they were past each other.

"Bastard."

"Scruffy waster."

Bitterness, an insidious enemy; its poison seeping in miniscule doses, drop by drop over time until it reaches saturation point, the point where the life that was, has gone.

43
August 1986, Top Car Park, Lindos

They stood hand in hand waiting for the bus. Both quiet, deep in thought. Anna spotted the bus first and clung to Vasilis.

"I don't want to go."

"Stay here, you don't have to go."

"I have to go just now." She kissed Vasilis. "I love you."

"Soon as I can, I will come for you."

The driver signalled to them to get on the bus. Anna could not help but cry when she saw the tears in Vasilis' eyes. But when she noticed that the driver's patience was wearing thin she moved to get on the bus. Vasilis grabbed her back – "Here, I nearly forgot," he said with a broad smile. He kissed a small stone and pressed it into Anna's hand. "Don't forget, if gravity is there then I still love you."

Anna cautiously threw it in the air and caught it again. She smiled and then blew him a kiss.

44
2002, DAY 8 – Lindos

Approaching the yacht, Anna was awestruck by the realisation that the 'boat' she had seen all week anchored in the bay was actually, on closer inspection, enormous. It is difficult to judge the size of any boat alone on a vast expanse of sea, as this gives an unreliable perspective. She scrutinised the yacht in increasing detail with every step that took her nearer. It was the craftsmanship that left her dumbstruck. She had imagined that the yacht would be like the old boat – just bigger, but there was no comparison. Every feature whispered 'quality'; oceans of wooden decking, the Jacuzzi on the top deck, the equipment on the bridge positioned inside Teak panelling. The six white sails that Anna had previously seen hanging from three masts were strapped down neatly and flapped lightly in the breeze.

"Oh Vasilis, it is absolutely fantastic! It's worlds away from that first little boat." Anna sounded excited, Hamish turned and stared at his mother, he went very quiet. "I absolutely love it. What do you say Hamish?" He looked at her somewhat suspiciously. "Well, what do you think?"

"It's very nice, Mummy." Hamish said eventually. Anna didn't notice his apprehension.

"Has it got a wheel, Captain Vasilis?" Anna asked "It must have a wheel!" she said dashing around.

"Anna, you know that boats don't have wheels!" Vasilis said, winking at Hamish.

"I mean a steering wheel; you know those big wheels with handles on for steering." Anna's exuberance continued as she waved her arms about as if manoeuvring such a wheel.

"Well, yes we have one of those wheels." He pointed towards the bridge.

"Come and get us on course, Hamish." Anna said, guiding Hamish in the direction of the wheel.

"The boat's not moving, Mummy."

"Yes, that's right Hamish! The yacht is anchored in the bay." Vasilis said smiling. "You are not very familiar with boats, are you Anna?" After a second or two Anna stood still, turned to Vasilis and started laughing.

"Oh Vasilis, that's so funny, do you remember?" Anna could not stop laughing; Vasilis couldn't help but laugh too.

"What are you laughing at Mummy?"

"Nothing really Hamish . . . well . . . along time ago . . . oh, it's a long story . . . I will have to tell you later."

When their laughter had subsided Vasilis showed them how to steer and then began his guided tour. He told them about the sails and the work that was needed to make the yacht move and keep it going in the right direction. He described the jobs of each crew member. All the Health and Safety issues were covered and he took extra time to be sure that Hamish knew what was ok and what wasn't. Hamish asked lots of sensible questions and Anna did not, her head was in the clouds. Hamish was beginning to wonder what had happened to his mother, she was behaving very strangely.

"Can we set off somewhere?" Anna asked. "To a desert island?"

"Maybe, but let me show you below decks before we think about moving." They made their way below deck.

Anna's steps slowed the further she got down the stairs, her eyes widened and her hand came up to cover her mouth.

"Wow!" she said, almost in a whisper. "It's like the Ritz!" Hamish hovered on the bottom step. "Gosh Hamish, isn't it beautiful?" She nudged him, but he stayed glued to the step. "What's the matter?" He lowered his eyes and pointed to his feet. "Oh Hamish, Sweetheart. Run up and grab a towel from the top deck!" she said sending him on his way and then "Bless him" as she realised that in his short lifetime one of the things that had been drilled into him was that you do not walk on pale carpets with dirty feet. The carpet, thick and plush, went from wood panelled wall to wood panelled wall; under button backed sofas and traditional chairs covered in Silks and Jacquards, with cushions galore; it went around pillars and up to rich brown, traditional hardwood cabinets; then under coffee tables, dining tables and chairs. Flowers in vases and a few choice paintings added a splash of colour to the neutral palette. A dining table stretched out across the width of the yacht set for twelve with wine glasses and silver cutlery, napkins and candles; flowers reflected their purples and yellows in the silverware.

"Let me get you a drink." Vasilis said, ushering them through to the galley. *A kitchen to die for,* Anna thought, every modern convenience, with bags of style and little touches of character.

"This place is amazing, Vasilis. How on earth did you make enough money to be able to afford this?"

"Hard work."

"Yes, but even with hard work . . ."

"This is the Master Cabin." Vasilis showed them into the room. "I built a successful business and then applied the same formula in a number of places all over the world. Italy, The Caribbean, Mauritius, Australia . . . and others. Most people want the same things when they are on holiday; sunshine, good food, interesting company, beautiful places to visit . . . and a little luxury. Jump up on the bed Hamish. Watch this!" Vasilis picked up a remote control and pressed a few buttons. The lights dimmed, a screen appeared at the foot of the enormous bed and music blasted from all corners of the room. Hamish giggled . . . and then Spiderman appeared on the screen.

"Wow!" said Hamish.

"Very impressive. I can see that you go out of your way to give your visitors a luxurious lifestyle with good food, beautiful places and all the other things, but how can you ensure that they have interesting company? Oh, I don't mean you!"

Vasilis laughed "It may not be as difficult as you think. It depends on the people that you employ, and maybe the way you treat them. I have never had a problem employing interesting people who have a passion for travel and who are genuinely interested in other people."

"I guess not."

Vasilis prepared their drinks, sat them on a tray and carried them up on to the top deck.

"Are you ready for a swim Hamish?" Vasilis asked.

"It's too deep for me here, isn't it Mummy?" Hamish replied.

"What about if I put you in a life jacket and we go into the Tender?" Hamish beamed and looked expectantly at his mother.

"I presume it's safe?" Anna replied. Vasilis gave her a look. "Yes, yes, of course you can. I will stay up here and fight off any pirates."

*

"It's not fair Daddy." Jo spoke to Will.
"What's not fair, Love?"
"Hamish gets to go on the big yacht and I don't."
"Ah, you just bide your time."
"I'm bored of biding my time."

*

One long blink and Tatti appeared before Algie. He melted a little more, if that was possible at 32 degrees.
"Do you want to go for a swim?" she asked.
"I'm glad to see you."
"Yes, I am still here. They decide not to go to holidays. Everyone is a little happier today, but I still decide to keep out of the way."
"I am definitely ready for a swim!" Algie prepared to go.
"Dad?"
"Shush Jo."
Tatti and Algie set off for the water.
"Dad, it's not fair." Jo tried again.
"Leave the love birds, Jo." Will whispered.

*

Lou, Stevie, Jack and Robert Reeve knelt in a circle around an elaborate sand castle, adding the finishing touches.
"Should we hire a pedalo and sail around that yacht fellas? Sometimes famous people stay on there, apparently."
"Apparently." Repeated Jack.
"We need to finish this Dad!"
"Well, yes, I mean when we've finished this."
"Ok" they replied in unison.

*

"Surprise!" Algie and Tatti splashed their way out of the water very close to the Tender. Hamish jumped.

"Ha, ha, made you jump!"

"Not me, I saw you a long time ago." Vasilis said.

"I suppose Captains have to be on the ball when it comes to things suddenly appearing on the horizon." Algie added.

"Like Ninjas?" said Hamish.

"My grandfather was a Ninja turtle," said Vasilis.

Hamish laughed and then looked serious suddenly. "He wasn't really, was he?" he said.

"I think Sally was, because she looks a bit like a turtle." Algie joked and they all laughed.

*

Anna reclined on a sun lounger. Drifting in and out of sleep, she picked up snippets of conversations from below. She was amazed how natural Vasilis was with Hamish and felt very relaxed and confident leaving them together. She was still reeling from the events of the last couple of days; events she would never have dared hope would happen. A wave of sadness came over her when she thought about Vasilis looking for her in England and of what might have been. But pulling herself together she knew it was silly to dwell on such things. She sat up, swinging her legs around and then steadied herself as she stood up to walk to the rail. Tatti was now in the Tender with Vasilis. Algie was in the water with Hamish. Vasilis had even managed to get Hamish to put his head under the water with a snorkel on. Unbelievable!

She spotted Lou with his boys on a pedalo, heading towards the yacht.

*

Vasilis had spotted them too. He waved.

"Hey boys, look, the man by the yacht is waving, let's go closer." They pedalled closer. "Is this yours?" Lou shouted to Vasilis as they got nearer.

"It is mine. Different to my last one, eh?"

Lou was confused. "Your last one?"

"Yes, remember the boat trip? Your leg? How is your leg?"

Lou looked again at the gentleman before him. He had not recognised Vasilis, but it was obvious now.

"Crikey! It's you! Vasilis?"

"Yes, how are you, Lou?

"I am good. That's some boat! How long have you had this one? You still doing boat trips?" Lou laughed as he said this.

"This boat is new this month."

"I'm glad my stupidity didn't get in the way of your ambitions."

"Not at all! Fuelled them if anything. How is your leg?"

"My leg is great thanks. It took a while to heal, but it's fine. Left me with a very manly scar." He took a good look at them both, "It has been a long time! For a minute there I thought that was Eva." Tatti pulled a face. "Sorry, Darling."

"My niece, Tatiani. Eva's daughter. Tatiani this is Lou, he stayed here years ago and ripped his leg on my old boat, before you were even born."

"Hi Lou."

"I would invite you on board but we have some passengers to pick up from the beach."

"No worries."

"I'm thinking of running a boat trip tomorrow. If you fancy it, bring all the family. Ten o'clock from here."

"Even the little ones?"

"Most definitely!"

"Count us in."

*

Algie and Tatti made their way to the beach to pick up the others. They rowed within a comfortable silence. Tatti broke the silence. "Do you think Lou was here just before I was born?"

"Well, I know he was here in 1986, was that just before you were born?"

"Yes. So it could be him."

"Who, what do you mean?"

"Maybe Lou was with Mama in 1986."

"All I know is that he had a holiday romance with Sally in 1986."

"Then it must not be him."

"Who? I don't understand what you mean?"

"He must not be my father."

"What do you mean, your father? I thought Yorgos was your father." Algie felt very confused.

"Yorgos is not my real father. My real father is English and no one seems to know who he is."

"Oh." Algie was shocked.

Tatti continued. "He would not be with Mama and Sally at the same time, would he?"

"I don't know. Maybe he would. Lou definitely knows your mother – I saw him speak to her last night, in the street, when I met you at the crepe shop. Lou knew her name, but she denied knowing him."

"Denied?"

"She told Lou that she didn't know him, even though he obviously knew her."

"You mean she lied."

"I don't know – I really don't know." Algie put his arm around Tatti.

The silence returned as they walked through the shallow water towards the beach.

"Come on Jo, do you want to see the yacht?" Algie grabbed his little sister. "Dad, Sally?"

"At last!" exclaimed Jo, stuffing everything into her beach bag.

"Will we get wet?" Sally asked.

"Not if you're lucky. Come on, quickly!"

"We're off to see the yacht, we're off to see the yacht . . ." They made up a 'we're off to see the yacht' song, on the way.

*

The MacFaddyans, Anna and Hamish Howard, Vasilis and Tatti sailed out of the bay in the yacht.

45
2002, DAY 8 – Lindos

Lou Reeve was in his element; surrounded by his boys, preparing the evening meal and his favourite girl in the world setting the table. He had been missing Jane this week, but tonight he was enjoying having them all to himself; showing the boys the joys of barbequing without Mrs Health & Safety spoiling the fun. Mel manoeuvred herself under his arm for an impromptu hug.

"Hey, Daddio! What's cooking? . . . Let me guess, you're doing my favourite cheesy filled burgers?" Mel said, nuzzling up to her father.

"Well, my darling, unfortunately not today. We've got fish, veggie kebabs and of course Donkey steaks." Lou winked at his daughter. The three boys stopped what they were doing.

"Donkey steaks?" Jack shouted. The other two joined in. "Yuk".

"You'll never want anything else once you've tried these."

"Well I don't want any." Jack said adamantly.

"Don't want any" the other two echoed.

"Looks like it's just you and me, Mel."

"Oh, what a shame, but I guess we'll manage to eat it all." Mel winked back at her father, with a big smile.

Lou and Mel struggled to keep a straight face whilst listening to the conversation that followed.

"I could never eat a donkey."

"I couldn't eat a donkey, their skin is too tough."

"I couldn't eat a lizard"

"Oh, I could eat a lizard."

"Lizards are poisonous!"

"No they're not! Dad, are lizards poisonous?"

"I think they might be, but you'd never catch one anyway, they're too fast."

"I bet I can catch one."

*

Algie walked Tatti around to the front of the yacht away from the others. They stood looking out over the vast expanse of water. Algie had thought it might be a bit like the scene in the film Titanic, but it was a different shape, you could not actually get to the point at the front.

"Ok here?"

"Yes." Tatiani replied. She looked so sad Algie just wanted to hug her. "I don't know what to do Algie. I feel like I will not have the time left, but I may be totally wrong about everything."

"I think you are not totally wrong. But you need to speak to someone."

Anna's exuberance continued, much to everyone's surprise.

"I can't say I've ever seen Anna quite so animated." Will exclaimed.

"Does that mean like a cartoon character?" Jo asked.

"It means lively and vivacious Jo, but I see the connection you're making."

"I have seen her like this" Sally added. "A long time ago. I hope things work out for her, she could do with some fun in her life." As if to sense them talking about her, Anna came over; there were guilty smiles all round but she did not notice.

"Vasilis is going to turn back now." Anna informed them. "It's been a short journey but at least you've all had a quick look and everyone's back here tomorrow on the trip."

"No problem Anna, it's been lovely. We're all looking forward to tomorrow."

"We haven't had any nautical nausea have we?" Everyone shook their heads.

*

Jack lay on the bed whist Emelda changed his nappy. He was the perfect child for those few minutes, until the job was done. The second she was finished he tried to roll himself over, but she grabbed him throwing him on back down on to the bed. "You don't get away that easily. I haven't had my cuddles yet. She nipped his chubby cheeks and kissed him. Jack giggled.

"Booperman" he said and she obliged. Laying on her back on the bed she launched him into the air so that he lay horizontally with his tummy on her feet. She held his arms out front in true Superman style whilst humming the superman theme. Jack just giggle and giggle. And then the finale – she appeared to drop him and catch him all at the same time. They rolled on the bed cuddling.

When all the fun and giggling was over he settled on the bed. She read him a short story, by which time his eye lids were heavy and the blinks became longer. She gently stroked his cheek. "I love you Jack, you're the best boy in the world."

Later, when all the boys were settled in bed, Lou and Mel sat out in the courtyard.

"I thought you would be going out."

"Oh well, if you want rid of me, it can be arranged!" Mel said, disgruntled.

"What, and sit here on my own? Of course I don't want rid of you! It's just that you've been out every other night."

"That's why I'm having a rest tonight . . . You could go out! You could meet up with your old holiday romance."

"What do you know about my holiday romance? Or any of my holiday romances, for that matter?"

"Nothing, except that Algie said his step mum knew you from years ago. You kept that one quiet Daddio!"

"Hey, we don't need to talk about that." Lou muttered

"Except that it was 1986 and I was three."

"Look here, young lady I don't need to explain myself to you." Lou was defensive and then went quiet. Mel looked sad. "Sorry, you're right Sweetheart." he said after a minute.

"Did you have an affair?"

"No, well . . . it's a long story." Lou sighed. He had not intended to say anything; it was water under the bridge.

"You will have to tell me now Daddio, you can't leave it like that."

Lou thought for a moment about where to start. "Your mum and I were about sixteen when we started going out. But we went through a rocky patch before you were born." Mel's face looked serious suddenly. "Things were not good; bad enough for Jane to think that you weren't mine."

"No way!"

"It wasn't until you were three that I found out that I was your Dad. It was two or three months after my holiday here. I shouldn't really be telling you this." Mel said nothing. "We got back together . . ."

"What because of me . . ."

"No. We got back together because we were meant to be, we were always good together. It was a little while after that I found out that you were mine. Jane got the tests done so that we knew for sure."

"God . . . I don't ever remember you not being there. It never crossed my mind. What was Mum thinking?"

"I would really appreciate it if you didn't talk to Jane about this."

"Oh my god, how could she not know? Presumably there was someone else involved . . . and anyway Dad, you and me, we are like two buttons on a jacket!"

"We are these days; you inherited my good looks, that's for sure." He kissed her forehead.

"Anyway, you didn't tell me about your holiday romance." Mel said.

"You didn't tell me about yours."

"Nothing to tell."

"I've nothing to tell."

"You liar Dad, tell all."

"Secret holiday romances should stay secret."

"Naarrr, tell all."

"No, that would spoil it." Lou sighed. "Anyway, how come you've been hanging around with sixteen year olds?"

"Don't change the subject . . . What do you mean sixteen year olds?" Mel thought for a moment. "Algie?" Lou nodded. "Oh my God! I thought he was in his twenties. Ooooo, that explains a few things."

"Too much information!" Lou put his hands over his ears and began humming loudly.

46
2002, DAY 9 – On-board the yacht, Lindos

Vasilis was ready and waiting when the families arrived the following morning for the boat trip. He greeted everyone as they stepped on board and directed them towards an array of champagne flutes with the obligatory Bucks fizz. 'No Fizz for you kids, just Bucks!'

Vasilis sensed Eva's anxiety when Lou and his family appeared. He had not told her they would be there, as he knew she would have stayed away and he made a point of introducing Eva to Lou. To Lou's surprise she acknowledged him, "I remember now" she said, eyes lowered, head down.

Once they had all been ticked off the list, he took them below deck to the dining room, ushering them around the long table. Vasilis drew their attention to the picture of the Titanic hanging on the wall – 'Ominous' someone shouted and laughter rippled through the room. There were gasps of surprise when the 'picture' changed to a black screen and then a hint of a groan filled the air when the words 'Health and Safety Information' appeared. Vasilis bristled, annoyed by their attitude to health and safety and threatened them with a test at the end. He ran through the 'man overboard drill' and pointed out where to locate life jackets and fire extinguishers. His intention was not to frighten anyone, but he stressed that no matter how beautiful today looked at this moment in time, things could change in an instance in the Mediterranean. He ordered Yorgos to check the flares.

Once he had covered the main points they could see that he had relaxed again and just when they thought everything was ok, sirens blazed, red lights flashed and Lou's face appeared on the screen. "If anyone sees this man making any attempts to leave this ship, especially over the side, let me know immediately – there is a reward." Laughter filled the room again.

He outlined the day, apologising for his decision not to go right around the island, making reference to time constraints and the prevailing wind. He held up his hand to stop any moans. "However, we intend to follow the beautiful east coastline of Rhodes heading north east. We will stop at Tsambika beach, just briefly, where you can swim and play – I know how you Brits love the sand! Then north again, swiftly past Mandraki harbour around the northern tip of Rhodes and full steam ahead to Symi. On Symi your lunch will be a leisurely Greek meal courtesy of Spiros, an old friend of Eva's. When we can tear ourselves away from the island of Symi we will call into Rhodes Town to see the early evening markets, then back to Lindos by eight o'clock. Our meal on the way back will be an 'Al fresco' affair on the top deck. Please make yourselves comfortable, we will be underway very soon."

"That sounds wonderful" Anna said gazing up at Vasilis in admiration.

*

Algie sat with Tatiani but watched Mel stretch out on a towel on the top deck of the yacht. He continually checked to make sure that Tatti was not watching him. He was confident that she would have no idea about his night out with Mel, but the vague memories he had of that disastrous evening, haunted him. Again Mel's breasts transfixed him.

'That bikini doesn't really cover her breasts. What's the point of bikinis anyway? They must just be for covering nipples.' Algie thought. He looked at Tatti again, she looked sad.

"Hey, you ok?" he asked. Tatti did not answer at first.

"Do you think I look like him?"

"Who? Oh, yes, Lou, erm . . . maybe a little."

"I think it's him. What should I do?"

"Oh, Tatti, I don't know. Do you want to get to know him?"

"Yes . . . No . . . I don't know."

"You need to know if it's definitely him. Can't you ask your mum? Or maybe your uncle?"

"Not Mama. But maybe Vasilis. Later . . . maybe."

Jo sat quietly behind them listening.

Algie looked around for Vasilis and found him handing life jackets to Anna and Lou for the little ones. After speaking briefly to Lou he disappeared momentarily, returning with a large old-fashioned life jacket which he took across to Mel.

"Mel, you need to put that on." Lou shouted across to her.

"What! You're kidding aren't you?" Mel screeched.

"Rules of the boat." Vasilis said holding it out for her to slip on, like you would a jacket. Mel had not noticed the fact that no one else was wearing one.

"I'm going to end up with a white chest" she said. Begrudgingly she put the jacket on, tying it as best she could. "This is ridiculous."

"It may seem ridiculous, but it is important. We don't want any accidents." Vasilis looked very serious. The others tried not to laugh.

"The amount of oil she's got on there, she'll just slip out of it anyway!" Anna said.

"I reckon she has her own built in buoyancy aids." Will added.

Mel struggled to sunbathe for a little while, but eventually gave up. She flounced about moaning.

"How come you're not wearing one?" she asked Algie.

"I didn't want to look stupid" he said, quickly taking a photo before she managed to untie it and throw it at him.

*

When Vasilis dropped the anchor and 'diving for champagne' was discussed, it was inevitable that the story of Lou's leg would be told. Tatti listened intently.

"Was Mama there?" she asked when they'd finished.

"She certainly was, she gave me a real telling off afterwards. I don't think she's forgiven me." Lou replied. He glanced around for her but she was nowhere to be seen.

"So, Mama, Vasilis, Lou, Sally and Anna, were all there then?"

". . . and me." Yorgos shouted from the wheel.

Vasilis outlined the next part of the trip. "I will launch the Tender and transfer you to the beach at Tsambika – those that want to, of course. If anyone is feeling energetic they can walk up to the tiny Byzantine church at the top. There, you will have fantastic views of the coastline down towards Lindos. And I must say – legend has it that if a woman is having difficulty having children then she should walk barefoot up the 350 steps to the monastery and pray to the Virgin, then she will be blessed with children. You will just have time to get up and back before we will have to get on our way . . . oh and as it's so calm today, if any of you older people fancy the jet skis, we'll get them out here. Algie you are big enough, Tatiani will show you."

"That's sounds better than a barefoot trip to a church – that's all we need!" Algie said.

"Maybe Tatiani could show me too." Lou said.

There was a chorus of 'me too's.

"Algie's only sixteen you know." Emelda blurted out.

"Yes, but he is big enough." Vasilis replied.

'Big enough for some people maybe.' Emelda thought to herself, managing not to say it out loud.

*

"Do you fancy walking up to the monastery, Will?" Sally asked.

"No, not really, I quite fancy the jet skis." He replied.

"Ok. Don't break anything."

*

"Sounds as if we should just get the toys out." Vasilis said, having considered everyone's preference. "We can dive for champagne first, but anyone who wants to try will need to come with me in the Tender so that we can move to a shallower area – it will be too deep here."

"See if you can get that." Vasilis threw the bottle over the side. "No life jacket wearers and one at once please." He had stopped the boat approximately a third of the way to Tsambika beach. It was reasonably shallow, but it would still be a challenge. Jo, Tatti, Alekos, Lou, Will and Anna all had a go, but it was Algie who managed to get the champagne.

Sally had decided to stay on the yacht. Settled on a sun lounger, she was enjoying a quiet read and the gentle breeze. For a brief moment she forgot about her worries, but they niggled their way back into her mind, her problem solving nature over-riding – what was she going to do about Will? She found this problem particularly difficult to solve, as she did not really know what she had done wrong and also, how could she convince Will when he didn't seem to believe what she was saying?

Eva stayed on the yacht with Yorgos. She couldn't remember the last time they had had any quality time together. She was surprised how much she loved him; he had certainly grown on her, this quiet, kind man. When Tatiani was little, Eva had resented him being there, even though he had made an honest woman of her. No-one had known that Tatiani wasn't his, she was so tiny when she was born they all believed that she was premature. But Eva had felt trapped, her world made smaller – she had been planning to travel, see the world. Spiros, the guy they were to visit on Symi was an old school friend. She had loved him when they were at school, he was so exciting and funny, but she knew, even then, that his relationship with drugs would have taken her into a different kind of life. Through the grapevine she had learned of his battle with alcoholism and more recently the cancer that curbed his hedonistic lifestyle. She smiled as she thought of him.

The pool on the Yacht became a playground. Hamish, Jack, Robbie, and Stevie were in their element playing with the noodles, rings and other toys around the pool. Mel was the first of the adults to take turns to watch over them and had to curb their excitement for everyone's sake, as the giggles, squeals and screams became unbearable.

Once passed Rhodes Town they moved away from the coastline out into open water and were joined by a school of dolphins at the bow of the ship. Anna shouted down to Hamish and they all ran to the front of the ship to watch them, cheering them on. The dolphins stayed with the Yacht long enough for the kids to get bored of watching them. Hamish, last to leave had been trying to give them names, but unable to find any distinguishing features had given up, deciding to call them all 'Mr Grey'.

*

"Land ahoy" someone shouted, but Vasilis warned them that they still had to travel the length of Symi and informed them of the expected arrival time. Eventually the Yacht slowed, turning into the wide mouth of the harbour, gliding, as if in stealth. The town drew closer, its cube-like buildings with shallow pitched roofs were scattered along the water's edge and up into the hillside facing them. Distinctly different from the Lindian houses, not only in shape but also in their colour – many were painted yellows and terracottas and a few in greens and blues. Dark green conifers punctuated the pale buildings, along with the occasional domed roof or church steeple. Boats of every shape and size were moored along the harbour side and quivered in the water. Over the radio the harbour master indicated to the crew where he wanted them to moor up and so working in silent synchronization Vasilis, Yorgos and Yannis brought the yacht to a stop and secured it in place. Again, unlike Lindos, the depth of the harbour allowed them to anchor at the harbour side and because of this, disembarking went smoothly and relatively quickly.

Spiros stood hands on hips at the gate; slight, with a fashionably unshaven face and short, silver flecked hair, his stern face broke into a smile when he saw Eva dashing towards him. He picked her up and swung her around, then linking her arm he directed her up the terrace towards the long thin table. Half way there they stopped and turned to be sure the others were following.

*

"Pizza and Beer – what's not to like!" Will shouted when he overheard Vasilis, reprimanding Spiros regarding the 'Greek' lunch. They all looked at Will. "Well, does anyone not like Pizza?" He said. No one spoke. "There you go, we're all happy. Come on Vasilis I'll get you a beer." Spiros looked relieved. Vasilis smiled finally.

"New Pizza oven." Spiros said pointing to the stone built domed oven in the corner of the garden. "I could not wait to try."

"Lucky for you they are happy." Vasilis said.

"We have the Greek Salad, we have the olives, we have the grow at home lemons and we have the Ouzo . . . and ladies and gentlemen in five minutes you will see the traditional Greek dancing." He turned to Vasilis and his crew. "You ready? Come on, while the oven heat up!" Momentarily he went inside and then the music began. Spiros, Vasilis, Yorgos, Yannis and one of the chefs from the restaurant stood in line. They danced, perfectly in step and surprisingly light-footed. Everyone clapped and cheered, the more they clapped the faster they went. The applause was phenomenal when they stopped.

*

Vines climbed up and over the simple wooden structure that covered the table forming an area of dappled shade for the diners. Attentive waiters took drinks orders and put colourful hand-painted bowls filled with salad out on the table. The diners hardly noticed, engrossed in their conversations. The pizzas were placed into the oven using a long metal paddle and shuffled to the back close to the fire that Spiros stoked from time to time. In no time at all the large pizzas began to emerge from the oven and were cut into a number of pieces and placed at various points along the table, so that everyone could start eating at the same time. Everyone ate their Greco-Italian meal without any further discussion of its nationality.

*

The kids sat together at one end of the table sporting a variety of tomato smiles and moustaches. Hamish even managed to keep a small cheese beard that waggled as he spoke. Alekos fiddled with the leaves of the fruit garnishing his dessert.

"What are those called, Anna?" Jo asked, pointing at the fruit in Alekos' hand.

"Chinese gooseberry I've always called them." Anna said.

"I thought it was Syphilis something." Emelda shouted.

Lou coughed over the top of her words. "No, no, no!" he shouted. "I think the name you are looking for is Physalis Peruviana, but Cape gooseberry is the more common name for them."

"That's it!" Jo said. "I used to think these bits were tissue paper, but they're actually leaves, aren't they?" she said this to Alekos.

"It is like thin paper" he said taking a cigarette that his father had left slowly burning away in the ashtray; he held it up to the leaf of one of the cape gooseberries in front of him. It immediately burst into flames. Taken aback by the unexpected flammability of the Cape gooseberry leaves, Alekos dropped the burning fruit on to the table. The burning fruit set fire to the collection of unpopular

Cape gooseberries that formed a nest for the napkin swan that Jo had made during the meal. Not only did the napkin swan suffer an unexpected cremation, but when the kids all jumped out of their seats in a panic, Vasilis' Panama hat tumbled off Alekos' head joining the inferno. Alekos got hold of Vasilis Panama hat, threw it on the floor and then stamped on it to extinguish the flames. Turning quickly to Lou, Vasilis urged him to put out the fire and Lou obliged, smothering the fire with a cover from a nearby seat. Everyone cheered. Alekos went red and handed the burnt and battered hat to Vasilis. "We will talk about this later." Vasilis said to the boy.

"Why didn't you just do that yourself, Vasilis?" Anna asked. "You were nearer than he was."

"I panicked, then I remembered that Lou's a fireman."

Lou's family all looked at Vasilis. "Daddy's not a fireman!" Robbie shouted.

"I always thought you were a fireman, you used to be didn't you?"

"No, never."

"Yes, I was led to believe he was a fireman too, for a while anyway." Sally said, giving Lou a sideways glance.

"That must have been some story we made up in 1986? Lads on holiday, eh?" Lou said laughing.

"Anyway, we need to be heading back to the Yacht soon. Fifteen minutes everyone." Vasilis said.

47
2002, DAY 9 – On-board the yacht

The journey back was a quieter event. Excitement, the food, or all the fresh air, had made the children sleepy. They were contented slouching on the cushion filled sofas, watching the dolphins, or playing the oversized games that Vasilis had brought out. Jo and Alekos played a large game of chess. It was not the motion of the yacht that made the game difficult, as magnets held the pieces in position, but their lack of knowledge of the game. Jo made rules up as she went along; admittedly she spoke with some authority and Alekos believed every word.

"Are you and Tatti actually brother and sister?" Jo asked.

"What do you mean? Of course!" Alekos replied, horrified. Jo, taken aback by his angry reply, back pedalled and started talking about step-families. They gave up on the game, so Jo decided to go off on her own and do some filming.

Anna said she would give Sally a guided tour; she had that excited expression, like a grin that was stuck, Sally could not help but smile. Anna spoke quickly and had a tendency to dash everywhere.

"Come on Anna, give me a second, I can't keep up in these flip flops!" Sally said.

"We haven't got long."

"Sorry I didn't realise. I need the loo actually, if you can direct me to the poshest one that would be good."

"Well that could be any of the ensuite bathrooms, if you go into any of the staterooms they are all exactly the same. Look here's one."

"Thanks Anna. I can find my way back."

The door closed behind Sally and she found herself in a gorgeous bedroom. She had imagined that the bed would be some kind of bunk, hanging off the wall, but it was more like being in a top hotel. Crisp white sheets. Sally had a thing about crisp white sheets. She would have clean sheets every night if she was a millionaire, not because she was a hygiene freak but because of the feel of them. She felt the sheets to check the quality of the cotton, not too crisp, not too soft. Sitting on the bed she caught a glimpse of herself in the mirror. *'The lighting is not very flattering'* she thought. The door clicked and she looked up to find Lou standing there. The room suddenly felt very small.

"What are you doing?" he said, grinning.

"Just checking out the quality of the bedding, actually."

"Do you think that's the best way to check it out?"

"Ha ha."

"No seriously."

"Erm no. It's best to get in, but I wouldn't want to mess the bed up."

"Vasilis has people to change beds."

"Even so . . . anyway I was on the way to the loo."

"It's been great to meet up again." Lou moved towards Sally. "Hug, for old times' sake?" Before Sally had chance to get away his arms moved around her and he enveloped her in a warm embrace.

"I really must go to the loo."

"Sure." He released her. "Will's a great bloke, by the way."

"He is." Sally smiled.

"Not so good on Jet Skis, but otherwise . . ."

"What he lacks in Jet Ski skills, he makes up for in other areas."

"Sorry that sounded bitchy of me I was just . . ."

"I know, don't worry" Sally laughed.

"I'll leave you to the toilet."

Sally waited until the door closed before dashing into the bathroom. As she sat on the toilet she remembered the effect Lou had had on her before – the shaking Labrador. Glad to have had those few minutes alone with Lou, she knew it was what she wanted – well needed, to test out her feelings, put her mind at rest. One hug. Now she knew without any doubt. There were not any of those old feelings. It was not as she had imagined. There was something missing. Will.

Jo was wandering around the ship collecting evidence. She spotted Lou in the corridor leaving one of the staterooms. She videoed him, just managing to catch his back view without being seen. She wondered why Lou had been in the stateroom. Curiosity made her open the door.

*

The Yacht sailed past the lighthouse at Rhodes Town just as two fishing boats left the harbour in the late afternoon sunshine. Algie tried to imagine the giant 'Colossus of Rhodes' with a leg either side of the entrance to the port. One of the Seven Ancient Wonders, supposedly; Algie decided that it was not possible.

Will noticed how different the place looks when you approach it from the sea, quite unlike the one he had visited earlier in the week. This is the welcome people would have received, he thought, the doorstep to the island, through this harbour. He noticed the substantial fortifications, the castellation's of the medieval castle – the Palace of the Grand Master of the Knights – and the Old Town city walls. The island had clearly been important and had obviously needed to defend itself.

Almost everyone had gathered at the bow of the yacht, excited by the busy port. They sailed between two deer standing on tall columns.
"One of them has lost its antlers." Hamish said.
"No it's a pair of deer" Will said, "This is a stag. A stag is a male deer and on the other side there is a doe, a female deer." Hamish started to sing . . . until he spotted the dolphin sculpture.
"Mr Grey!" he shouted.
"Misty grey" Jack shouted pointing.
Sally noticed the three stone built cylindrical windmills on the harbour wall, with their little terracotta coloured pointy hats, she got out her camera.
Anna noticed that Vasilis' yacht was the most impressive yacht in Mandraki harbour, and there were some seriously fine yachts in there.
Vasilis gave them just an hour to visit the markets.

*

The MacFaddyans, Anna and Hamish wandered the markets together. Sally watched Jo. She had noticed that Anna seemed to take a lot of Jo's attention. Anna appeared oblivious, but Jo was by her side all the way, asking her this and that. She noticed that Jo had even started to slap her thigh when she laughed, just like Anna.

Jo had been surreptitiously trying to film people, but had found this difficult. She decided that they should get back to the boat early so that she could film everyone as they returned. It was hard work convincing her family to go back early, especially when they had little time as it was. In the end she developed a 'tummy ache' which got them back to the yacht a little before the others and which miraculously disappeared when they got back. She filmed them all getting back on board. Even Eva, who had kept out of sight for much the day, apart from lunchtime, had been into town with Yorgos.

*

Sally realised that she had been neglecting Jo. She called her over and pulled her onto her knee.

"You having a good holiday?"

"Yep, really good. Boring sometimes, but it's better than being at home."

"Have you finished making your film?"

"Ner, not yet."

"What's it about?"

"Oh, nothing much."

"Nothing?" Sally said. Then after a minute. "Is it about Anna?"

"No, why?" Jo snapped.

"No reason . . . you know you are very special, don't you?"

"What do you mean?"

"You are special. You are lovely, just the way you are, you don't need to be like anyone else."

Jo looked annoyed and jumped off Sally's knee. "You're just jealous because I like being with Anna." She stomped away. Sally almost laughed; that hadn't gone quite how she had expected. She decided that things could not get much worse. Then Algie came over.

*

Sally found it difficult to take in what Algie was suggesting. *Was it really possible? Did I not see the signs, have I misread everything? Is nothing as it seemed?* She went through her memories, searching for clues. There were signs, when she thought about it. She wanted to ask Lou. The desire to know was creeping out of control. She could feel her blood pressure rising. She considered the implications – selfish ones, she realised that she was just one of probably a number of girls that Lou had been with during that holiday. She went over and over things in her mind. She looked at Tatti and then at Lou. How could she not have seen the resemblance before?

'*Go away*' Sally thought when she saw Lou coming over to talk to her. '*Not now.*'

"You ok, Sal?"

"Fine" she snapped.

"Are you sure, you don't sound fine."

"No really I'm fine." she struggled to be civil. He seemed to get the message and left her alone. Will overheard the conversation but said nothing.

Vasilis and Anna stood chatting in the kitchen whilst putting the final touches to the food. It had all been ordered and picked up from Rhodes Town, there was very little to do.

"It's a shame Zak didn't come today, he would have loved it."

"Why didn't he come? Was he too busy?" Anna asked.

"I guess so."

"How do you get a job picking up donkey poo anyway?"

"Seriously?" Vasilis started laughing.

"What?"

"It's not his job, Anna."

"What do you mean, why does he do it then?"

"I thought a gardener like you would have worked that out."

"What, you mean he just picks it up to put on his garden?"

"Exactly that."

"Well that makes more sense. There was I thinking the poor man earned a living picking up poo." She laughed too. "It must work, whatever poo does to gardens, his garden is stunning."

"Well he looks after a few gardens – just as a hobby though."

"How does he earn a living? Oh, I suppose he's retired."

"I'll let you into a little secret. Zak is a very wealthy man."

"Yeah?"

"He was orphaned in the mid 1940's" Vasilis began, "and was taken in by an Italian Industrialist who had settled in Lindos after falling for a local girl. They lived in the Captain's House on the corner where I live now. Influenced by the Italian designer couture that she had seen on her visits to Italy, the Industrialist's wife tended to dress Zak in starched expensive clothes and his friends had made fun of him at school. Needless to say Zak hated the clothes and after countless 'accidents' with various garments she eventually gave in, letting him wear what he wanted.

"The Industrialist was killed in the 1950's in a quayside accident in Italy and his wife inherited what was rumoured to be an enormous sum of money. I guess more than a million English pounds, which was a lot of money then. The money all went to Zak when she died in 1975. Zak and my mother were always friends, even though my father didn't get on with him. When I left the village it was Zak's links to the boat building company in Italy that took me there. He helped me financially too, lending me money which I quickly repaid as the business grew. I've been lucky." Vasilis said. "Zak has always supported me – 'gives me something to think about' he always says."

"You would never think he had any money to look at him." Anna said.

"That's true. Apparently people in Lindos decided that the money must have been lost or frittered away. But my mother knew the truth – that it was all just hidden away."

"That reminds me. I've been wondering who 'Maria' is – you called the yacht 'Maria.' It's your Mother's name isn't it? I learned today."

"That's right." Vasilis said, then he went quiet. "I learned something today too."

"What's that?" Anna asked, but Vasilis remained silent. "What did you learn?" Eventually he spoke.

"When I tried to find you, in England . . . I didn't spend the whole two weeks looking for you." He looked very serious. Anna nodded for him to continue. "I spent some of the two weeks around Oxford . . . looking for Lou."

"Why?"

"I thought that he was a fireman, so I spent a bit of time contacting fire stations trying to find him. But I never found a trace of him."

"Because he's not a fireman."

"No, apparently not – as I found out today."

"That's quite funny. But I don't understand why you were looking for him."

"Well, even though Eva would never tell me, I always thought that he was the father of Eva's baby. In hindsight, I could have got myself into real trouble, I don't know what I was doing really because Eva and Yorgos had married by then and so it's probably a good thing that I didn't find him!"

*

It was breezy on the top deck, but they all preferred to put on an extra layer and stay up there than go inside to eat. The meal was a casual affair. Vasilis, determined that they would experience the Greek food he had intended, served Dolmades, Souvlaki, grilled swordfish, Lamb Kleftiko and Moussaka, along with salad.

"Souvlaki and beer, what's not to like!" Will joked.

When the meal was more or less over, they lolled about on the cushions feeling overly full. Anna appeared with a guitar.

"Come on Will, give us a tune" she said. Will declined, but he was under so much pressure that he gave in. After a terrible, tuneless start, he re-tuned the guitar and as he played and sang, the kids danced and everyone joined in.

Sally moved over to the railings, unable to shift her mood. The vast expanse of ocean only exaggerated her feeling of lonely isolation. As the yacht moved around to approach Lindos bay, the sun slipped over the horizon and the cool blue sky turned warm pink and orange hues. Sally found its beauty overwhelming. As the white buildings of the village came into view again they reflected the colours of the setting sun. The yacht slowed and the tempo slowed as Will began a song that nobody seemed to recognise:

Long fringe and dungarees
Her Dad keeps honeybees
Drawn to the mystery of Sally
Wet coat that smells of dog
She's got no dialogue
Intrigue and mystery, that's Sally, Matchbox Sally.

Sally knew the song; it was embedded in her memory. She could picture them both in the flat on George Street where she lived when they first met. She had heard the song develop from a simple guitar riff, had commented on the beautiful melody. Then a week later he had sung the lyrics that he had been writing in secret, this song about the pair of them. Sally could not hold back the tears.

48

2002, DAY 9 – The Villa, Lindos

Will noted that Sally had snapped out every word she uttered to just about everyone that she had spoken to on the boat trip. He knew this was not really like her, but it annoyed him. Whatever it was that was bothering her, she should not take it out on other people like that. She was being selfish and thoughtless. Just occasionally she did it, letting her mood seep out and taint the atmosphere of whichever group of people she was in. Heart on her sleeve. He knew that she was always devastated to find that she had upset anyone and that she always went out of her way to make people feel comfortable, but she was often quite hard on the kids – although she would say 'firm but fair'. Will guessed that whatever was on Sally's mind, it had nothing to do with the kids today. He guessed it was something to do with Lou Reeve.

"Algie, what makes Tatti think that Lou is her father?" Sally asked. Will was surprised how quickly his suspicions were confirmed.

"Two things really – one, because he was here at about the right time and two, because her mother has been in a ridiculously bad mood ever since Lou arrived in Lindos. She even tried to take them away on holiday in the middle of their main holiday season. Also, I was looking at them today and they do look quite similar."

"Have you thought about what it means to you, Algie?"
"No?"

"Well, Tatti and Mel would be sisters – half-sisters."

"Oh no, you're right! And there are funny little things about them that are similar. Things like they both have green eyes, like proper green eyes. Until this week I'd never met anyone before with proper green eyes. Their hands are nearly identical, as well. I bet Tatti hasn't thought about that."

"Well I've got video of everyone, so you can look at that to check. Look at Lou and then look at Tatti." Jo said, handing them the camera.

"How come you took that video, Jo?" Will said.

"Oh, I just wanted pictures of everyone."

"Really."

"I still don't think this is what you would call hard evidence, Algie." Will said after everyone had looked at the clips.

"Oh and she pretended not to know him in the street."

"Well that's certainly a little strange, but I still think it's a long shot."

"So, you two don't remember them being together then?" Algie directed his question at Anna and Sally.

"There was just one occasion, on the beach one evening. We were hiding in the bushes . . . sounds bad now I've said it out loud. Anyway, long story, they may have been together that night. It was the night that we saw Lou for the first time, in fact, it was in Manolis restaurant. Then we saw them together on the beach later." Anna said.

"It could have been anytime, we wouldn't have known." Sally added.

"Who's gonna ask Lou?" Algie said hopefully.

"I think we need to keep out of this, for the whole Estathio family, it's their business not ours. It caused a massive rift in the family that still hasn't healed; we must be careful. I'm sure we can patch up Sally's ego." Anna looked serious as she spoke.

"You can leave my ego out of this thank you, Anna." Sally said, bitterly.

*

Algie tapped his fingernails on the table.

"Pack it in." Will said.

"What?" Algie replied.

"Stop drumming, you're driving me mad!"

"Sorry I didn't even realise I was doing it. I was just thinking, surely Tatti has a right to know who her father is."

"Does anyone have a right to know? You could say that a man has a right to remain anonymous?" Will said.

"I think a man loses his right to remain anonymous when he has sex." Anna joined in.

"Yeah, that's the gamble you take when you have sex." Algie said.

"I think people should at least have a right to know who their father is, even if they don't get to know them." Sally said.

"What if the woman doesn't know who the father is?" Will said.

"I think she would know – at least between one or two people." Sally added.

"What about Sandra, you know, lived next door but two, in our first house?"

"God yes, they would have to round up half the village and do DNA tests!"

"Actually, maybe men should have a right to remain anonymous because women can trick men into having sex with them – they ensnare them and wham bang it's all over." Algie said. "I agree with Dad." They all stared at Algie.

"Ensnare, are you from 1948? And I think the phrase you're looking for is 'wham bam thank you man' – I changed the last bit for the role reversal." Will replied.

"Whatever."

"I think it's probably more likely to be the other way round." Sally jumped in.

"Works both ways." Will said.

"Anyway, I think Tatti does have a right to know." Algie said.

49
2002, DAY 9 – Lindos

Manolis met Zak in the street, it was about the same time, in about the same place as usual, but Manolis had to look twice in this instance because extraordinarily he found Zak sitting on the bench near Yolanda's Bar.

"Idle waster" Manolis muttered as he walked past. There was no reply. "Idle waster, I say." He raised his voice, but continued to walk. Again there was no reply. Manolis stopped in his tracks, swinging around. Briskly he strode back towards the bench, his hands in fists. "Not even a grunt, eh?" Manolis shouted. His face pushed to within inches of Zak's. Zak stared an empty stare. "Pphhah!" Manolis punched out the 'P'. Then he whispered. "You know she picked the right one."

50
2002, DAY 9 – Lindos

Tatiani watched her mother for a minute before she went into the room. She was surprised when she scrutinised her closely just how sad and tired she looked and felt a pang of guilt because she had not even noticed. She sat down next to her mother. "Have you got something to tell me?" Tatti asked. Eva visibly jumped.

"What do you mean?"

"Who is my father?"

"This again, Tatiani? I told you, it is best if you never know."

"Best for who though? Best for you, maybe."

"Maybe."

"I need to know, Mama. It won't change anything. I will always love you and Yorgos, you are my parents."

"Maybe. But it will change things." Eva signed. "This is not how I intended to tell you."

"So you did intend to tell me one day?"

"Well, no actually. Until this week I never intended to tell you."

"So I wonder what changed your mind this week?" she smiled at her mother. "It is Lou, isn't it?"

Eva let out a long sign. She visibly wilted. Tatti waited. "You're right . . ."

"So, it is Lou."

"You're right about one thing – maybe you do need to know. The problem is that it affects so many people's lives."

"But it is the most important thing to me, and it must be important to my father."

"What if he doesn't want to know?"

"Don't you think I've thought about that?"

"What about the rest of his family?"

"At least they know who their parents are!"

"What about your Grandpa? It might just finish him off!"

"I still think it is more important that I know."

The resignation showed on Eva's face, she knew she was beaten, there were no more excuses. "Before I tell you, we need to come to some agreement."

"Ok."

"I will tell you who your father is, I have never told anyone. However, I think we need to discuss the implications of telling him and for now I would like you to promise not to tell him."

"But what if he is going home soon?"

Eva smiled. "Even if he is going home soon."

Tatiani waited expectantly, her heart began to beat quickly. "Mama, tell me!"

"I just need your promise."

"Ok, I promise."

Eva looked serious again. "Your father is Lou Reeve."

51
2002, DAY 9 – Lindos

Vasilis studied his sister's face, the lines sharpening his focus on his own age. He remembered endless days in St Paul's Bay and Sundays, family days with Mama and Papa, uncles, aunties and cousins. There were always competitions, maybe fishing or swimming and then the meals, lengthy affairs with everyone helping, proud to do their part. And most of all he remembered the laughter. Any cross words or raised voices would be Grandma, when someone picked at their food or ate too quickly. Vasilis tried to remember the last impromptu family gathering – not the funerals, or weddings for that matter, which often carried tension with them, and sometimes regrets or disappointment. It was certainly before the summer of 1986. The summer that brought so much joy and love, then took it all away.

"What do you want to happen? What's the best ending for you?"

"That's too hard Vasilis. I don't know."

"Is there no way that Tatiani can get to know Lou, and you and Yorgos can cope with that . . . and in any case, does it matter how you two cope, isn't it more important for them to get to know each other?"

"You're supposed to be on my side." She managed a smile.

"I am. I think if you do anything to stand in your daughter's way you will be doing to her what father did to you. Haven't you got to let her make her choice?"

"What do you mean? Do you think she will choose to live her life near him?"

"No, no, no! I just mean let her choose whether he is in her life . . . and of course, he may choose not to be part of hers."

There was a noise at the gate.

"Hey, my friend, a drink before bedtime?" Vasilis called out to the old man when he appeared in the gateway. "Stay." He whispered to Eva when he sensed her movement. Zak jumped, swayed slightly and then clung to the gatepost. "Ah, too much already, I see!" Vasilis sprang across the yard.

He reached for Zak's arm, but was taken aback by the eagerness in his old friends grasp. Breathing heavily, he stumbled across to the table. Vasilis placed him beside Eva on to the bench. Zak tried to speak, tapping his chest with his fist.

"Hey, get your breath."

"I need to tell you . . ." Zak spoke at last.

"Get your breath"

"Water."

Vasilis dashed to the kitchen and straight back out with a glass of water, holding it to his lips. He drank the water eagerly.

"Not good" he said, banging his chest.

"What happened?"

"No breath" was all Zak could say.

"Take your time. Big slow breaths."

*

"You had me worried for a minute there, old man!" Vasilis smiled at last relieved that Zak was breathing more comfortably.

"Hey, not so much the old man!" Zak coughed a little as he spoke. "Your father is a silly old fool."

"What has he done now?"

"Ah . . . nothing." Zak said with a sigh. Vasilis waited, but Zak shook his head.

"Eva has a dilemma Zak."

"Yes?"

"Does she let Tatiani get to know her real father?"

"Of course."

"That simple?"

"Yes."

"But imagine the upset it will cause with father and the family!"

"Maybe, but it does not really concern them."

"But it caused such a rift, especially with father."

"Well, he is a hypocrite!"

"Why? What do you mean?" said Eva.

Zak suddenly looked a little unsure. He glanced at Vasilis. "Well you're going to have to tell us now!" Vasilis said.

"Surely you know?"

"Know what?" They said in unison, raising their voices.

"That your mother was expecting Vasilis before they got married."

"I don't believe you!" Eva said, eyes wide.

"It is true." Zak looked at Vasilis. "We both loved your mother. I wanted to marry her, but so did Manolis. She couldn't decide." Eva and Vasilis smiled. "I cared for her, I respect her. I make her happy. I wait patiently. Your father showed no respect, he make her pregnant and then she feel like she has to marry him." Eva gasped. "I said 'no don't do it, I will look after you both'. He promised her the world and she married him. My heart crack and break, but I live all my life watching her with him . . . I know she was happy because she told me. But he did not deserve her."

"So, they really did have to get married because Mama was pregnant?"

"Yes."

Eva covered her face with her hands. "I don't believe this! How could he do this?" she stood up and began to pace around. "He put me through all that pain, anguish and fear when I had Tatiani, and all the time he had been through it himself. How dare he, how dare he?" she shouted louder.

"I never knew" said Vasilis.

"Me neither. This isn't a joke is it Zak?"

"No joke. I am sorry to say this." Zak said, taken aback by the vehement reaction.

"No, you have helped me to decide, thank you, thank you, thank you." She kissed his cheek and made for the gate.

"Wait Eva! Don't be too hasty." Vasilis called to her.

"Don't worry! I won't harm him."

"Just wait a minute." Vasilis caught her before she managed to shut the gate properly.

"I need to think."

"Come back, have another drink. You can think here." He smiled at his sister.

"I've only just got my sister back. I don't want to lose father, not before we've sorted things out." Eva gave in and returned to her seat.

"I just can't get over what you said, Zak. Why would he treat me like that when he had been through it himself?"

"I think he not want you to make the same mistake."

They sat in silence for a while.

"I am sorry about father. I presume you never really got on?" Vasilis broke the silence.

"Never got on! We were best friends. From as far back as I can remember Manolis was in my life, like brothers we played together, swam and worked together, laughed, cried and fought together" Zak sighed.

"No!"

". . . Until we both fell in love with your mother."

"But that does not make sense. If he married Mama, it is you who should be annoyed." Eva said.

"You would think so. However, Manolis always think that she loved me more. He once found her in my garden – I always help her with plants. It was always in his mind after that. But really she loved him very much."

"Are you still planning to go to see Father?" Vasilis asked Eva. "Isn't it a little late?"

"No, it is not him I need to speak to. But now it is too late to speak to anyone. I must go." Eva said standing up.

"Are you ok?"

"I will be ok. Good night."

*

The two men sat out in the courtyard until the music in the village stopped. Zak had found his breath and was chatting animatedly.

"I love your father too. He is such an oaf. He was the biggest boy in school, I was the smallest. We used to laugh so much. I just remember laughing so much. We used to get up to mischief. He had the strength and the courage. I had the ideas . . . and I had speed . . . and I could get into small spaces if that was ever necessary. The only time we did not laugh was when we were eating and when we played the game."

"The game?"

"You never heard about our game?"

"No."

"We played this game – for years! My parents and your grandparents did not get on and so they did not like us to play together. We used to meet away from the centre of the village so that no one would see us. Every day we bumped into each other in the village and so we would pretend that we did not get on. Usually we just ignored each other. Sometimes we challenged each other to pass something across secretly. Sometimes we tried to make people think that we hated each other; if our parents mentioned it we scored points. It was fun."

"That's so funny!"

"At some point after your parents got married it seems Manolis stopped pretending. I don't know when. I just thought he was very good at the game."

"What if you met outside the village?"

"We never did." Zak continued. "Your Mother made excuses for him. She tried to get us back together. But it never happened. Time went on. The only consolation for me was your mother. She was a wonderful woman – but you know that."

"I will always regret . . ." Vasilis began, but Zak jumped in.

"Never regret anything. Your Mother was always on your side. It was Manolis who drove you away. She always said that she would have done the same as you."

"Thank you Zak. Thank you for everything you did for Mama."

"Not necessary." He smiled. "Back there in the village, I thought I was going to see her tonight."

"Who?"

"Your Mother."

"Don't you dare!" Vasilis said as he hugged the old man.

52
2002, DAY 10 – Lindos

Lou sat in Yolanda's bar watching his daughter and her brother. He could see that they were bickering as they walked up the street towards him. He wiped the palms of his hands down his shorts and subconsciously corrected his posture; he then ran his hand through his hair, ruffling it. As she got closer he scrutinised her, realising he was seeing something very different this time. The girl that looked so like Eva, on closer examination looked like his mother; the smile, the teeth, how did he not see that before. Her stature was Eva's, petite, doll-like, delicate. Colouring too, except for the freckles, again like his mother and those green eyes – Reeve green eyes! Tatiani smiled as their eyes met. Her brother went into the bar opposite, settling down in front of the big screen with some of his friends. Tatiani began to weave her way through the tables; Lou stood up to greet her, ordered her a drink and sat down opposite her at the table.

"I know this is a big shock for you." Tatiani said. "I have been waiting a long time to find out who my father is. I have had a little bit of time to get used to this. I am sorry for the shock." Again she smiled a beautiful smile.

"It was a shock. Before Eva came to see me this morning, I had no idea. But, I am very pleased to meet you Tatiani, I hope we can get to know each other."

"We do not have long."

"No that is true, but I will come back to see you soon."

53
2002, DAY 10 – The Party, Lindos

Tatiani and Alekos had spent the last hour preparing food and setting up a long table at Manolis' restaurant, ready for the party. Balloons, ribbons and candles made it look very special. Eva was already flustered because there was a big party, but considering the guests made her extremely nervous. First to arrive were the MacFaddyans. Eva noticed that Tatti seemed excited; she was interested to see her with Algie, as they had managed to stay out of her way on the yacht trip.

Manolis stood in his usual place outside the door. He bristled a little when he spotted Anna and Hamish walking down towards the restaurant, but managed a civil welcome, directing them through to the others. He was busy doing this when Vasilis arrived with Zak. Shock then anger spread across his face. Eva saw them and dashed to the door.

"Welcome home Vasilis, come in Zak." Eva said, stepping in front of Manolis. Tatiani and Alekos 'high fived' in the kitchen doorway.

"I thought you were dead." Manolis muttered to Zak under his breath. Vasilis overheard. He sent Zak to the table then went to speak to his father.

"None of that tonight, father. I am very happy to see you and hope we can all put these things behind us. Tonight is about building bridges and fresh starts." He hugged Manolis. Shocked by the warmth from his son, Manolis softened and eventually managed a smile. He nodded.

"Pa, come and carve the meat!" Eva shouted. She noticed Lou and his family arriving and dashed around to see them in. She greeted them all with warm smiles, directing them around the family's table. She was so friendly that, for a moment, Lou wondered if it was in fact a twin sister, the change in her persona was so striking. Yorgos had also noticed a change in his wife.

Once they were all seated Vasilis stood banging his spoon on the table.

"Welcome everybody, to the house of Estathio. It is wonderful to have you all here around this table. I never thought I would see this day. I hope you will all help us to celebrate Anna's 40th Birthday. Happy Birthday, Anna!" Vasilis said, raising his glass. They all stood up and shouted a chorus of 'happy birthday Anna's'.

Yorgos came out from the kitchen when he heard Vasilis. He stood grinning. Striding forward after the cheers he hugged his old friend, slapping his back. "Hey, my friend, great to see you back in this house." He spoke in Greek, tears filling his eyes.

The music was turned up and once Manolis had carved enough meat he grabbed Vasilis, pulling him out of his seat and shouted for Yorgos. Everyone clapped along to the music. It was years since they had danced together – Eva, Tatiani and Alekos were amazed. Tears flooded down Eva's face.

"Hey Mama, everything is going to be fine!" Tatti reassured her.

"I know my baby, I know!"

Hamish, Stevie and Robbie tried to dance too, much to everyone's amusement.

They brought out the food and everyone tucked in. There were endless bottles of wine, plate after plate of food, course after course. Spirits were high and there were many smiling faces around the table.

"It seems strange that we have been invited to this big family do." Mel said to Lou.

"Not really, it's Anna's 40th birthday party, that's why we were invited, I think they just wanted lots of people here."

"Maybe."

"There . . ." Lou began, but decided now wasn't the time.

"What?"

"Nothing important, I'll tell you later." He pointed to Jack who was now standing on the table trying to do the Greek dance.

"That's my boy!" shouted Mel. "Can someone grab him, before he falls?"

*

Sally was quiet, she loved the atmosphere, it was a wonderful party, the best party she had been to for years, but Will was still being funny with her and she really did not know how she was going to turn things around. She just hoped that everything would get back to normal when they got back home. Lou looked lovely, Sally thought. She noticed that there was some eye contact going on between Lou and Tatti. Anna looked happy too; it had been a long time since Sally had seen Anna look so happy. She hoped that Anna and Vasilis could make up for some of the years that they had lost.

*

Algie helped Tatti to serve the meal and after a special request Jo had been allowed to help too. Tatti had found a suitable apron for her – she was in her element. She worked hard at the names of the Greek dishes, practising time and time again in the kitchen so that when she put the food on the table she pronounced it correctly. She got a round of applause every time she got the name right – she loved all the attention she was getting.

Yorgos watched Lou closely.

Anna was very happy.
"I'm so happy I think I might pop!" she said to Sally.
"I'm glad you're happy, but don't pop until you get home or there'll be a right mess in here! You wouldn't want to spoil the atmosphere." Anna slapped her thigh and rocked on her seat. This made Sally laugh, her top lip stuck to her gum.

*

As the last dishes were set on the table, the music was turned up again and the Greek dancing began in earnest. Alekos joined in this time, dragging Zak up there too. Manolis was surprisingly light footed for someone with such a large frame, although at one point he teetered just a little too long before setting off back in the other direction. The end of the table was at risk, everyone held their breath.

"She's too young for Algie." Mel look disgruntled as she watched Algie and Tatti together.
"I think they make a good couple." Lou said. "Remember, he's too young for you."
"Never heard of a toy boy, Father? I just don't see what he sees in her. Goofy teeth and . . ."
"Yes, like your Grandmothers."

"Well yes, but that's different. And she's got freckles!"

"What on earth is wrong with freckles?"

"Well, nothing but . . ."

"Before you carry on, there is something I need to tell you."

"Oh my God! What?"

"I have only just found this out myself. I didn't intend to tell you just now, but maybe you should know. Do not say a word to your mother before I get chance to speak to her!"

"What Dad, this is sounding serious." The smile dropped from Mel's face. "I won't say anything to Mum. You haven't had an affair have you? Oh my God, it's that holiday romance isn't it? Was it just for old time's sake or are you in love?"

"Mel, shut up and listen!" Lou took his daughter by the shoulders as he said this. "Apart from my 'Holiday Romance' with Sally back in 1986, I also spent one evening with Eva."

"Who the fuck's Eva . . . what, that Eva?" Lou nodded and Mel just said "Oh" and then eventually "She doesn't look your type."

"Does anybody ever need to be anyone's 'type' for just one evening?"

"I guess not."

"The thing is, it turns out that the evening was more eventful than I thought."

"Yeah?"

"I have just found out that Eva had a baby." Mel just stared. "My daughter. Tatiani is my daughter."

"You're having a laugh? Dad that's not funny!"

"Do you think I would joke about something like that? I just found out this morning. I think I'm still in shock."

"But Dad that means . . ." Mel stood up and shouted, pointing at Tatiani. "Are you saying she's my sister?" Lou pulled her back into her seat.

"Shush!" Lou said quietly, but it was too late.

For a moment Manolis looked puzzled, but then the realisation transformed his face. "It was you!" he pointed at Lou. He clambered over the table, food, crockery everywhere. "It was you!" he shouted again reaching out towards him. Lou prepared to run. Manolis lurched forwards to grab his shirt but Lou managed to dodge him and Manolis fell on to the floor.

"Are you ok?" Lou asked tentatively, moving back towards him. This time Manolis swung for him. Vasilis was there in a shot holding him back. Yorgos, grabbed hold of his punching arm.

"Did you hear what he said, Yorgos? He is Tatiana's father."

"I know, I know" he said to Manolis, whose face was like thunder.

"You Knew!"

"No, I just found out last night!" Then Yorgos spoke to Lou. "Why did you have to bring this up now!" he punched Lou on the chin.

"Give him one from me." Manolis shouted, still being held by Vasilis, helped at this point by Will.

"Calm down everyone!" Eva came through from the kitchen.

Eva asked Manolis to go through to the kitchen. Will and Vasilis began to guide him in the direction of the kitchen, but he pulled away from them saying he didn't need dragging there. Yorgos followed them in.

"What on earth did you do that for?" Eva said to Yorgos. "You are as bad as he is." Nodding towards her father.

"Well, why did he tell everyone tonight?"

"I don't know, but you need to get back out there, apologise to your daughter's father and get the party atmosphere going again!"

Yorgos did exactly as he was told. He explained to Lou that it was part of a Greek custom and that it was customary for them to follow this with a dance. He turned up the music again, pulling Lou up to dance. Lou was no fool, but obliged. Quiet, mild mannered Yorgos, got the party going again.

*

Eva sat with her father in the kitchen. For a while neither said anything, Manolis inspecting the floor and Eva staring out of the window. Eva looked at her father, half waiting for the right words to appear in her mind, half wondering how things ever got to this.

"Feel better now, do you?" Eva asked eventually.

"Better?" Manolis replied.

"Now you know. Does it really make that much difference? All those years you hated the English because of one man's mistake. Well, one man and one woman's mistake."

"You were just a girl."

"Same age as Mama when she got pregnant, I believe." Manolis looked puzzled.

"Don't pretend you don't know what I am talking about. How could you treat me like that Pa, when you and Mother had been through a similar thing? How could you?"

"I don't know what to say . . . it was different."

"Not that different."

"We loved each other."

"I needed your love and support."

"We looked after you. We've always looked after you all."

"Yes, but at what price?"

"Eva, I am sorry."

"Sorry?" Eva looked thoughtful for a moment. "It's a little late for apologies, and anyway it is Vasilis you need to speak to. Do not let your relationship with Vasilis suffer anymore because of ridiculous prejudice."

"Yes?"

"Yes. Come on, we have a party to finish. Let's build some Anglo-Greek relations. I love you Pa."

"I love you, too."

"Hey. Also, I believe you and Zak were old friends."

"Pphaah! Useless bastard. I can stretch my apologies only so far."

"Pa!"

"Well, he is a fool . . . and he smells of mushrooms."

54
2002, DAY 10 – Lindos

Sally found Will. He was standing out on the top of the restaurant, looking out over the rooftops of Lindos, the Acropolis lit up behind them. The tip of his cigar glowed briefly, then the smoke crept out of the corner of his mouth and away. Will only became aware of Sally when she kissed the back of his neck.

"Peaceful, isn't it?"

"Sure is."

"What are you thinking about?" Sally asked. Will remained silent for a while, the cigar appearing to take his attention. Then eventually he spoke. "I was just trying to work out how they got those stones up there."

"Ah! I can't help you with that one. Weren't they already up there?"

"Maybe, but not that shape."

"Of course, yes." Sally thought she had better shut up.

They stood together a long time. It was Sally that broke the silence. "I love you Will MacFaddyan."

"I know." Their silence continued. The music seemed loud again. "Where have you been?"

"I was out in the garden . . ."

Will interrupted "I didn't mean that."

"Ah." It was Sally's turn to be quiet.

"I thought I'd lost you Sal."

"No, no," was all she could manage at first, her eyes full with tears. "It all started to slot together a couple of days ago." She slid her arms around him, underneath his jacket. Will raised his brow for her to continue. "I felt very mixed up. No matter what I did I seemed to make things worse. You seemed to misinterpret everything I said and did. Just when I felt like I was making sense of things you seemed to become more and more distant." She hesitated a moment. "I went to the church."

"Did God give you a sign?"

"Don't you take the mickey – this isn't easy! But, yes, he kind of did."

"Really?"

"As I walked into the church, the smell of the flowers wafted towards me. I was hoping for a dark, cool room with a delicate floral fragrance that would calm my migraine, but instead I found myself in a hot, dry, musty room and had a rather strange reaction. I was suddenly overwhelmed, I couldn't stop myself from crying; it didn't make sense. I nearly threw up. My stomach turned upside-down. I sat down in the church until I felt better and gradually worked out what had happened."

"Go on."

"Well, I think the last time I experienced that smell – the flowers, was when I went to see my father after he had died, in fact, the only time I saw him dead, laid there in the Chapel of Rest. I remember trying to drag myself into the room to see him. The room was full of flowers, many of them lilies. I hate that smell." Will hugged his wife. "What amazed me was just how vivid the memory was, how strong the emotions were, and so quickly, totally overwhelming me. I sat there a long time and did a bit of thinking."

"Yes?"

"Will, I'm sorry." He looked puzzled. "I know it sounds pathetic, but I think maybe . . . coming back here

– the sounds, the smells, well just the place really, has tweaked some old emotions. Then seeing Lou, just seemed like a ridiculous coincidence. I got swept up in some old memory."

"He meant a lot to you didn't he?"

"Well, that's the funny thing. It was just a holiday romance. It was lovely at the time, but eventually I tucked it away in a box in my mind marked 'Holiday Romance'. I have fond memories of him – it's the one old relationship that I carry no baggage with, no hard feelings – just warm fuzzy feelings. But, he was not the love of my life; we are very different people. If I had met him in England, I don't think we would have ever got together. And now I know that I maybe wasn't quite so special to him, on his holiday, he clearly had other things going on for him, I thought it would change everything, but in fact it changes nothing.

"I do think that he was really important in my life. He appeared in my life at a time when I was battered and bruised, metaphorically speaking, the people I had been out with had knocked my confidence, tried to change me, wanted me to be something I wasn't. He treated me right when he was with me; he was the first person to really make me feel special; he seemed to love me, just as I was. It was something I hadn't really experienced before. That one brief holiday romance was enough to convince me that somebody could one day love me, the way I wanted to be loved. He let me be me. He gave me enough confidence to wait for Mr Right, the man who would not try to change me and love me just the way I am."

"I love you, Funny Lady."

Part 2

55
2014, Lindos

The sea before me, as flat as a lake. Waves making their way up the gentle slope of the beach break in an energetic display. I feel the temperature of the early morning sun increasing by the minute. An outcrop of rock on my right, forming a natural conclusion to the beach, rises sharply to the white walls of the village, then higher still to the Acropolis above. In places, I can just make out the winding donkey path that forms the main route from the village to the top. The semi-circular beach sweeps beneath me from the rocks, intermittently protected from the sun with the all-too-regimented rows of parasols.

I can hear laughter, heart-warming, soul-soothing laughter; in the distance music from the snack bar; birds overhead; a donkey braying; water lapping against the stationary pedalo at the water's edge.

I feel the sun warming the sun cream covering my body and drop my hands into the sand by my side. I lift the silky top layer and let it slip through my fingers, or I can burrow into the warm sand with my hands reaching down to the cool, damp sand beneath. I relish the breeze, not cool in itself, but cooling, stroking and massaging . . .

Sally stopped; she decided that she did not need to do this because she was calm enough. She ran through the itinerary for the next day in her mind, using it like a checklist of the things that she needed to do. She felt excited and nervous. Her mind darted about and she found herself wondering how different she would feel if Algie was her own son. It was something she had done from time to time, ever since she had finally acknowledged to herself that she would not have children. It was impossible to imagine how she would feel about her own child. She thought she knew, but yet she could never know – maybe what she felt was only a tenth of what a mother really feels – a hundredth even. And then she did it again, her mind went back to September 1986 she experienced the horror of the bleeding; the stuff that fell into her hand and the sadness overwhelmed her. It was a sadness that had grown over the years, but one she controlled, kept it in a box, within a box, within a box.

"Hey, couldn't you sleep?" Sally jolted into an upright position, startled by the voice. Shielding the sun with her hand she thought that she recognised the silhouette. "Sal?" he said again.

"I thought it was you – but just wanted to be sure. I could ask you the same question. How are you doing anyway?" she asked Lou.

"Better than you by the look of things" he replied.

"I'm ok . . . just thinking too much!" Sally wiped her eyes.

"Not like you Sal." Lou said laughing. "You're not worrying about Algie and Tatti are you?"

"Not at all." Sally managed a smile. "Anyway, you wouldn't be laughing if you knew what I was thinking about."

"Why, what are you thinking about?"

"Sorry that was a silly thing to say. I can't tell you."

For a while neither spoke. Lou settled on to the sun bed next to Sally.

Eventually Sally spoke. "I think everything is organised. I'm really looking forward to it. Looks like Hamish has made it – last minute as usual. Have you seen him?"

"Not yet."

"He's only been in Australia for six months, but he's already picking up the accent."

"Is that a permanent move – Australia?"

"Extended holiday with his father, after his exams. I think he plans to stay in Lindos with Anna and the family for a while now. He's really missed his little sister. How's Tatti?"

"Calm and happy – as ever. I can't imagine anything ever ruffling her feathers."

"Do you think they will be ok – Algie and Tatti?"

"Of course! It's funny; I can't imagine not having her in my life."

"She is lovely . . . and so determined. I remember Algie telling us about her plans to teach – that was years ago and there she is practically running the local school. And her vision for the restaurant . . . well their vision for the restaurant."

"I like to think of it as our vision!"

Sally started to laugh. "I'll always think of you as a fireman. But you're right, you have all worked hard to get the new restaurant up and running." Sally said. "Lindos has gone up market, you'll have a lot of competition, there are so many wonderful restaurants, and the accommodation too, I've noticed a change just since I was last over. But I think the restaurant will do well. Algie and Tatti are such characters, but hopefully not quite like Manolis!"

"Lindos was always great, it's just evolving."

"I'm looking forward to tomorrow. I was just wondering if I would have felt any different if Algie had been mine." *'Shit, why didn't I just keep my mouth shut?'* Sally thought.

"I always forget they're not yours?"

"Don't let their mother hear you say that!"

"Is she here?"

"She certainly is, haven't you heard her?" Sally laughed. Then serious suddenly. "Do you ever worry that you haven't brought your kids up right?"

"I can't say I've spent much time thinking about that."

"I do. Always have. I used to worry myself to death about it. I took the responsibilities of Step-motherhood very seriously. I read tons of stuff and asked other people. I think that sometimes I was looking for the bit that said that I had a right to . . . I don't know . . . time . . . space . . . but ninety-nine times out of a hundred it always said their needs came first. I tried hard to do the right thing, but I know I didn't get it right, I shouted . . . and I was selfish at times. Will has always been so selfless; his kids have always been his priority."

"They are a credit to you all."

"I love them both dearly, but I think they turned out like that despite me."

"How come you never had kids, Sal?"

Sally took a deep breath. "That's a very personal question."

"I guess so. Sorry."

"I don't mind really . . . It just never happened. Some things are just not meant to be."

"I imagined you'd have loads of kids."

"So did I . . ." Lou listened intently. ". . . I was pregnant once. I was just thinking about it when you arrived . . . I lost it at ten weeks. I will never forget that feeling. The baby would have been the same age as Tatti if it had lived."

"So about 27 years ago."

"Time doesn't change the feelings."

"I guess not."

"It was 1986." Sally watched Lou closely as she said this. "I met someone on holiday, didn't take precautions and . . ." She saw the realisation wash over his face.

"Do you mean . . ?"

"Yes Lou, it was yours. The only time I was pregnant – it was your baby. I miscarried the day before your note arrived. I had only just found out that I was pregnant, having buried my head in the sand for a number of weeks." Lou remained silent. "I've never told anyone, not even Anna. She felt so guilty for dropping your address in the canal I just didn't have the heart to tell her . . . and it all seemed as if it was meant to be that way. I had no way of contacting you." Lou stayed silent. "Can we keep this to ourselves?"

"Sure." The word came out gruff.

"An eventful holiday." Lou did not respond. "Hey, Mr. Super-sperm!" Sally thumped his arm gently.

"Sure. Sorry you had to go through that Sal."

56
2014. The Big Day, Lindos

His teeth gently crushed the large green olive, releasing that unfathomable dry oily substance. *Food of the Gods,* Will thought. He was becoming a real connoisseur, but it was always going to remain a mystery to him that he could enjoy this food that he had hated so much in the past. It's almost like an addiction. The more you eat them, the more you like them. He smoothed the wrinkles out of the crisp white tablecloth and his hand moved over Sally's. "Hey, Funny Lady" he squeezed her hand. Sally smiled at him leaning forwards to kiss his cheek; she wiped away the oil running down his chin.

"Should we move over here?" Will asked.

"I'm not sure about that." Sally said.

"Why not?"

"Well, you know, Greece is going through hard times at the moment, we don't know what will happen."

"Maybe we could take a risk, Sal. How would you feel about that?" Will smiled.

*

Algie walked into Emelda when he came out of the toilet. "You know I have a thing about married men. Algae."

"Good job you have a husband then." He pinched her cheek. She slipped her arm around his waist and swung around him. He steadied her, gently pushing her in the right direction. "By the way, congratulations little brother

. . . half-bro-in-law." Algie thanked her and walked back into the bedroom.

*

"Caught you!" Algie shouted. Tatti jumped, she was standing with her back to the door in her underwear. Before she had chance to turn around he took hold of her and threw her onto the bed. "If we're quick we could consummate the marriage."

"We could" she smiled "but it would be nice to take a little more time."

"You're right we don't need to hurry back, no one will notice."

"No I mean . . ."

"Only joking Mrs MacFaddyan, there's no rush, we have all night." He tempted her with a long kiss. Tatti eventually broke away.

"Come on, everyone will be waiting for us, I need to finish getting changed."

"Ok, ok." Algie said sulking like a small child, but only for a second. "See you in a minute." He pinched her bottom before leaving the room.

*

Jo poked the lens of the camera around the doorframe. *Pure gold* she thought, capturing Vasilis with his ten year old daughter on his knee. She got the shot but the click of the camera got their attention; she clicked again.

"Where is Anna, I want to do some family shots next?" Jo said. "I'll get the tripod. Eleni, can you find your Mum and Hamish?" The girl dutifully jumped off his knee and ran outside. "Where would you like to do these photos Vasilis, the garden or on the roof?"

"Let's do them in the garden just now Jo, but I would really appreciate it if you would do some shots for us on the yacht – another day."

"Sure."

Anna appeared, she looked tanned and beautiful. Slimmer these days – too thin some people thought – after her travels with Vasilis.

"Before we do the photos, could you just give Zak a hand, he wants to sit outside in the square – says he needs some air?"

"Yes, of course." Vasilis said, jumping up immediately.

*

Vasilis found Zak. He was surprised how light Zak seemed as he helped him up from the chair. He gently manoeuvred him out of the restaurant, into the square and felt guilty when he realised just how frail Zak had become whilst he had been gallivanting around the world with Anna.

"We'll have to squeeze you on the end of here, Zak." Vasilis said and the couple sitting in the middle of the bench moved up to make room for him. Manolis was having an after meal snooze at the other end of the bench. Vasilis squatted down at Zak's side so that he could speak to him easily.

"Are you comfortable?"

"Of course, this is my favourite place to sit."

"We will have to get a name plaque for you!"

"Only when I've gone."

"Hey, don't say that!"

"It's been a wonderful day, thank you." Zak smiled.

"You don't need to thank me. It is me who should thank you." Vasilis squeezed Zak's hand in an uncharacteristically intimate fashion.

"You are the son I never had. Your family is mine. Thank you."

*

Eva tugged at the hem of her turquoise silk shift dress as she perched on the arm of the chair. It had been a long time since she had splashed out on an outfit and never in her life had she spent so much on a pair of shoes – more comfortable than she expected, she was still wearing her designer shoes, even after dancing. Yorgos chatted to Lou. This unlikely friendship had grown over the years and the 'daughter' they shared had done much, over time, to build their mutual respect for one another. Eva and Jane, on the other hand, were never going to be big buddies, but got on well enough to keep the peace. This was probably exacerbated by Lou's occasional jokes about his own attempts to cement Anglo-Greek relations. When Lou had eventually found a way to tell Jane about Tatti it had not gone as well as he had hoped and Jane's initial reaction had been to move out. But just as they had done a number of times before, they had eventually worked things out.

When the time came for the Reeve family photos, Jo sent Eleni to collect people again; in this instance the teenagers Robbie, Stevie and Jack. Eleni hesitated. "They won't bite you!" Jo said laughing. The boys turned up five minutes later looking like a 1960's pop band in their matching suits.

*

"Kalispera!" Hamish greeted the locals respectfully. The eighteen year old looked older than his years. Dazzling, he turned heads wherever he walked. A beautiful innocent face transforming with a wicked smile.

The wedding celebrations had spilled out into the Main Square, all the villagers were there. Manolis still at one end of the bench, Zak at the other. The couple separating them got up to go for more food, leaving them alone on the bench, a large space remained between them.

Manolis muttered to himself, smiling and waving to everyone whose eyes he managed to catch. Happy to see his Granddaughter married, he toasted them with a drink. "Estathio good looks" he said to anyone and everyone. He could hardly believe he would ever feel happy to see Tatiani marrying that English boy. The drink caught in his throat and he began to cough.

Zak was quiet, he had enjoyed the day as well. His favourite people gathered together again; Vasilis and Anna back from their round the world trip, Tatiani and Alekos . . . and of course Hamish back from Australia. He watched the tall blonde. Tired, he nodded as he began to doze, jolting back into position, his eyes wide for a moment, until he nodded again.

As Manolis coughed, his face turned crimson and beads of sweat lined up on his top lip under his moustache. Spluttering, he sprayed saliva. He leaned forward moving his hand as if to pat himself on the back; heads turned and faces began to look concerned. He continued to cough, making gravelly, rasping sounds, fighting for breath. Open mouthed he displayed his furry white tongue and yellowing teeth. He suddenly had everyone's attention and a small circle of people formed around him, patting his back, bending over and peering into his face. He held them back with his hand signals, but together they pulled him up to standing. Eventually things became calmer, the coughing subsided, his breathing slowed, crimson turned to pink and then brown. He covered his mouth with his hand and hankie as he turned to find his seat again.

"What are you staring at?" he muttered to Zak. He waited but there was no answer. The concerned crowd dispersed leaving him with a glass of water and he sat for a moment steadying himself.

"I say, why are you staring, haven't you seen a man coughing before?" he turned to Zak, but the face had not moved. He slid along the bench and nudged the old man, whose arm dropped and hung loosely by his side. Manolis shook him gently, his face distraught. Carefully he closed Zak's eyelids. "Don't leave me, my friend!" He said, putting an arm around him.

**

Zak stretched, basking in the warmth of the sun and watched the heat rippling as it lifted off the surface of the square. The square was empty. He contemplated taking his jacket off, but a light breeze made the heat bearable. It really was very comfortable.

He got up from the bench, turning to look at the sea. From this distance the sea was silent, but he could still imagine the rush of the surf on the beach. This, he thought, like the rock beneath the Acropolis, never changes. For a moment he was reminded of Sunday afternoons before the people came.

A sound behind him made him turn.

"Hello Maria, it's good to see you. It's been a long time."

"Hello my friend. Did you enjoy the wedding?"

"Of course. Did you see your granddaughter?"

"Tatiani looked beautiful – I felt so proud, she is just like Eva. Vasilis so handsome . . . Estathio good looks – Manolis is right."

"He is a great big oaf . . ."

"Leave him be." She said calmly. "He always said that you were too small, that you should put donkey shit in your shoes!"

They stood and laughed together.

"It's nice and quiet." Zak said.

"Yes. Don't you get fed up of all the tourists? I wish they had never come here."

"Do you really Maria? I don't think Lindos would be the same without them, quieter of course, but they bring it to life. Without the tourists the younger generation would move away."

"I still say better without."

"I still say better with. And, anyway you can't unchange things."

"Ah, you see – that's why I picked Manolis . . . he never dared to disagree with me."

"I know why you picked Manolis. You picked him because you loved him, I always knew that. I only wish you had told him enough times to convince him. Silly old fool."

"Oh, what I would give for a hug from him . . ."

"Enough of him. Come and look at this garden, I've been very busy." He linked her arm and they walked out of the square towards the Captain's House.

* * *

About the Author

Sarah Bailey Southwell was born and brought up in North Yorkshire, England and now lives close to the North Yorkshire Moors with her husband and dog.

This is her first book.

You can contact her at sarahbaileysouthwell@gmail.com

Acknowledgements

Thank you to *all* my family and friends for their time, support and encouragement. But special thanks must go to Rachel, Sarah, Lara, Anna L, Sue P, Pat, Rachael, Anna and Sally.

Thank you to Zach for his help with the original cover and also to Mick and Charlotte for their nautical advice.

But most of all I need to thank my husband for his encouragement, advice, love, support and patience.